Singlets and Secrets

Singlets and Secrets

UNVEILING AIDEN
BOOK ONE

How Hard Would You Fight
For True Love?

JOE
CHIANAKAS

BESTSELLING AUTHOR OF *RABBIT IN RED*

an imprint of
Roan & Weatherford Publishing Associates, LLC
Bentonville, Arkansas
www.roanweatherford.com

Library of Congress Cataloging-in-Publication Data
Names: Chianakas, Joe, author.
Title: Singlets and Secrets/Joe Chianakas | Unveiling Aiden #1
Description: First Edition. | Bentonville: Mad Cat, 2023.
Identifiers: LCCN: 2023944945 | ISBN: 978-1-63373-843-0 (trade paperback) |
ISBN: 978-1-63373-844-7 (eBook)
Subjects: | BISAC: YOUNG ADULT FICTION/LGBTQ+ |
YOUNG ADULT FICTION/Coming of Age |
YOUNG ADULT FICTION/Loners & Outcasts
LC record available at: https://lccn.loc.gov/2023944945

Mad Cat trade paperback edition August, 2023

Cover & Interior Design by Casey W. Cowan
Editing by Laura Lauda & Amy Cowan

To Bri.

No, I love you more.

Acknowledgements

MY BIGGEST ACKNOWLEDGEMENT is reserved for my husband, Brian. When I first met him in 2007, I had no idea how amazing life could be. I grew up in a conservative community, raised by a Catholic family and Catholic schools, and at that time teenage Joe never thought he could have love and relationships like the ones in these books. But I do. It took time, patience, courage, and a desire to put my happiness and well-being above stereotypes and closed-minds. To my young readers: You will find joy. Coming-out, especially in certain parts of our world, is still very scary. Find inspiration and hope in these stories, and when you're ready, take a giant leap forward and speak your truth. Great things don't typically happen unless we take a risk. If there is anything worth taking a risk on, it's true love and happiness! And if you lose people on that journey, I'm sorry. That's so painful and unfair. But it is better to be loved for who you are than to be loved for who someone else wants you to be.

Brian was the first to read this book, and he loved it with an enthusiasm I hadn't seen before with my other work. It inspired me to work harder on this novel, revising and editing for a long time, to make it the best that I could make it. I love you so much, Bri. When you believe in me, I feel like I can do anything.

Second, to my "hometown" editors who helped me before I even had an agent or publisher: Tami Blanco, Tracy Walper and Elise Zwicky, all who helped make this a better story!

Third, to my wonderful agent, Amy Brewer and her former co-agent, Patty Carothers. Patty fell in love with this story and eagerly wanted to represent it. When Patty resigned as an agent, Amy continued celebrating it with an unstoppable enthusiasm. And of course to my team at Roan & Weatherford. I worked with publishers in the past, and I have self-published, as well. All I ever wanted was a true team that worked together to make the best books we could. I am grateful to finally have a home at R&W. Special thanks to Laura Lauda and her editing of this story. It has evolved into something I'm very proud of. Thank you also to Amy Cowan for your line edits, and to Casey Cowan for the great cover work, for believing in me, and for giving my book series a wonderful home.

There are many other friends, creatives, and literary professionals in my life that deserve thanks, too, for helping me get to this place in my literary career. You are never far from my mind, and I hope you know you are appreciated.

Singlets and Secrets

1

A Singlet of Unfortunate Events

"AIDEN ROTHE, ARE you here?" Coach Krake asks. He holds a singlet in his right hand and a clipboard in his left. Krake's chest looks like a brick wall, and his broad shoulders could total a vehicle. He's been the wrestling coach here at Washington High School for longer than I've been alive.

Freshman year has been rocky. It's not that I give a crap about wrestling. I just want to get tougher. I've always been the skinny kid who bruises in gym class. When I was little, I asked my dad if I could take karate lessons. Of course, he said karate was for wussies and told me to play a real man's sport like football. I didn't want to.

But all my junior high friends did, and they have turned into football-playing jocks. It's October, I have no new friends, and I'm as skinny as I was when I graduated eighth grade.

So here I am.

Staring at the singlet, I doubt my decision. Who in the hell would wear that? It's white spandex, and my scrawny body will look ridiculous in it.

"Aiden Rothe?" Coach Krake asks louder. I step forward on a squishy wrestling mat, and a cloud of teen B.O. makes me cover my mouth. Coach's nostrils flare like he enjoys the smell. "When I call your name, you move. Immediately. Understand?"

I nod, grab the singlet, and dart to the locker room. One at a time, each of the future Washington Hornet wrestlers gets assigned a practice singlet and goes to dress. I pick a locker in the far back, open it, and hide behind the door. The locker room makes me gag. I cough into a fist, trying not to think too much about the nasty odor, which I can only describe as hot, sweaty poop. My toothpick arms race against time to get this stupid thing on so I can get out of here and so no one sees me nude. Will there be other wrestlers as little as me? I don't know what I'll do if I have to face a big guy.

With the white spandex from hell covering my body, I look in the mirror. The spandex clings to every crevice. Grimacing, I try to pick it out of my butt. Then I run my hands along the side of my head. My hair is buzzed short on the sides, but on top I wear it in a short, spiky style. The spikes look like little leafy-brown curls, but I think it's too short. The only thing I really like about myself is my eyes. They're emerald green and bright as the sea.

"Hey, new kid. Hurry up. Coach doesn't like to wait." It's the junior varsity captain, Mateo Hernandez. Mateo's also a freshman, but legend has it that he came out of his mother's womb wrestling. What would he be wrestling as a newborn? An umbilical cord? Placenta? I shudder at my own thoughts.

According to the rumors, Coach Krake worked privately with him all last summer. Krake selected Mateo as JV captain before our first official practice.

Mateo's incredibly attractive. He has thick, wavy hair, parted down the middle and covering his ears. A tiny bit of stubble grows on his chin, and when he moves, his shoulders and arms rip with muscles. It's simply not fair for a kid his age. That's why I'm here. Not because of him, specifically, but because I want to get strong like him.

"I'm coming," I say.

Do I really want to do this?

I shake my head. It's not only about being tough. Maybe it sounds stupid, but I want to find a place where I can make a friend or two. Being alone sucks. I'm tired of browsing social media and feeling jealous of what everyone else is doing. If I have to wear this stupid uniform to find some friends, well, so be it.

When I return to the wrestling room, everyone stands on the edge of thick, black mats. I think about all the sweat those mats have absorbed over the years. I can't wait to take a shower at home tonight.

Coach Krake stands in the center, wearing a red Washington Hornets polo and black athletic shorts.

"Mateo. Jordan. Come show them how it's done," Krake commands.

Mateo runs a hand through his thick hair and jumps in a wrestling stance. He faces Jordan, a short, heavy boy.

Coach blows his whistle, and Mateo wraps a hand around the back of Jordan's neck. Jordan tries to swat it away, but Mateo is too quick. Mateo steps in with his right foot, his hip thrusting into Jordan's gut. In a split second, Jordan's up in the air, and Mateo flips him over. Landing on Jordan, Mateo's right arm locks under his head, pinning him.

"That's it," Krake shouts. "Nice work."

Mateo stands and smiles.

"What do hornets do?" Krake asks.

"We sting!" Mateo answers.

Krake faces the rest of us. "Hornets don't wait to attack. Hornets sting fast. When that whistle blows, you don't wait. You sting your opponent hard and fast. Got that?"

We nod, and Coach Krake's lips curl into a sinister grin.

"Mateo, you take that half," Krake instructs. "Jordan, you take the other. Show them how to sting."

I'm in Mateo's group. We get paired with a partner close to our own weight, and thankfully there are a few other scrawny kids like me. Mateo shows us how to throw.

I attempt the throw with my partner, but I fall forward on my knee.

"What's your name again?" Mateo asks.

"Aiden."

"You can call me Mat. Come here." He puts his right arm on my shoulder and his left grabs my elbow. "Like this." He steps in with his right foot and spins. I inhale a whiff of his cologne. It's musky and masculine—the only good thing I've smelled today. He drives his hip into my groin, lowers his stance, and thrusts hard into me. His right arm grips the back of my neck. He scoops me up and tosses me down.

"Nice form, Mateo," Coach Krake says.

I stand slowly. Then everyone laughs at me.

Some kids cover their mouths. Others point.

Mateo's gaze sweeps the room and then settles on me. His eyes lower, and his eyebrows lift with surprise.

I look down.

Oh, no! This stupid singlet! I have a boner, and this stupid thing shows everything.

The kids keep laughing at me.

Coach Krake groans. "Aiden, is there any particular reason why you have an erection?"

What? How do I even answer that?

"I'm asking you if you happen to fancy another boy grabbing you," Coach Krake barks. He steps closer to me, and it's like staring at a truck about to run me down. "This school's got policies that keep me from asking you certain questions, but that don't mean I think it's okay. So, I'm asking you. Am I gonna have a problem with you on this team? In the locker room… with my boys?"

My face turns beet red.

"No, sir," I mumble. I feel vulnerable and exposed like I'm standing here naked, and every single person in my high school is pointing and laughing. It's every nightmare come true, and my knees wobble.

"Louder!" Krake commands.

"No, sir," I shout.

"Good. Now go do one hundred push-ups and take a cold shower.

Next time I see an erection on my mat, it will cost you one thousand push-ups. You understand?"

"Yes, sir." Tears well in my eyes, and that's all I need—to cry in front of all these boys, too.

I throw myself on the mat face down so no one can see me. I struggle with the push-ups. Coach Krake doesn't say anything to the other wrestlers who keep laughing at me.

My ears fill with the laughter of dozens of boys, all directed at me.

2

One on One

"HIT THE SHOWERS!" Krake yells before I've finished all my push-ups. I'm only at thirty-six. I'm never going to make it to a hundred.

I stand, all wobbly, arms shaking, black spots dotting my vision, and limp back with the team. A stream of tired wrestlers exits the room.

"Not you," Krake shouts. "You don't shower with my wrestlers."

"But you said—"

"Quiet!" he yells. "I'm not gonna let you take peeps at my boys."

What the hell am *I*?

"What do you want me to do?" My body shakes when I speak. I should quit. I should walk right out of here and never look back. But if I do that, then they'll all know.

"Mateo, you wait here," Krake continues. The rest of the team has left. "This school may have its bend-over backward to diversity bull," Krake says, "but I won't allow it on my wrestling mat."

Krake glares at me, and my stomach turns into a knot. I catch Mateo's wide, warm eyes—is that sympathy? Will he stand up for me?

"Mateo, you know what to do," Krake commands.

"Yes, Coach."

Coach blows the whistle.

"What is—?"

I'm not able to finish my question.

Mateo grabs me and throws me like before. My body slaps against the mat like a whip.

"Get up!" Krake yells. "Again."

I stand, digging my feet into the mat to keep my knees from buckling. It doesn't matter. I don't stand long, as Mat tosses me again.

"Ninety-eight more times." Krake cocks his head toward Mateo. "Throw him until his abnormal desires are destroyed. We're doing you a favor, kid." An icy smile covers his face. He believes what he says.

How can anyone be so cruel?

"You can't—*ow!*" I cry when Mateo tosses me. I can't find the strength to stand any more, but he pulls me up every time and whips me down again.

"Good." Krake's grin lingers, and I want to punch him. I've never thought that way about another adult in my life, but I want to punch him in the mouth! "I'll leave you to it, Mateo. Not one throw less than one hundred." Coach laughs and walks away.

"Please!" I beg Mateo. "No more." I rub my stiff neck.

"Man, you got off on the wrong foot with Coach," he tells me. He relaxes, his shoulders dropping.

"It just... ugh! It just happened! It didn't mean anything!" I defend. It's the truth. Isn't it? My temples pulse, and I close my eyes.

Mateo puts his hand on the back of my neck, but now that Coach Scumbag is gone, he's much gentler about it. "Dude, I've been wrestling my entire life. It happens. I know." He cracks a subtle smile.

Relief washes over me. Thank goodness *someone* understands.

"Coach is hard," he continues, his voice a little deeper. "But he'll make you tough. We're the best team in the state for a reason, you know."

"I'm quitting," I say. His arm remains around my neck, but he doesn't throw me. It's almost like a hug, and I welcome it—anything but another throw.

"After one day?"

I take a deep breath. Mateo isn't nearly as sweaty or gross as me, and I can still smell his cologne. Clearing my throat, I try not to get distracted. Oh, if I got another boner right now—I blink and swallow hard. "Why should I put up with this?"

"Why are you here in the first place?" Mateo asks. He lets go of me. His eyes move up and down, examining me.

I'd answer, but my brain feels like a broken puzzle.

"Here. Sit down for a minute and chill." He leads me to a rolled-up mat and waits for my answer.

I consider telling him my goals to get stronger. But that would reinforce his defense about Krake being the best. "I dunno," I say instead, taking a seat next to him. "I just wanted to fit in somewhere. Clearly, I don't fit in here."

Mat shakes his head, his thick, beautiful hair bouncing. "No. Today you have the chance to prove yourself. You come back tomorrow, and you earn respect. With the team. With Coach. Quit, and they'll never respect you," he says.

"Is Krake always this mean?" I ask. My gaze sweeps the wrestling room, making sure we're alone. The door is closed shut. Black mats fill the room. White walls covered with motivational posters surround us.

Mateo laughs, and even his laugh is attractive. His mouth opens, revealing perfect white teeth. I catch myself smiling even though I don't feel happy. "Yeah. But like I said, it makes you tough. Seriously, dude. I'm not here because I like touching half-naked guys." My eyes fix on Mateo's chest, as one of the singlet's straps falls down his shoulder. I look away quickly. That's the stuff that will get me in trouble again. "I'm here," he continues, "because I know if I work my ass off over for the next four years, I'll get a full scholarship to any college I want. Krake can do that for you."

"But he's a jerk," I say, keeping my eyes down.

"He doesn't care what color you are. But he is a little, well, homophobic, I guess." My eyebrows raise at his word choice. "Aiden, are you... no, never mind."

My heart beats like a machine gun. I know what he was going to ask, and I'm glad he didn't.

I know the answer. Of course, I do. But I'm not even ready to say it to myself, let alone out loud to someone I barely know.

Mat stands and offers me his hand. I take it, and he pulls me up. His touch is magnetic—there's a strength even in his grip. "We've got a few more throws to do," he says gently.

"Oh, please. *Please,* no," I beg.

"Coach's orders. You don't get tough by disobeying Coach. You get stronger." He puts a hand behind my neck and another on my elbow. He's gentler about it, though.

When we finally finish—after more throws than I could count—Mateo tells me, "Just think. A month of training like that—no throw is ever gonna hurt you."

I'd nod, but I can't move my neck.

"Will you come back tomorrow?"

I want to quit, but his gorgeous brown eyes drown out all logic. Looking at him takes away some of the pain, like my body numbs. I've never had this feeling before. I don't know if I like it. I mean—I love it. But I don't know if I can trust my body or the words that may come out of my mouth.

I swallow hard, burying those thoughts. "Yeah, I'll come back."

"Good," he says. "That's how you earn respect. See you tomorrow."

He slaps me on the butt on the way out. I look down to make sure I don't show any visible signs of excitement. Although everything hurts, a small smile stretches across my face.

3

True Colors

THE NEXT MORNING I let the hot water from the shower soak my neck. When I get out, I stare at my body in the mirror. Flexing my muscles, I release an awkward laugh. Well, it's better to laugh than cry. One day when I flex, maybe I'll see something more than arms as flat as pancakes.

I put on jeans and a simple gray T-shirt. I don't want to wear anything that attracts attention. I style the top of my leaf-brown hair in an attempt at cute spikes. Then I put in my contacts—at least I no longer have to wear glasses.

Flexing my stomach, I lose my smile. For as skinny as I am, I should at least have abs or something, but no.

"Why are you here?" Mateo had asked.

It's not just about finding friends, and that's a good thing, as I'm off to a rock-star beginning. Who will want to be friends with the kid who got a boner?

I brush my teeth, and those sure aren't perfect, either. The dentist says I need braces. Mom can't afford that, though, so I don't smile much in public.

Would karate have been this tough? I'll never know, given I never had a chance to take lessons. I hear Dad's voice in my memories.

"Karate is for wussies."

And when he got drunk, which he did a lot—*"Karate is for pussies. No pussy son of mine is gonna wax on and wax off."*

Dad had spoken like that a lot before he left Mom and me. I can still picture him—long, messy blonde hair covered by a stupid hat. It was a fedora, I think. He wore it in public, and I never understood why. Sure, it covered the hair he never washed, but it made him look dumb.

I never did take karate lessons, but I also sure as hell never joined the football team.

I walk downstairs, and Mom makes some scrambled eggs.

"Oh, honey. You look terrible!" Her sky-blue eyes examine me, and her ash-blonde hair shakes as her head turns side to side in disapproval. "I don't like this wrestling business. Not one bit." She puts her hand on my cheek. "Bruised all over. Why are you doing this?"

It's the question everyone wants to know.

"I dunno, Mom. I just wanna do something."

"Isn't there like a club you can do? Something that doesn't involve physical violence?" she asks. The eggs smell like they're starting to burn, but she doesn't take her eyes off me.

"It'll be okay, Mom. It was our first practice. I gotta get in shape is all." Taking a seat at the kitchen table, I stare at the skillet, where smoke starts to rise.

She sighs, grabs a spatula, and flips the eggs. She puts them on a paper plate with a side of toast. "I don't know. If you look like this much longer—or it gets worse—you're done. You hear me?"

I nod slowly, trying not to wince at my stiff neck.

After breakfast, I hop on the school bus. Putting in my earbuds, I want to listen to some music and not think for as long as possible. I start to rock out to a new band I like, closing my eyes and enjoying the lyrics. "I wanna be normal. I wanna be sane," the singer repeats, and the song soothes me.

Then something wet hits the top of my head. I turn around and some guys laugh at me from the back of the bus. I recognize one of them—the red-headed kid is Logan. He's on the team. The other boys play football, I think.

I better earn their respect for showing back up this afternoon.

I get hit again by a spit wad.

This time, I snap around angrily. "Quit it!"

Red-headed Logan stands up. "What are you gonna do if I don't? Get a boner?" He laughs so hard he snorts. "I can't believe we got a fag on the wrestling team. No one's gonna wanna wrestle you!"

Fag? Really? What are these guys—some idiot wannabe jocks in an old '80s movie? I wish I were brave enough to say the words out loud.

I swallow back my anger, and it rolls into sadness. My eyes burn, and I want to scream at them.

I thought the world was better than this. Even in grade school, we had people talk to us about big ideas like inclusivity.

Some people never got the lesson. Or do they just not care?

I sink into my seat and cross my arms, wishing I could just disappear.

When we finally arrive at school, I race off the bus. Grabbing my books from my locker, I dash to my first-hour class. I'm ten minutes early, but it's better than sitting in the commons and waiting for someone to pick on me.

"Good morning, Aiden," Mr. Samuels greets me. He takes a sip from his coffee cup that reads *I put the Lit in Literature.*

"Hi."

"You're quite early today." He sets his coffee down and narrows his eyes. "How are you feeling?"

He must see the bruise on the side of my face. It took me about fifty throws to learn how to take a fall.

"I joined the wrestling team."

"Going well?" He flashes a sarcastic smile.

"It's going," I mumble. Mr. Samuels walks to my desk. I wish he'd leave me alone. When he approaches, I look up—way up—he's quite tall. He wears a purple short-sleeved shirt that fits tight against his muscular, dark skin along with black dress pants. He's got to be in his thirties, I'd say. Not nearly as old as some of the other teachers.

He examines my face. "What did your mom say about this?" He knows about my home life because of some personal essays I've written. I've never held back on how I feel about my fedora-wearing, drunk father.

"She's not thrilled."

"I wouldn't be, either."

"It's what I have to do to get stronger. What doesn't kill you and all that."

Mr. Samuels scratches the side of his face. "I don't like that saying. What doesn't kill you messes you up, too. Why do you feel you need to be stronger?"

I picture Logan in the back of the bus and all the kids who laughed at me.

"I dunno. I guess I'm tired of feeling weak."

Mr. Samuels crosses his arms. Underneath the purple polo, his thick muscles flex. Why is it so hard for people to understand that I'd like to have that, too?

The first bell rings, letting us know we have five minutes until class begins. Fortunately, Camila enters the classroom and sits right next to me, interrupting Mr. Samuel's awkward staring.

Camila's my only real friend.

But she's more than that, too.

Camila's my girlfriend.

4

Girlfriend

"WHY DIDN'T YOU call me last night?" Camila asks. A few adorable freckles spread around the cutest dimples. Her dark hair frames her face, and her light brown skin glows. Her eyes sparkle, and her smile is the perfect one I'd like to have.

We've been dating since the homecoming dance last month. And, by dating, I mean I see her at the Friday night football games where we sometimes hold hands. During the week, we text funny GIFS and tag each other on hilarious memes.

"Practice kicked my butt." I look over at my English teacher, who has returned to his desk to grade papers.

"I tried calling you." She pouts at me, and I have to force back a smile. When she pouts, her dimples look even cuter.

"I'm sorry." If there's one thing I've learned over the past month, it's that you just need to say you're sorry a lot, even if you don't understand why.

"That's okay." Relief washes over her. "So, how was your first day wrestling? I can't wait to come cheer for you in a match!"

I grunt. "Bring a body bag."

"Huh?" Her dark eyebrows narrow.

"I'm not very good."

Camila crosses her legs. Although the weather is cool, she wears shorts, which creep up, revealing more of her thigh. Something catches my eye. Trust me—it's not anything dirty. There's a bruise, and it looks fresh. Camila tugs at her shorts, covering it up. Why is she bruised?

"You'll get better. It was only your first day," she says. "Why do you wanna wrestle? You never struck me as a wrestler, especially because the boys have to wear that weird thing. What's it called?"

"A singlet."

"Whatever. Isn't it all a little—no, never mind," she says, her lips tightening and forming a straight line.

"What?" I can't help but smile a bit, even if what I think she is going to ask may be somewhat accusatory.

She whispers, "Isn't it all a little gay? Boys grabbing boys?"

I laugh, but I choose not to answer. Especially because right as Camila asks me the question, Mateo walks into our first-period English class.

Unlike me, he looks refreshed. There's not a bruise on his body, not even a little one like Camila has on her thigh. My mind wanders, watching Mateo stroll into our classroom. He wears a Washington Hornets Wrestling T-shirt, and his shoulders nearly burst out of it. His thick hair is parted in the middle and styled so that it barely moves. He nods at me, a tough-guy bro-nod.

Camila catches my eye, and I blush. The last thing I need is for her to see me staring at Mateo. At least with a girlfriend, I stand a chance at redeeming myself with the team and guarding my true self.

I reach for her hand and make sure Mateo sees it. "Hey," I say, trying to think of something else to talk about. "How's, um, how's Tisha?"

Camila shakes her head enthusiastically, and I know I picked the right subject. "That's what I wanted to talk to you about last night! She's dating some scumbag."

"Oh?" I ask, my eyes wandering back toward Mat. He wears shorts, and he sits a couple of desks away from me. My gaze moves down to his legs, which are thick and hairy like a man's. I look at mine, and they look like a little girl's legs. Smooth and skinny. I hate them.

"Did you hear what I said?" Camila asks.

"Huh?" I clear my throat.

"Where is your head?" She sighs. "My best friend is dating some loser, who happens to be on the wrestling team with you, by the way. And you don't even listen!"

"I'm sorry." I need to pay attention. Tisha hangs out with us at the football games, and if she's dating someone on the team, that could be good for me. Someone else to see that I have a girlfriend. "Who is she seeing?"

"That creep, Logan. He's so vulgar," Camila tells me.

My stomach drops, and the bell rings.

"Good morning, class," Mr. Samuels says. I stare at our teacher, but I'm not listening.

I picture how a Friday night double date will work if the other guy in our foursome is calling me a fag and throwing spit wads at me on the bus.

Can this week get any worse?

AT LUNCH, I sit with Camila and Tisha, and I literally hold my breath whenever Tisha looks up.

Please don't let Logan sit with us.

No one answers my prayer because a minute later, the little jerk sits next to Tisha.

"Hey, guys," Tisha says. She plays with her braided hair and smiles all flirtatiously when Logan arrives.

I try not to puke.

"I want you to meet my boyfriend!" she squeals. I put my arm around Camila. I adjust my hand, and then she leans in closer to me. I can't see her shoulder—she wears a long-sleeve shirt, even with shorts. Is her shoulder bruised, too, or something? "This is Logan," Tisha speaks. My skin crawls, as I turn my attention over to him. He looks me right in the eye with an incredibly cocky expression. "We've met," he says to me. He grins, and it's a cheesy know-it-all-look. "Is that your... *girl?*"

"I'm Camila," she says and moves even closer to me. Thank goodness. I need to keep her close.

I ignore him. Tisha's a nice girl. Innocent, sweet. She wears a smile that fills me with jealousy. I'd love to feel that way about someone else. She looks so happy, too. Suddenly, I feel protective. I've never had a sibling but seeing Tisha's happiness fills me with what I can only describe as a brotherly kind of concern. I don't want to see her hurt. I don't think she's even had her first kiss.

Of course, neither have I. Not really. Camila and I have pecked on the lips, but we've never made out, never kissed passionately. Plus, there's this whole other side of me that kind of gets in the way to kissing her for real. It doesn't stop me from snuggling close right now, though.

We've all got secrets, I guess. But if Logan tries to hurt Tisha—

What will you do?

My own voice mocks me. I can get my ass kicked, I suppose. That's about the only thing I'm good at.

Logan's eyes narrow, and he flashes a sinister smile as if he's reading my mind. Then he whispers something into Tisha's ear that makes her giggle.

When the bell rings, Logan takes Tisha's tray, acting all nice. I know it's pretend. No one who does crap like he did earlier is a good guy. We stand, and he bumps into me ever so slightly.

"See you at practice, homo," he whispers.

5

Got Your Back

AFTER SCHOOL, I head to the locker room. The floors must have been cleaned—the smell of strong bleach hits my nostrils, but it's still not enough to cover up the stench of teen body odor.

Just walk away. Quit! I don't need this!

Boys in a sea of singlets line up against lockers, and a cacophony of laughter and chatter bounces off the walls. They go out of their way to avoid me, though, making exaggerated movements to step around me.

Everyone except Logan, that is. He walks right up to me, wearing an icy smile I'd like to smack off his stupid face. He glares at me through narrow, green eyes.

His mouth hangs open like a dog. "So. You got yourself a bitch, eh? Whaduya call it? Fag hag?"

My face burns. "Don't call her that!"

"Ooh. The truth gets under your skin, huh, homo?" Logan cackles and spit flies out of his mouth.

I step closer toward him. He's bigger than me, but who isn't? I'm not going to let him talk about Camila like that. "You call me whatever you want. But leave my girlfriend alone."

"Or what, big boy?" He licks his lips.

"I'll start by telling her all about you. You know she's best friends with Tisha." That wipes the smirk off his face. He pulls at one strap of the singlet, and it snaps back hard against his chest.

"You say anything about me, and I'll kick your ass." He steps closer, and I feel his breath. It stinks of peanut butter.

"Hey, Logan!" Mat shouts. "Dude, if you wanna make out with another guy, that's your choice. But do it after practice. C'mon. We're late." Thankfully someone here can give Logan a taste of his own terrible medicine.

Logan's face turns as red as his hair.

"Screw you, man," Logan says. But his voice is soft. Mateo's our team captain and the superior wrestler. How much will Logan challenge him?

"What did you say?" Mateo quickly gets in Logan's face. Mateo puts his hands on his hips, and his biceps twitch. He's not only the authority—he's much bigger than the little jerk, too.

Logan looks down and kicks his foot at the concrete locker room floor. "Nothin'. Sorry. Be right there."

"Uh-huh," Mat says. "Get going, then." Logan marches out of the locker room. The other wrestlers quickly turn away and follow him out. Mat turns to me, his brown eyes warm and empathetic. "You, okay?"

No, I'm *not* okay. I'm forcing myself to be here to prove a point— that I'm not a quitter, and that a bunch of jerks won't get under my skin. But they have. I don't say any of this. I just shrug.

"Logan's an ass. Let me teach him a lesson today." Mateo rubs the little stubble growing on his chin. "You'll like it."

"Okay." I can't help but return the smile. Mateo's so cute, and he's the only one of us that looks good in a singlet. I just have to make sure I don't show any visible form of excitement.

"Let's go." I follow Mateo out. We make our way through bright white halls, move past a gymnasium, and head toward the corner of the school where we have our own special facility. Coach Krake stands at the entrance to the wrestling room with a whistle around his neck.

He wears his red Hornets polo, and I wonder if he ever does laundry or has any other clothes.

"You boys are late," he says through gritted teeth. "Let's all start with one-hundred burpees as a reminder that we begin promptly at 2:45. Not a minute after."

Everyone groans and glares at me. Not Mateo. Me. Naturally, this is *my* fault. I can't seem to start on the right foot.

By the time we finish the burpees, I can't feel my arms. But it's time to practice basic throws again, Coach instructs. "Mateo. Show them again how it's done."

"Logan," Mateo says. "C'mere."

Logan approaches hesitantly, green eyes trying to read our Captain.

"The secret is all in hip placement and balance," Mateo tells us. "Watch." He grips Logan by the back of the neck, and then he spins one-hundred and eighty degrees. When he turns around, Mateo slams his hip right into Logan's groin. Logan's face explodes, and I cover my face so no one can see my grin. Then Mateo snaps him over his shoulder. Logan crashes on the mat, and Mat moves right into a pin.

"If you do it like that, you knock the wind out of them. Then you slam right on top for a pin, and they'll have no stamina to kick out," Mateo says. He looks at me, flashes a smile, and his right eye twitches—not quite a wink but enough of one that I know that was just for me. My stomach flips, and my chest feels warm. Every second I'm around Mateo, I like him even more.

After a pause, Mateo adds, "Coach taught me that one."

Why does he have to compliment that jerk?

Krake grins. "Nice form. That's right. Knock the air out of them on every throw. Then they can't breathe. If they can't breathe, you'll get the pin. Now line up by weight. I want fifty throws from each of you."

I get paired up with another small kid like me. "I'm DeMarcus, but my friends call Demented," he says with a smile. I brace for a look of disgust or judgment. But I don't see anything like that from DeMarcus. He offers his hand.

I shake it. "Aiden."

I grip him, practice the form of the throw slowly, and toss him down. Then I offer my hand and pull him back up.

"Not bad. But if Krake is watching, you better throw harder than that," DeMarcus says. He smiles at me, and I instantly like him. He's got bright white teeth that shine against his dark skin. His hair is buzzed short, and he has cherry-red lips that reach to the corners of his face when he smiles.

"Thanks."

"Everyone will forget about yesterday, you know. It'll just take time," he says, as I prep for another throw.

"How do you know?"

"Um, do you remember Pledge Penis?"

"Oh, yeah." I laugh. "In seventh grade, some kid wouldn't stand for the Pledge of Allegiance. His teacher made him, and it turned out he had a boner and was hiding it. I can't believe I forgot. That was so funny."

"Yeah, to you. Not to me. I'm Pledge Penis," DeMarcus says, but he laughs a little.

"No way!"

"*Yes* way."

"When did people forget?"

"I owned it and laughed at myself, and some kid called me demented. I thought *Demented* was a better nickname than Pledge Penis."

I give him a warm smile.

Krake walks over and watches us, his dark eyes moving up and down. DeMarcus nods at me. I swing my hip in and throw him with as much might as my body allows.

It's not very good, but DeMarcus helps by selling the throw. When he lands, he releases a loud groan and holds his stomach like he's been hurt.

"Not bad, kid," Krake says. "Keep it up." He walks to the next pair. No jokes. No insults.

I help him up, but that catches Krake's attention. "He can get up on his own. Don't you help anyone up once you knock them down. You got that, new kid?"

"Yes, sir," I say. DeMarcus hops up. Krake nods and moves on to the next pair.

"Why is he so mean?" I ask DeMarcus.

"I dunno."

"Thanks for, uh, faking a little extra pain."

He chuckles. "You do the same for me, all right?"

"Absolutely. I got your back."

We each finish fifty throws, and Coach Krake blows his whistle. "Time for one-on-one." He looks around the room, his eyes settling on each one of us for a brief moment.

Then his lips curl into a nasty grin, and he raises his eyebrows as if delighted at whatever he's thinking.

"Aiden. Logan," he announces. "You two are up first. Let's go!"

Oh, no.

6

Logan vs. Aiden

"I'VE BEEN LOOKING forward to this," Logan whispers. My skin crawls with disgust.

"Touching me?" I retort, glaring at him. "I bet you have."

He scowls and runs both hands up the sides of his red hair to make spikes. He tries to look tough, but it makes him look like a little kid.

I can do this. He's just a stupid boy.

Krake blows the whistle. Logan moves in quickly.

"Let's get some excitement in here," Mateo calls out. "This half of the room—you all shout for Logan. This half, Aiden."

"C'mon, Logan!" His half is a lot louder than those who are supposed to cheer for me. They pound on the thick mats with their fists and feet, and it sounds like drums. "Go Aiden!" Well, at least one person is on my side. *Thanks, DeMarcus.*

I kick at Logan's shin and attempt to trip him, but he hooks my leg. Then he lunges in and sweeps my standing leg, knocking me hard on the ground. The wind blows out of me, and Logan jumps on top for a pin. A sharp pain sears through my ribs. I can't breathe, and my eyes fill with hot tears.

Logan gets the pin, and his half of the room screams, along with a handful of applause by wrestlers who were supposed to root for me.

Logan doesn't offer to help me up. "That's my boy," Coach Krake says. "Notice how Aiden couldn't breathe. Logan snuck in a punch to the ribs. Now, if a ref sees that, you'll get penalized. But if you make sure the ref is opposite of you, that's a great strategy. Curl your fingers into a tight fist."

Krake lifts his right arm to demonstrate. "Logan—demonstrate this again on Aiden as I walk the team through the strategy." Logan scoops me off the floor with his left arm as Krake instructs. "Then on the way down, you slam your knuckles into your opponent's ribs. If he can't breathe, he won't get out of the pin. Show them." Without warning, Logan shoves me back on the floor and jumps on top of me. Then he hits me in the ribs, and a sharp pain rushes through my midsection all the way to my ears.

Krake bends down and whispers in my ear. "Don't worry. We'll destroy whatever disease is inside of you. One throw at a time. I'll make you all better. You have my promise." His hot breath smells like tobacco, and my stomach churns. Tears blur my vision. God, I can't cry. Not in front of everyone. When they stand, neither offers to help me. "Time for endurance training, Everyone line up at the edge of the room. Suicides and burpees!" He cackles and wipes spit from his mouth.

I can't move. Mateo approaches, his eyes black with anguish, and offers me his hand.

"Leave him," Krake commands, his stare cold and unfeeling. "He can get up by himself."

"Coach, he looks—"

"I *said* leave him," Krake interrupts Mateo. "In fact, for every second Aiden stays on the ground, that's five extra minutes of endurance training for everyone else. Starting now."

I roll to the side and put my hands on the floor. My ribs roar.

"One. Two. Three." Coach counts methodically, an icy smile hovering on his face.

It takes everything I have left, but I rise to my feet.

"Quicker than I thought," Krake says, and it almost sounds like a compliment. "Line up."

There's no way I can run, let alone do a burpee. I waddle to the edge of the room, placing a hand on my side. My breath comes up shallow, and each inhale makes me wince in pain.

Coach blows his whistle, and the rest of the team sprints ahead, completing the first suicide. I force my legs to jog, but I can't move my arms. The team begins the first round of burpees. I jump down with them, but the moment I place my hands on the floor, I yelp.

"What is it?" Krake asks, rolling his eyes.

"Coach, my side hurts. Bad." Hot tears break free and roll down my face.

He stomps over to me, grabs my singlet, and pulls it down off my shoulder. His eyebrows lift in mild surprise. I gasp at the sight of my body, embarrassed that everyone can see.

My ribs are black and blue.

"Should have known you'd be as fragile as a Barbie doll," Krake mutters. "Probably cracked them. Well, looks like you'll be on the sidelines 'til they heal. Mateo—get the school nurse."

"Yes, Coach," he says and runs out of the wrestling room. "You two, help him up and get him off the mat. Everyone else—line back up. We still have training to do."

DeMarcus and a kid named Jeff sit me on the edge of the room on a rolled-up mat. "You okay?" DeMarcus asks. His lips form a straight line. There's an obvious concern in his eyes.

"I dunno," I say. "It hurts a lot."

"That was pretty crappy what they did. First Logan, then Coach both slamming and hitting you like that," DeMarcus says.

"Hey," Jeff snarls at both of us. "That's our training. Get tough or get out." I've never really hung out with the guy as a friend, but we were assigned a class project in eighth grade. He seemed nice then, but his tone shocks me now.

"I wanna train, too," DeMarcus tells him. "But we don't have to hurt each other like this."

"Coach is just making us strong." Jeff pulls at his singlet, which fits tightly against his pale white skin. Blue eyes look me up and down, and they're filled with disgust. "When we have a real match, you think anyone else is gonna be all nice and gentle? He's tough on us so that we're prepared. He's won more wrestling titles than any other coach in the region."

DeMarcus rolls his eyes but doesn't say anything. I'd laugh if it wouldn't hurt. Somehow DeMarcus hasn't been brainwashed like everyone else. At least not yet.

The school nurse runs into the wrestling room with Mateo, and she shakes her head disapprovingly. "I've told the principal a hundred times that this shi—stuff is bad for our students." She sighs. "Let me take a look, honey." She gets on one knee to examine my ribs. She's an attractive lady with thick, dark hair. Lots of boys like to joke about pretending to be sick so she can examine them. A few kids in the back snicker at something as she touches me. "Oh, boy. I recommend getting you to First Care and getting an X-ray. Okay?"

I hate doctor's offices, but it's better than this hell hole.

"I'll call your parents."

"It's just my mom," I tell her. "She'll be getting off work soon."

"Okay. I'll drive you." She stands, puts her hands on her hips, and glares at Krake. "Hey, Coach. We're going to First Care. Again."

He tilts his head back and laughs.

"Oh, Nurse Bradford. Why don't you take Aiden to a real medical professional? You know, someone who has a little more experience than passing out Tylenol to cramping girls."

Blood rushes to Nurse Bradford's cheeks. "Oh, I'd have some words for you if there weren't so many kids around. Guess I'll just share them with the principal."

"You do that." Coach lifts up a hand and waves. "Bye-bye."

"I need one of the other students to help," she tells him. "To help lift him up and take him there."

He smirks. "Fine. Mateo. Go with them."

"Yes, Coach."

Mateo puts a beefy arm around me and helps me out of the wrestling room.

So much for earning everyone's respect.

7

A Dinner Date

"GOOD NEWS AND bad news," the doctor says. She's young and wears a shiny blue polo over khakis.

My eyebrows raise.

"Nothing broken, only bruised. That's the good news."

"And the bad?"

"They'll need at least a week to heal. No practice for a week." Her face remains expressionless. She sits at a computer and punches in some data.

"Oh, no," I mutter with a laugh.

"I can see your disappointment. We'll wrap up the paperwork and get you out of here in a few minutes, Aiden." The doctor leaves us alone.

I had asked Mateo to join me in the room, and Nurse Bradford stayed in the general waiting area. Mom will meet us here as soon as she can.

I lift up my shirt again and look at the black and blue. "I'm glad they're not broken," I mumble. "I don't want Logan or Coach to think I'm that brittle."

Mateo's eyes glance at my ribs, and his face melts with sympathy. He brushes his thick hair, still parted in the middle, out of his eyes. "Yeah."

"Thanks for coming with me. Can I ask you something?"

Mateo walks over to the patient bed, where I sit on a rolled-out sheet of sanitary paper.

"Is it always gonna be this bad?"

"You keep showing up, no matter what. You take a beating but come back. In time, you'll earn their respect." He puts his hands in the pockets of the shorts he threw on before leaving school. We both put some clothes on over our singlets. I'm pretty sure my head could be pouring out blood, and I'd still not want to wear that stupid thing in public.

"What if I don't want their respect?" I cross my legs. At first, I cross them completely, one leg hanging over the other. That's too feminine, I think, and adjust so it's only my ankle over my knee. "What if it's not worth it?"

"That's your call. What else will you do?" His eyes glance at my legs. *Does the way I cross them make me look gay?* I pull at the bottom of my T-shirt, frustrated at my own thoughts.

"Nap. Netflix. Eat. Who cares?" I laugh, hoping he'll return it. He cracks a small smile. "My first two days have been absolute chaos."

"I hope you don't quit." His brown eyes soften, and his smile grows. Oh, just a little thing like that—the way his lips part and reveal those beautiful teeth—makes butterflies dance in my gut.

"Why?" I ask softly, hoping he'll say something perfect. *Tell me you like me. Really like me. That would be amazing.*

He puts a hand on the bed close to me. My tummy flips like I'm on a carnival ride, butterflies acting more like hornets raging war with my hormones. "You've seen these guys, Aiden. Wrestlers can be assholes. Lots of, I dunno, testosterone, anger, and people just wanting to fight. That's not me. I'm not in it for those reasons. It's nice to have someone else like me."

Like *me?* I swallow hard. I feel high like I could float away. How similar are we? I put a hand on my tingling stomach, trying to calm it.

There's so much about him I want to know, but I want to be careful about what words escape my mouth. "Why do you do it?" I ask, my voice nearly shaking. I'm nervous as hell—have I finally found someone who's like me? And who might possibly like me back?

"I told you." He shrugs. "I'm good at this. It's my ticket to college."

"There's gotta be other ways to get to college."

"Maybe."

The door swings open, and Mat steps away from the bed.

"Oh, honey. Are you okay?" It's Mom, and her face washes with a mix of concern and frustration. Her ash-blonde hair looks messier than usual, which means she's had an extra crazy day at work.

"Yeah. Just bruised."

"I tell you, I don't like this wrestling. Not at all." She looks over to Mateo. "Who are you?"

"That's Mateo, Mom." He extends his hand.

"Hi, Missus Rothe."

"Not a missus anymore. But nice to meet you, too." She studies him closely. Their eyes lock, and it gives me a second to look at him carefully, too. It's really not fair that someone should be so athletic and so handsome. He steadies his breathing, his shirt clinging tightly to a ripped chest. Dimples form when he smiles.

A nurse enters the room with the paperwork and hands it to my mother. We both take our eyes away from Mateo. I feel flushed and warm, dozens of different emotions hitting me. I'm not used to feeling so much at once. "You're all set. You can check out up front," the nurse tells us.

"You can send this bill straight to the school. Don't you think so, Aiden?" Mom asks.

"Yeah, drop it off in Coach Krake's mailbox. He'll love that." I roll my eyes, but Mateo laughs. It's contagious, and it gets me laughing, too.

"I think this coach and I will have a conversation about how he treats my son," she says out loud but not to anyone in particular.

My smile vanishes. "Please, no, Mom."

"Mateo, why don't you join us for dinner? It's our way of thanking you for staying here with Aiden while I was at work," she says, ignoring my plea.

"Cool. I'll text my parents."

Mom checks out, and Mat and I follow. Nurse Bradford left, apparently, when Mom arrived.

"Where would you boys like to eat?" she asks. "Let's go out. I don't feel like cooking."

"Do you like Mexican?" Mateo asks. "My uncle works at Hacienda. Great food, and he'll give us a discount."

I sure like Mexican. It's hot and spicy, and if it tastes as good as it looks... I feel my cheeks redden at the thoughts, and I look out the car window. What the heck is wrong with me?

"Sounds wonderful. Hacienda it is."

Mat and I both sit in the back since Mom has a work bag overflowing with papers in the passenger seat. My eyes dart to his thick legs.

He catches me looking at him, and I turn away. My ears burn. Get a grip, Aiden!

When Mom parks at the restaurant, we hop out. Mateo takes the lead and greets the host in Spanish. She sits us at a nice booth in the back.

A server brings us some water, and we look over the menu.

Then I hear a boy's laughter that immediately makes me sick. Tisha and Logan sit two booths over, apparently on a date.

Crap.

I lift the menu up high to cover my face, hoping they don't see us. In all the restaurants in this stupid town....

8

Someone's Always Bigger

"OH, NO," MOM says. She puts down her phone and presses her hands against her temples. "Ugh!"

"What is it?" I ask.

"UGH!"

"Mom, what?"

"Oh, you know that hiring committee I'm on? I had rubrics to fill out for each interviewee, and those have to be turned in tonight. I forgot and left them on my desk." She reaches into her purse and hands me her debit card. "You guys get dinner on me. I'll be back as soon as I can. Aiden, just order me whatever you get. Get it to go. I'm sorry." She rushes out of Hacienda.

"What's your mom do?" Mateo asks.

"She works at a children's advocacy place."

"That's cool."

Logan glares right at us. At this moment, I wish I had superhero powers to turn invisible.

"Ignore him," Mateo whispers.

"What's good here?" I ask, trying to do what Mat says.

"Everything."

We eat chips and salsa and do our best to ignore Logan's stare. Eventually, Logan and Tisha get up to leave, and I breathe a sigh of relief.

But Logan stops at the door and talks loud enough for us to hear. "Tell your mom hi from me," he tells Tisha.

"You sure you don't wanna ride with us?" She laces her hands together, and her face reveals disappointment. She's beautiful, even in her sadness, perhaps more so. Her dark hair is straightened and not braided today. The white in her eyes shines against her darker skin. Logan doesn't deserve her. What does she see in this jerk?

"No, I'm gonna join Mat and Aiden. I'll get a ride." He kisses her on the cheek, and I wanna puke.

Without asking, Logan slides in next to Mateo. Logan's green eyes widen, and he nearly drools, as if he's been holding back a hundred insults he couldn't say while Tisha was here.

"So, you two dating now?" Logan asks. He laughs at his own question, and his tongue hangs out of his mouth like a dog. "I didn't know you swung that way, Captain."

Mateo's right hand lunges at the back of Logan's neck. Mateo's fingers dig into skin, and Logan groans. "Who do you think you're talking to?" he asks. Even Mateo's knuckles look like muscles. "And knock it off with your B.S." He lets go, and all the color runs from Logan's face.

"I wonder what Krake would say if his star JV athlete was hanging out with the Washington High homo." Logan laughs again. None of this is right. Mateo is a nice guy, doing what a team captain should be doing. How the hell does getting one boner make me gay? It could happen to any guy!

Regardless, when I'm ready to be me—to speak my reality—it should be under my terms. Not some jerk's.

Mateo reaches for Logan's neck again, but Logan slides out of the booth. "Oh, hey." Logan sneers. "Look who decided to have a team meal," he says and gestures toward the parking lot.

It's the *varsity* wrestling squad.

Mateo's face turns pale.

"What the hell, man?" Mateo glares at the red-headed jerk.

"If you end up jumping to varsity, I thought they should know who they'd be wrestling with." He crosses his pale arms and cackles. "Maybe I'll get the nod to replace you as JV captain. Wouldn't that be great, Aiden?"

What makes a person so cruel?

"I haven't done crap to you," I say. I rise out of the booth, and a couple of servers stare at us. "Why are you such an ass?"

He scowls at me.

The door opens, and it's Tanner McQueen, the varsity captain. "Outside. All of you. Now."

Tanner's ripped from top to bottom. He's at least a foot taller than Mateo. Mat's only a freshman, and although he's rumored to become the best the Washington Hornets wrestlers have ever had, Tanner Mc-Queen is the best.

Mateo walks outside, and I follow. His legs shake, and Logan's lips curl into an impossibly large grin.

The varsity team stands behind Tanner.

"Logan texted me that there's a problem with JV," Tanner says. "What's the problem?" His voice sounds stupid, like he's been hit in the head too many times.

"The problem is that we have a homosexual relationship between our captain and this twig," Logan quips. "I think that's an unnecessary distraction if our team wants to win the state championship again."

Mateo glowers at Logan. "First, that's not true," Mateo states firm-ly. "I'm here because Aiden got hurt in our practice."

"This doesn't look like the nurse's office," Tanner barks. He laughs like he's made a joke, and I have to force my eyes to stay still or they'd roll into the back of my brain at his stupidity.

Mateo sighs. "Logan is lying to you."

"Mateo's telling you the truth," I say and step forward.

"We're a championship team," Tanner declares. He says the word slowly, expressing each syllable, like an idiot. "Champ-i-on-*ship* teams require strict diligence from their leaders. No distractions or"—he shakes his head, glaring at Mat—"whatever this is."

"This is bull," Mateo says.

"What did you say?" Tanner's shaved head contrasts with Mateo's thick, dark hair. Mateo's ripped, too. But Tanner's taller and bigger.

"I'll take care of my team," Mateo says. "You take care of yours."

"That's what I'm doing," Tanner tells him. "I think we need to teach you a lesson about who's in charge."

9

Parking Lot Showdown

TANNER LUNGES AT Mateo, but Mat steps to the side. Tanner looks like a semi-truck that lost control of its brakes, and he skids on the pavement.

When he does stop, he turns slowly and licks his lips. "Oooh, this is gonna be fun. You're as good as they say, huh?"

"Better," Mateo replies, and he crouches in a stance. My heart leaps into my throat. Tanner has at least fifty pounds on him, not to mention three more years of experience.

"We'll see about that." Tanner rushes Mateo again. He locks his fingers around Mat's neck and pulls him close. Mat's feet dig into the parking lot ground for stability. Tanner moves in for a throw, but Mat blocks it, his forearm knocking Tanner's hip away. Tanner laughs, moves in to attempt the throw again, but no—it's a fake-out. Tanner spins to the front, kicks his right leg in between Mateo's feet and sweeps him. Mat falls hard, and I gasp. There are no wrestling mats out here to protect his back or his head. Mateo grits his teeth, and when Tanner lands on top of him, Mat rolls quickly, flipping Tanner over.

Mateo's on top! Even though Tanner has fifty pounds on him, Mat flips him over. Mat locks his arms around Tanner's neck, embracing him tightly for a pin, but Tanner's too strong. He breaks free and shoves Mat off him. Mateo flies about three feet in the air.

Mat lands on his feet, but now a few of the other varsity guys grab him, locking arms behind his back.

I run toward him. "No!" I yell, and Logan kicks me in my stomach. Falling forward, I throw out my arms, and I scratch my hands and knees on the concrete.

Logan pulls my hair, and I scream. "Which side's your bad one?" he asks.

Being that I've just gotten out of the doctor's office, I pray that he'll hit me anywhere but there. I don't answer, but I place my hands over my right side.

"Good to know," he says and spits at me.

Mateo yells, and I climb onto one knee. Tanner slugs him in the stomach with an uppercut and then hits him in the side of the face with a hook.

"Coward!" I yell.

That gets his attention.

"You mean the senior captain of the wrestling team can't handle a freshman one-on-one?" I ask, spittle flying out of my mouth.

He laughs and struts over to me. My arms tremble, but at least he leaves Mateo alone. "Oh, I can handle him, but this is more fun. You should have kept your mouth shut, homo." Tanner pulls me up. "Hey, Logan. Wanna practice that throw I showed you?"

"Hell, yeah," Logan answers through laughs. He grabs me and swings me around. His stance is wide, each foot outside my own. It's a throw I don't know, and I flip over his hips. I land hard on my back. Mateo roars, breaking free from the varsity wrestlers holding him.

He slugs Logan in the face.

Then Mat faces Tanner, and they lock arms again. Tanner throws a knee into Mat's stomach, flips him over his shoulder, and lands on top of him.

Tanner elbows him in the face. "This is your warning, idiots. Our team has standards, and you're living well below them." He spits at

Mat. "Even if I, uh, understood your choices or whatever—" His face twitches like he's trying to think of the words he wants to say. "You're a distraction to the team's goals. We win. We don't date each other. Understand?" He doesn't wait for a response. Instead, Logan and the others raise their hands and give Tanner high-fives. Then they walk away.

I want to puke.

The varsity squad and Logan get in their cars. Engines come to life, and tires squeal. The smell of burned rubber lingers in the air as the jerks peel out of the parking lot. Mateo scrambles to his feet and helps me up.

"Thanks," I say.

His face is beet-red. "I'm not gay, you know." He says it harshly, and it scares me.

"Um," I stutter. "I never thought you were."

"Yeah, but *they* do." He looks fiercely into my eyes. "Because of *you.*"

Nausea rises in my throat. "I'm not gay, either."

It's a lie, one I've told myself over and over again. But it's a lie I'm willing to tell if I can keep Mat on my side, and maybe keep us from getting beat up again.

He looks me over. "Yeah?"

I nod. "Yeah."

He shrugs and looks down the street. "Those guys are a bunch of douchebags."

"That's sayin' it rather nicely," I tell him, and it makes him chuckle.

He takes several deep breaths, staring down the now empty road. "You okay?"

His beautiful brown eyes widen, and I wish I could tell him the truth about me. He should know what he's really fighting for—not defending me against a lie but standing up for me against hate.

Isn't the truth worth fighting for?

"They at least didn't get my ribs. But now more of me hurts." More of me than I can honestly tell him. "You gonna tell Krake about this?"

He snorts. "You crazy? Krake would be on their side."

I shake my head. "Then I'm done with this. Look, man, I get your reasons. You're good. You could have taken Tanner if it was a fair fight, and he's incredible. But I'm done."

He frowns. "I wish—I dunno." He clears his throat. "I could help you. Private training. Just you and me. What about revenge? You quit now, and Logan will give you hell for the next four years of high school."

"Maybe I could move."

"Yeah, but every school's got a kid like Logan." Mat moves closer to me. His right hand reaches for me like he's going to put an arm around my shoulder. Then he puts his hand in his pocket, but he steps closer. His shoulder almost brushes against me.

My heart races. I like Mateo. I *really* like Mateo. My body turns warm, and I have to look away. "You'd really work with me one-on-one?" I ask, my voice way too high.

"Hell, yeah. I want to see you kick Logan's ass." He removes his right hand from his pocket. It approaches me, slowly, and then it settles over my shoulders. His hand squeezes my shoulder, only for a second, and then he lets go.

It wasn't a long touch, but my heart is beating so fast I'm sure Mateo can see it.

I laugh, and it sounds lame. Not manly or attractive at all, but he doesn't seem to notice or mind.

Swallowing hard, I try to get a grip on my emotions. I have to admit I'd like to kick Logan's ass, too. Me standing on top of that loser bully giving him a dose of his own medicine—yeah, that would be a pretty nice sight to see. "Okay. I guess. But, I dunno, if it gets much worse—"

"How much worse can it get?"

10

Mom Knows Best

"IF YOU THINK for one second that I'm letting those punk-ass idiots get away with this, then you're loony!" Mom yells. I sit in the backseat next to Mateo, who keeps his head down. Mom came back a few minutes after the varsity team and Logan left. The fact that we were just hanging out in the parking lot immediately aroused her suspicions, and we couldn't wipe the dirt off our clothes fast enough.

"We're going to the principal right now. I've got a bill to drop off and a hell of a lot to say!" The car accelerates with her anger. The seatbelts lock tightly against our chests when Mom brakes at a stoplight. Mateo looks at me with wide-eyed concern—perhaps somewhat for our lives if Mom continues to drive like this, but mostly because I know he doesn't want this story to get back to Krake.

"Mom, please. We're fine!" I beg, tugging at my seatbelt.

"Fine? You're not *fine*. Something's going on here. First, a visit to the doctor." She hits the accelerator, and the car peels out. "You could have had broken ribs! And now—what happened in that parking lot?" She glares at me through the rearview mirror.

"Nothing. Please drop it." Sweat trickles down my face. "I promise. We're okay."

"And what about your parents, Mateo? Will you be lying to them like my son is lying to me now?" Mom doesn't hold back.

"Missus Rothe—"

"I told you I'm *not* a missus," Mom snaps.

"*Miss* Rothe—" Mat's voice cracks.

"And I don't go by my jerk ex-husband's name. It's Miss *Gardner.*" Her hands tighten around the steering wheel, and she takes a sharp right turn, heading straight to the high school. My only hope is that everyone's gone by now. It's after six in the evening.

"*Lo siento.*" The color rushes away from Mateo's face, and he bounces a knee. "I'm sorry, Miss Gardner. My parents will be upset, yes." Mat looks at me for help.

"Mom, you don't understand. It's like being a tattletale. This will only make things worse. You want me to get hurt more? Because that's what will happen if you make a big scene about this."

She opens her mouth wide and forces a laugh that sounds creepy and demonic. "Oh, really! No, I don't care about what people think of tattletales. If something is wrong, you do something about it." I open my mouth, but she catches my eyes in the rearview mirror. "*Period!*"

Mom pulls up outside the school, and I pray we don't run into Coach Krake. How awful would he make our lives? And even if I just quit, Mateo won't. This could really put him in jeopardy. We follow behind Mom, and she pulls on the main office door from the entry hallway.

Locked. Thank goodness! The lights are off, and Mom peers through the window.

"Guess everyone's gone home for the day," I say with too much cheer.

She looks around for any sign of life. "Where's this wrestling room? I want to see if anyone's there."

I reach for her arm. "Mom, please. Just trust me on this. I know you think you're doing the right thing, but Mateo's our JV captain. He's got a lot more riding on this than me."

Mom shakes her head. She opens her mouth to answer, but another voice interrupts.

"Can I help you?" The door opens after all, and my heart pounds.

Please don't let it be some authority who will make this worse, and let Mom just be quiet!

We turn to face the man who opened the door. Then he says, "Hey, Aiden and Mateo. What are you doing here so late?" Then he catches my mom's eyes. "You must be Aiden's mother." His eyes widen, and I can't help but think that Mr. Samuels is looking at Mom the same way I first looked at Mateo. Mom blushes, and I'm grateful for the distraction. He offers his hand. "I'm Lloyd Samuels. I teach English here."

"Oh." Mom shakes his hand, and her face reddens more. "Nice to meet you. I'm Miss Gardner. Susan. Call me Susan."

"Can I help you with something? I was here late grading essays. If I take them home, they don't get done." For a man who spends so much time reading and grading, Mr. Samuels is in great shape. Mom's eyes lock on his thick biceps, and my face burns—is she *checking out* my teacher? She looks at me, and I beg her with my eyes to keep quiet. "Um," she starts. "Well... I was looking for the principal."

Mr. Samuels glances over his shoulder. "I'm sorry. It looks like they've all gone home for the day. Is there anything I can help you with?" He turns from Mom to Mateo and me. "Boys, you look a little rough. Did something happen?"

We both shake our heads.

"Well, Aiden got hurt in practice. They both had a rough practice today," Mom says. I breathe a small sigh of relief. If that's all she says, then maybe we'll be okay.

"Wrestling." Mr. Samuels rolls his eyes.

"I don't much care for it," Mom says.

"Well, don't tell Coach Krake, but I don't, either."

"Really?" Mom asks. "Why not?"

Oh, please! Let us go home.

"I don't want to talk down something that's brought this school a lot of recognition," Mr. Samuels says. "Mateo, everyone says you're the next star."

"No, please. Tell me more. Is it safe for my son?" Mom asks. "I have some serious concerns."

"Well, for starters, I don't like any fighting that's just about fighting. There's no self-defense to it. It's just about roughing each other up."

"Uh-huh," Mom says, her head nodding too enthusiastically. "What else?"

Mr. Samuels folds his arms. "As I said, I don't want to talk about it negatively. At least not here." If he weren't so dark-skinned, I'd have sworn he was blushing. "But what about over dinner sometime? Care to grab a bite to eat and we can talk more? For the sake of Aiden, of course."

Is my English teacher asking my mother out on a *date?*

"I'd love to. When are you free?" Mom's eyes sparkle, and she holds back a smile.

My stomach flips. I'd groan, but I feel completely paralyzed. My mother absolutely can*not* go out on a date with my English teacher! That's just—weird! *Gross!*

Mat looks like he's holding back a laugh. My mouth opens wide to say something, and then he puts his hands over his mouth. He's covering a smile—I know it! I'd smack him if I could move, but this conversation has me in complete shock.

An uncomfortable feeling washes over me. The last thing I want my mother to do is to create a situation that results in me getting bullied even more. I wish I could pull the plug on today and have a restart.

11

A Special Boyfriend

THE NEXT MORNING, I enter Mr. Samuels's class hesitantly. Students move desks around, the steel legs screeching on the linoleum floor.

Camila groans when she sees me, and it makes my heart drop. Her eyes darken with disappointment. She huffs, but even with a frown, her dimples crinkle, and her freckles dance.

"You don't reply to my texts, and you're late. What's going on?"

I glance at her chest. Not because I'm particularly interested in what's under her shirt but rather what's on it. There's a fist in the center. An all-caps word surrounds the fist, but I only make out three of the letters—*ECK*. The rest is covered by a thin hoodie, which she zips all the way up when she catches me staring.

"Sorry. Rough practice. Fell asleep early. Barely could get out of bed today," I reply, my voice soft.

After adjusting her hoodie, she reaches for my hand and holds it. Her eyes show compassion, and she gives me a warm smile, her dimples even bigger. What does she see in me? We've never even made out, and I'm such a crappy boyfriend. I saw her texts last night, but I wasn't in the mood to talk to her.

"Oh, babe. I'm sorry." Her brown eyes narrow as she studies me. "You do look a little rough."

"I know." The bell rings, and Camila releases my hand. I catch Mateo's glance from the corner of my eye, but he turns away. How does seeing me with Camila make him feel? If there's any chance he's like me, maybe he'll be jealous.

"What are you thinking about?" Camila asks.

"Huh?" My cheeks immediately burn. "Oh. Nothing. Sorry."

Camila tilts her head to the side, still trying to figure me out. She runs her hands through her raven-dark hair and turns away.

I get it. I don't know who I am, either.

Mr. Samuels begins class, but he never holds eye contact with me for long. Is he embarrassed, too?

When class ends, he calls for me. "Aiden, can you stick around?" He wears a yellow button-up shirt that makes his skin radiant. "Just for a minute."

My stomach tightens.

"Do you have a study hall?"

I do, but I consider lying. He must want something, and if I don't have the time for him—no. I nod. He could look up my schedule, so there's no use lying.

"What hour?"

"Sixth."

He raises his eyebrows. "Oh, that's the same as my prep period. Would you come to talk with me?"

Of course it is. I should have lied.

"What about?" I mumble, staring at the white, shiny floor.

"You're not in trouble," he says calmly. "I don't want to make you uncomfortable. That's why I want to speak to you."

"Okay," I say. Mr. Samuels writes me a pass to visit him during study hall. What choice do I have?

AT LUNCH, I sit next to Camila. She plays with the zipper of her hoodie, which is all the way at the top of her neckline. Tisha sits across from her, and that means I'll have to see Logan again. Tisha looks very beautiful, and it makes me a little ill. I know who she's trying to impress. She wears a sleeveless dress shirt. Her arms are smooth but firm, a gorgeous light tan to her skin. I want to tell Camila and Tisha the truth about Logan. I'm nervous, though, because it could intensify his hate for me, or even worse, maybe Camila and Tisha wouldn't believe me. Then not only would Logan be pissed, but I'd hurt everyone's friendship.

I have to hang on to Camila. She's so pretty and nice, and most importantly—oh, I hate myself a little just for thinking this—our relationship protects me.

Logan approaches, his green eyes lock eye contact with me, and he sits without even blinking.

"Hi, love birds," he says facetiously. "I bet you two spend every night together." He gives me an I-know-you're-full-of-it laugh. "I bet you're the kind of couple that begs the other to hang up the phone first. Aren't you?"

I try to swallow the lump in my throat. Jesus, what is his deal? Guilt weighs heavily on my chest. Camila fidgets nervously. He's hit a nerve, and my skin heats with anger.

I reach for her hand. "Actually, I haven't been the best at that recently. Maybe I need to spend less time worrying about wrestling, so I can spend more time on my girl." I force my most charming smile, and it works. Camila's eyes soften, and she leans into me.

"I would like that," she says.

I kiss Camila on the cheek, right on her cute dimple. "Can you and I eat alone today? The courtyard is open, and it's a nice day," I say.

Camila's eyes brighten. "Aww. Yeah, okay. A lunch date it is." She turns to Tisha. "We could use some catching up time. He's been so busy with wrestling."

"Well, *I* haven't had any problems spending time with *my* girl," Logan snaps.

Tisha shifts uncomfortably. Is she disappointed that we're leaving? Or is she, perhaps, not thrilled to be alone with Logan, after all? Maybe she *does* sense something about him. But how can I know for sure? "You do you," she tells Camila. Something's off with Tisha, but I'm not sure what. She looks away, and I follow her gaze, which locks on the cafeteria wall clock.

Camila heads toward the courtyard, and Logan gives me the middle finger discreetly. One day I'll break that middle finger off and shove it in his ass. I glance at Tisha one more time before leaving. She scratches her slender arm. I wish I knew what she was thinking.

Once we go outside, I feel instantly better. Just not having that jerk's dragon eyes in my vision makes the world feel lighter.

We take a seat in the shade, away from the other students who gathered outside today. "Are we okay?" Camila asks. Her hoodie breaks open, and I catch a glimpse of that fist again, showing only the letters *ECK*. My mouth opens to ask her about the shirt, but then the serious look in her eyes pulls my head out of my butt. Who cares about some T-shirt? I have to be a better boyfriend.

I take a deep breath and consider how to answer her question. She puts her elbows on the concrete table. Camila wants the kind of closeness that Logan and Tisha appear to have—even if they've only been dating for days. We've been going out for months, but we've never acted like a real couple. I've told myself I've got age on our side—no one expects a lot from a fourteen-year-old, do they?

"You deserve better," I say, and my arms tremble. "And I'll do better," I follow up. "If you'll give me a chance."

That brightens her smile, and she sits up straighter on the outdoor bench. "Of course!" She reaches across the table, and I give her my hand. "You're sweet, Aiden. Why don't we do a movie?"

"This weekend?"

"No, tonight. After practice. I'm tired of waiting to see you just on Friday nights."

Movie nights? Just the two of us? That will involve cuddling, and—oh, no—it will lead to making out, won't it? She'll want me to kiss her, and not just a quick peck on the lips, but like full tongue in mouth and—

Stop thinking.

If this is who you want to be, this is what you have to do.

"I would love that. Just you and me." I force a smile, but I'm pretty sure I just killed a piece of my soul.

12

Study Hall

SIXTH PERIOD ARRIVES, and I give the study hall monitor—a cranky, quirky dude named Mr. Christ, not pronounced like Jesus, but rather like it rhymes with mist—my pass. He examines it closely, and he even smells the note.

"Hmm. Just so you know I'll be checking with Mr. Samuels to make sure you arrived, and not only that but at what time you arrived and what time you leave his classroom." Mr. Christ stares at me like I'm a criminal trying to impersonate someone else.

Geez, dude, I'm leaving study hall not prison.

Slowing down as I approach Mr. Samuels's classroom, I think about what it would be like for a teacher to date my mother. I'm no expert on dating, but Mom *does* need someone. She works hard, and she sees some friends maybe one weekend a month. We used to be a lot closer when I was in grade school. It's not that I don't want to hang out with her. It's just that I usually have other things on my mind. Like watching *Love, Simon* over and over again. Or doing Google image searches of the actor—in incognito mode, of course—hoping he'll be shirtless.

Don't start thinking about that now, or you'll need to walk down the halls with a notebook over your crotch.

Mom needs someone other than me, but does it have to be my teacher? What if he slept over? That would be so freaking awkward.

I open his classroom door. He sits at his desk and drinks a Diet Coke. "Afternoon," he greets me.

"Hey."

"Want a soda?"

"Sure."

"I've got Diet Coke and Mountain Dew. Most afternoons I have one Diet Coke. But when I need an extra kick, I reach for a Dew." He smiles at me, and it's weird having an adult who is my teacher trying to talk casually with me. He folds a red grading book shut and places it on top of a stack of papers. Pushing those to the side, he looks at me, waiting for a response.

"Mountain Dew, please."

He hands me one, and I pop the can and take a big gulp. "You're a very polite young man."

"Thank you, sir." I don't tell him why—Mom wanted to raise a son that wasn't like his deadbeat father.

"How's wrestling going?"

Is *that* what he wanted to talk to me about?

"It's rough."

"It would appear so, by the looks of you." His lips form a tight line.

"Yeah, and it's only been two days." I take another gulp of Dew.

"Your mother clearly doesn't like wrestling." He laces his hands together and putting them on the desk. It's classic teacher-conference mode. Suddenly, I'm nervous like I'm being questioned for doing something bad. My leg bounces.

"It sounds like you don't, either."

He nods, unlaces his hands, and taps his fingers on the desk. "I enjoy wrestling for entertainment. I grew up in the days of The Rock, you know. That was story and show, just entertainment. But this kind of wrestling—well, it's more about fighting than sport, it seems to me," he says, narrowing his eyes. "And it's certainly not about entertainment, unless—"

He doesn't finish his thought, and I don't understand the difference. "What do you mean? What's the difference between fighting and sport?"

His forehead crinkles, and he scratches his chin. "Sport's about discipline and growth."

"Krake is all about discipline."

"Yeah, not that kind of discipline. I guess, I would say discipline is about improving who you are without hurting anyone else." He crosses his arms, and I realize that he's nervous, too. It makes me relax a little, seeing his hands move from one position to another. "If you have to hurt someone to improve who you are, then that's not sport. That's another form of bullying."

"Then how is wrestling a sport?"

"It *is* a sport. I don't mean to say that." He breathes heavily through his nose and takes a sip of his Diet Coke. "I've said too much already. Never mind that."

"Do you mean—" I can't think of the words, but I picture Tanner and the varsity team hurting Mateo and me, Logan laughing and then kicking me in the stomach. Coach Krake breathing like a bull, teaching us tricks to keep our opponents down on the mat, and ridiculing me. "Do you mean, like, it's more about how the sport is coached? Like there are people who are in it for the wrong reasons? Not for sport but to hurt people?"

"Exactly. You're a bright kid. I won't tell you what to do, outside of this classroom, anyway." He cracks a smile. "But be careful. Kids become who their mentors are. You know what I mean?"

"I think so." I finish my Mountain Dew.

"But I didn't bring you here to talk about wrestling."

My stomach drops.

"I came here to make sure it's not weird if I take your mother out," he says. "On a date."

"It's definitely weird."

He chuckles. "Okay, maybe that was the wrong word choice."

"It's funny that even English teachers use the wrong words," I joke.

He laughs harder at my comment than he should. "Yes. We are fallible, as much as I'd like to think otherwise."

I don't know what *fallible* means, but I smile.

"What I mean to say is—I'd like to take your mother out on a date. I know it will be weird. But I don't want it to be"—his lips tighten, and his eyes narrow—*"inappropriate.* I know it will be strange, but will you be okay with it, Aiden?"

He didn't have to ask how I feel about it at all, and it definitely earns him points. It seems that most adults do what they want without asking how others feel, especially teenagers. I think about everything. Mr. Samuels has been a nice teacher and a good guy.

"It's okay with me," I tell him, thinking about all the extra time I may have to do internet searches in private.

"Excellent. So, what can you tell me about your mom? Favorite foods, favorite things to do, that kind of stuff?"

"You tell me how much extra credit I get for answering, and then we'll talk."

Mr. Samuels tilts his head back and chuckles. It's a nice, deep laugh. "How about I provide you with a Mountain Dew anytime you need one?"

"All right," I say, and I tell him a bit about Mom.

13

Practice, Day Three

THE GOOD NEWS is that I don't have to practice today, due to my bruised ribs. My doctor's note is my golden ticket, and I'm out for the week. The bad news is that Coach Krake doesn't let me go home. I'm forced to sit on the mat and watch.

My mind wanders, and I do my best to snap to attention whenever Coach or Mateo teach technique. The thick, black mats sink under Coach's weight, and I try to concentrate on Mateo. If I'm ever going to hold my own, I need to know this crap. When I look at his thick shoulders and tight butt—there are some good things to these stupid singlets, especially a physique like Mateo's—I get distracted too easily.

My gaze shifts to Coach. There's certainly nothing attractive about him. He focuses on takedowns. The wrestlers pair up, and the move is to grab both of your partner's legs with your hands, just below the kneecap, and tug hard. That sends the opponent falling on his back.

DeMarcus pairs up with Jeff, and I cringe when Jeff executes his takedown. He's rough, and his attitude reminds me of Logan's. Jeff's eyes burn with a competitive spirit. He has a slender neck, thin jaw, and milky white skin that contrasts with dark, short hair. DeMarcus has bigger muscles. Nicely defined biceps rip on his dark skin, and when he smiles, he's absolutely adorable.

I root for DeMarcus, but he's too gentle. Krake gives him fifty push-ups and tells him to get tougher, while complimenting Jeff's aggression. DeMarcus completes his push-ups with enthusiasm, but something in his eyes tells me he wishes there was a better program or a better coach. Maybe I'm projecting—I sure as heck wish there was something better than this.

Mateo and Logan avoid each other. Does Coach know anything about what happened with varsity?

As if to answer my question, he makes a special announcement. "Today, you get a unique opportunity. We're gonna have a scrimmage with the varsity team."

The color washes out from Mateo's face. Tanner and the rest of the varsity jerks jog to the center of the wrestling room.

"Tanner! Mateo!" Krake yells, and they approach the center. Tanner scowls, but Mat doesn't back down. "You'll be the coaches today," Krake says. It may be my imagination, but both wrestlers look a little relieved. If Mateo were to take Tanner in front of everyone, that would sure be embarrassing.

For the rest of the practice, I wince as each JV wrestler gets pounded by a varsity guy. They're all unfair matches.

I catch a fair number of glares from the varsity team, too.

When the scrimmages end, Coach says, "All right. Mateo, you take JV for conditioning. Varsity, it's you and me for now. JV—dismissed."

"But what about a battle of the captains?" It's Logan who asks. Of course it is.

"How could I forget?" Krake cackles. "But not today, team. Next Friday, we host a public scrimmage. It's our annual season opener. I will post who you will wrestle soon, but our main event, which is sure to draw plenty of public attention, is Tanner versus Mateo. Friday! So, let's not spoil it tonight."

"Looking forward to it," Tanner says loudly and licks his lips.

"Me, too. One-on-one. No one else to help you." Mat speaks calmly, but sweat runs down his forehead.

Krake looks at each of them and laughs. "I look forward to it, too, men. Now, Mateo, you take these boys and whip them into shape. Tanner and varsity—with me."

I follow the JV team to the weight room. Catching up with Mat, I ask quietly, "Are you scared?"

He glances to make sure no one else is watching. "Yeah. A little." He clears his throat. "Okay, a lot."

"But you can win. Think of what that would do to his ego!" I say.

"And to all the jerks," he adds. "It's just a scrimmage match, but I don't think I've ever wanted to win something more badly."

"I wish I could help you train."

"You can." His words surprise me. "I could use someone to encourage me." We're at the top of the stairs that lead to the high school's weight room. The rest of the team has already gotten to work.

Logan's on a pull-up bar, and his biceps twitch with a golf ball size bulge. Maybe it's not much, but he gets stronger every day. I can't do a single pull-up, and he must have completed a dozen.

Teaming up with another wrestler named Anthony, DeMarcus takes off his shirt. For a young kid, he's already got nice pecs. Anthony spots him, and jealousy stirs inside me. I swallow hard.

"Can you meet me tonight?" I turn my attention back to Mateo. "I don't wanna practice around anyone else. But I could use someone to hold me accountable."

"Yeah, absolutely!" I can't believe Mat wants me to help him. "Oh, crap!"

"What is it? You busy?" He frowns, looking genuinely disappointed.

I forgot about Camila. We're supposed to have a movie night.

I look at Mateo's face, his brown skin, those dark, hypnotic eyes. I can't say no to him.

"No. I'm not busy. When and where?" I smile, thrilled to spend another evening with Mateo. But another piece of me dies on the inside.

I have to lie to Camila again.

14

Mateo's Dojo

STARING AT MY phone, I think of what to text Camila. I type a phrase, then delete, then repeat. I'm at home now, chilling in the living room. Mom pulls her car in the garage.

I am SO SORRY, I text. *Mom saw my test score in Algebra and is making me study. No going out till I bring up my math grade. I SUCK. SORRY.* I end with a heart and a crying face emoji. Then I put my phone away and don't wait for her response. No matter what, it'll make me feel bad. I can't give up a one-on-one with Mateo. I'm gonna help him kick Tanner's ass next Friday, and that's what's most important right now. Of course, there are other reasons I look forward to helping him.

Mom marches inside carrying a stack of folders. She walks right past me into the dining room, tossing the folders on the table.

"Lord, how I am gonna get through all of this by seven?" I think she's just talking to herself, but I answer anyway.

"What's at seven?"

"Crap, Aiden." Her cheeks redden. "I didn't tell you, did I?"

"Tell me what?"

"Sit down." I'm already sitting on the sofa in the living room across from the dining room table. "Never mind. Let me join you." She takes a deep breath and puts a hand on my knee. "I know this may be weird, but I have a question to ask you."

"It's okay, Mom." I laugh a little. "Let me guess. You have a date with Mister Samuels?"

"How did you know?" The red in her cheeks deepens.

I shrug. "It's fine. Will you just warn me if he stays the night? I don't wanna run into my English teacher if I'm wearing nothing but my underwear."

"Oh, honey." I wouldn't have thought it was possible for her to get any redder, but her face is a beet now. "That won't happen. I mean—of course, I would tell you. But, if that would happen it would be a long, long time from now." She fans herself with her hand and stands. Then she kisses me on the cheek. "Thank you for being so understanding. I love you."

"Love you, too." Will you be this understanding with me, if I ever get the courage to tell you who I really am?

Running her hands through her messy hair, she sighs. "I really need a shower."

I check my phone. I have a text of nothing but cry-face emojis from Camila. I reply back with the exact same number of cry-faces plus a broken heart.

Then I text Mateo. *On my way.*

I hop off the sofa and run to my bedroom. I reapply some deodorant, probably too much. My pits are caked with white—it looks like a blizzard under my arms, but they smell good. I put on a clean T-shirt. At first, I grab a Hornets shirt, but I don't feel like showing school spirit. I ditch it for a shirt Mom bought me the last time we went to the mall. It's a gray shirt with a retro Nintendo Game Boy design.

Then I run to the bathroom door. Without opening it, I shout, "Mom, I'm going to Mateo's to study. Be back before you are, I'm sure." She yells something back through the running water, but I can't make it out. I go into the garage and get my bike.

I ride to his house, and nothing could wipe the smile from my face. I haven't had a best friend since last spring. David. He and his family

moved away, and we didn't end on the best of terms, anyway. I spent
the summer before high school pretty much just watching movies and
hanging with Mom. Then when school started, I somehow got a girlfriend. It all kind of happened by accident. I don't know why Camila
likes me, but I'm lucky that she does.

Now, I have the chance for a high school best friend. A friend who's
tough, too, and isn't afraid of the bullies. A friend who… no… I shake
the thought from my head. *Let's not go there. Just focus on friendship!*

The thought returns. I can't stop it.

A friend who is maybe—just maybe—like me? I mean, *really* like me?

No, he can't be. He *told* you he wasn't gay.

Yeah, and you said the same to him! Maybe you're *both* liars!

Maybe? *Maybe.*

But unlikely. I know.

Shut up, stupid brain!

I bike to Mateo's faster. My side hurts a little, but not too bad.
When I get to Mateo's, his dad opens the door. "Nice to meet you,
Mister Hernandez." He shakes my hand.

"Mateo is in the basement." He leads me to the door, and I take
the stairs two at a time.

Mateo stands shirtless with his back to me. He's got earbuds in,
and he picks up a weighted bar and puts it over his shoulders. Then he
squats, over and over.

Sweat trickles down my forehead, and I swallow hard. Don't get
excited. I pull my Game Boy T-shirt down over my crotch just to be
safe. He has back dimples right above his rear, and they deepen with
each squat. The muscles around his back bulge against his tight spine
with each motion.

What does he need me for?

He sets down the weight and looks over his shoulder. Taking out
the earbuds, he says, "Hey, Aiden!"

"Hey," I say, my voice cracking. "Hi."

"This is my training room. You like?"

He's got a bench, a lot of dumbbells, some weighted plates, and even a couple of wrestling mats. "Wow. It's like your own wrestling dojo."

He laughs. "I like that. Mateo's Dojo. You know, I took karate when I was a kid."

"Oh, yeah?"

He nods. "Yeah, just for a bit. Then I signed up for wrestling."

"And no more karate?"

He shakes his head. "Once Krake saw me in action, I guess I was kinda a natural, you know? He told my parents all about the scholarship opportunities for college wrestlers. Told them with my talent and his coaching, that I'd be able to go to any college I wanted for free." He shrugs. "You can imagine my parents took me out of everything and put me in wrestling full-time."

"You know, I wanted to take karate when I was a kid. My dad said it was for pussies."

Mateo flinches. "That's pretty mean to say to a kid."

"Yeah."

"What all happened with your dad?"

I take a deep breath. There's a lot I don't like to think about. Maybe I'll tell him a little. That's what best friends would do, right?

15

Curious Questions

"HE LEFT WHEN I was young." Should I tell him how he had beat up Mom one night when he came home drunk? Or about how he had kicked me in the stomach when I came out of my bedroom, crying and begging for him to stop?

I can still smell the whiskey on his breath and see the droopy eyes, the skin under them puffy and red. He'd adjust his stupid fedora, say something inaudible, spit flying from his mouth, and then kick me right in the gut.

"He's a bad guy. I haven't heard from him in a few years. He used to hurt my mom and me. It's good that he's gone."

"Oh, man. I'm sorry."

"It's okay. I mean—you know what I mean." I force a smile, and I risk a quick glance at his beautiful pecs. That certainly helps. "Anyway, we got a job to do, right? How can I help?"

He scratches his flat stomach. "I'm focusing on legs and core. A strong core supports everything else. Strong legs will give me the stance I need to prevent Tanner from taking me down. But I need a partner for the core work." He lays down on the mat. "Will you hold my legs down? And count for me? It's like a crunch but with a twist. I need to do two hundred, no excuses."

My hands grip his ankles. He wears gray shorts and nothing else, and they're a bit revealing. I focus on the number of crunches and try not to get distracted.

It doesn't help.

He breathes hard, and the muscles in his core twitch with every rep.

Why do I have to feel this way?

It kind of sucks, actually. Why can't I just be a normal dude who helps out a buddy? Why can't I be more disappointed that I bailed on Camila? Instead, I'm staring at Mateo's beautiful, shirtless body while I hold onto his ankles.

"How many so far?" he asks, breathing hard.

"One-seventy," I tell him. "Almost there. C'mon!"

"Thanks." He grunts through the final thirty. I close my eyes—it's torture to look at him and torture not to look at him.

"Two hundred!" I shout. He collapses on the floor, and I let go of his ankles to stretch out my shirt so that it covers any potentially embarrassing situations. There are some unfortunate moments I certainly do not wish to re-experience.

When he finally finishes his training—after eight more exercises that take another hour—we collapse on his wrestling mat. Mateo is sweaty from head to toe, but it doesn't make him less attractive.

"So, tomorrow night? Will you come back?"

"Yeah." I'd do this every night, even if it's self-torture.

"Thanks, man," We sit in silence for a bit, moving so that our backs are against the wall, legs spread out on the wrestling mat. We sit shoulder to shoulder. Then he asks me, "So, you and Camila. What's that like?"

The question takes me by surprise. "She's nice."

"She's hot. How'd you score with her?"

I shrug. "Actually, it was because of a poem."

"A poem?" He raises his eyebrows teasingly.

"Yeah. For Mister Samuels's class. Remember that creative writing assignment when school started?"

"Oh, yeah."

"I wrote a poem. When Mister Samuels passed them back, she asked if she could read it. She liked it, and we started talking. She asked me out. To a football game."

"Cool." His dark eyes are wide with excitement and curiosity like he's trying to figure me out.

"Yeah." *I guess.*

Ask me something else. Tell me what you like. Tell me it's me.

"Have you two, like, you know—made out?" He blushes when he asks, and it makes me chuckle.

I consider lying to score some bro-points. But I don't wanna lie to Mateo if I don't have to, at least about anything besides my sexuality. "No. Not yet. We've kissed a little. But that's all."

"Nice."

"What about you? You have a girlfriend?" My face burns even asking him the questions. There are things I want to know and things I'm scared to know.

Hope is a powerful drug. I'm scared some of his answers could take that away from me. Right now, hope's all I got.

"No. I was going out with like two girls last year. It was just one of those things where we said we were going out. We never did anything but talk and text." A look of disappointment flashes across his face. "I wish I was as lucky as you. Camila's hot, dude."

"Thanks. You know, uh... you could get any girl in our class." *Or a boy like me, if that's what you wanted.* "Especially after you kick Tanner's ass."

"Yeah?"

I study Mateo's face. Does he not realize how attractive he is? And athletic? If amazing people like him have self-doubt, what chance do the rest of us have?

Or, just maybe, it means we're all a lot more similar than I've ever realized. "No doubt. Mat, you're—you know, you're very, uh, good lookin'. For a dude, you know." I make a fist and pound it against his shoulder. He blushes. I want to put my arm around him so bad it hurts, but I lace my fingers together, putting my hands back in my lap. "You could have anyone you want." I swallow the lump that suddenly forms in my throat.

"*Gracias.*"

"Is there, um, anyone at school you like?"

He shrugs. "It's weird. Like, I'll think someone is hot during school. Then I go to wrestling, and practice wipes me." He takes a deep breath, and a mischievous smile grows on his face. "Sometimes I wake up to these really good dreams, though." He laughs.

"What kind of dreams?" I dig my fingernails into the palms of my hands. I know what kind of dreams. I just want to hear him say it.

"Have you ever had, um, well—you know, a wet dream?" He whispers the question, looking at the stairs.

"A few." My smile stretches to my ears. "Who did you dream about?"

He wipes his mouth. "I can't remember. You know how dreams are."

"You had plenty of energy tonight, even after practice."

"Yeah. That's because I'm determined to beat Tanner." He crosses his arms, his classic look of focus and determination back in his eyes. "Can you imagine? A freshman beating a senior?"

"It would be legendary."

"Yeah."

I wish it wasn't a school night. Maybe then he'd ask me to spend the night.

"What are you thinking about? You've got a big cheesy grin."

My cheeks burn. "Oh. I was, uh, I was—I was picturing Tanner's face when he loses to you. That's gonna be priceless."

Mateo laughs. "Thanks for believing in me." He puts his arm around my shoulders. I think I'm going to die. My heart slams against my chest, and my arms tremble. But it's brief—he takes it away. It was just a touch of friendship, I guess.

The door creaks above the basement stairs. "Mateo, it's getting late for a school night," his mother shouts down at us.

"Okay, Ma, I'll be up in a minute," he replies. "Say about seven-ish tomorrow? You'll come back?" He stands, offers me his hand, and helps me up. I smile at the irony—even after all that practice, he's got strength I've never known.

He pulls me up to my feet. "Yeah."

"Thanks, Aiden." We stand face-to-face for a second, but it feels like an eternity. What would it be like to kiss him? To feel his lips press against mine as he pulls me close with those strong arms? He turns and walks upstairs, and I follow.

I guess I'll never know.

16

*Hashtags
and D-Bags*

I SIT WITH my arms folded on my desk and my head stuffed firmly into the crook of my elbow. It's first hour with Mr. Samuels, and when I got up to leave for school this morning, it hit me harder that my teacher and my mom had a date.

Isn't that weird? I don't even know if I can look Mr. Samuels in the eye!

I also need to face Camila. I thought about what I could say all morning, and the lies made my stomach ill.

A finger presses into my shoulder repeatedly. It digs hard and deep, and I'm scared to see the face on the other side of that finger.

Raising my head up slowly, I exaggerate a yawn. To my luck, there's even a little drool on my chin. Maybe she won't give a tired boy too hard of a time?

"So, how was studying last night?" Camila asks. When she's done poking me, she crosses her arms.

I gulp. What did I tell her? Oh, yeah—that Mom wouldn't let me go because of a bad math test and was making me study at home.

I clear my throat. "Fine. Boring. But fine." I flash a subtle smile. "I missed you."

She huffs. "I saw your mom, you know. Last night." The freckles on her nose crinkle with her anger.

"Huh?"

"I went out to eat with my parents since you canceled on me. We ran into your mother at the same restaurant."

How small is this town?

"Oh. That's nice," I mumble.

"It was weird because she was with our teacher." Camila shrugs. "Anyway, she got up to go to the bathroom, and I followed. Just wanted to say hi and be polite, since she's my boyfriend's mother and all."

Oh, no.

My skin turns cold.

"Yeah. What do you think happened when I talked to her?" She taps her foot on the ground. How do I dig myself out of this mess?

"Look, I'm sorry." I shake my head. "I had to practice, and I knew you'd be mad if that was my excuse."

"You can't practice! You're out for the whole week!"

"I mean—" I scratch my head. If I could tell her the truth, it would be better for everyone. *You see, I have a crush on Mateo. I like you, but I don't LIKE you.* Yeah, that would go over great. "I mean, it's even more important that I have extra practices this next week since I can't really practice. I'm learning technique. Form. Mateo is helping me."

The bell rings, and she sits at the desk next to me. "I don't like this," she whispers. "I'm not saying I wouldn't have been disappointed, but you have to be honest with me."

"I know. I'm sorry." I put on my biggest puppy face pout.

"Make it up to me tonight?"

Mateo wants to practice all week. Hot, shirtless Mat working out in all sorts of ways with me. I could do that or have a movie night with Camila.

"Um, so if I'm being honest," I mumble, "I really need the one-on-one until my ribs heal completely. So I don't get behind."

She crosses her arms again. "Fine."

Mr. Samuels walks in. "Sorry, I'm late, kids." He looks the opposite of how I feel. There's an extra bounce to his step and a wide smile on his face.

When class ends, Camila races out of the room before I can say anything else to her. Instead of trying to chase after her, I turn to Mateo. "*Hola,*" he greets me. He wears a black Nike shirt that clings to each muscle of his arms and chest. The *Just Do It* slogan taunts me in more than one way.

"'Sup?" I try to act cool, but the sound that comes out of my mouth makes me cringe on the inside. It's so hard to be real, especially when you're pretending to be someone you're not.

"I'm sore, man." He laughs. We stand outside of Mr. Samuels's class, not in a hurry to go to second hour. "You wore me out. Still on for tonight?"

"Yeah,"

He leans against the wall on one arm, high by his head. "I might ask one more guy. I need someone to fight. Someone big like Tanner."

No one-on-one? My heart drops and my voice cracks when I speak, and I hope he doesn't hear my disappointment. "Who would that be?"

He shrugs and moves out of the way as a few kids walk into Mr. Samuels's room. "That stupid varsity team. They're all jerks. Look at this." He takes out his phone and opens up his socials. "I posted a pic last night after you left." My eyes widen at the picture. It's Mateo, still shirtless, flexing and taking a selfie. He looks fantastic. He added *#readytorumble* after it.

"That's a good one."

"Thanks. But look at the comments." He hands me his phone, and I scroll through the feed. I recognize some of the names. They're straight off the varsity roster.

Mateo #readyforaman
#readytotakeitinthebutt
homo

I thrust the phone back at him. I can't stand to read any more crap like that. "That's so dumb. Ugh. They're such d-bags."

"Yeah. So, I don't know who to ask. Got any big friends?"

I shake my head.

"Maybe I can help you." We turn, both surprised at the voice. It's deep, masculine, and all too familiar—it's the voice we've heard in hundreds of classroom lectures.

"Huh?" Mateo asks.

"I couldn't help but overhear. I have a pretty decent judo background. It's not the same, I know. But I'm also bigger than both you and Tanner. How would you like to beat up your English teacher?" Mr. Samuels asks, as a mischievous grin forms on his face.

17

Rock vs. Water

"I'D LIKE TO join you, too," Mom tells me that afternoon when I inform her that Mr. Samuels will be wrestling my best friend.

While I'll enjoy watching Mateo in action, she'll enjoy Mr. Samuels. *Gross.*

"But Mom—"

"No buts. It's a school night, after all. If I give you permission to go, I'm coming, too. That's my final decision." She stacks some paperwork together on the dining room table. Her hair looks surprisingly styled.

"Fine," I mumble and roll my eyes.

"I know we've only had one date, but I learned a little bit about your teacher's past. You might be surprised."

Whatever.

We drive over to Mateo's house. Mr. Samuels sits in the living room and chats with Mat's parents. They laugh, and Mr. Samuels stands promptly when my mom enters. Everyone introduces themselves.

"Please be gentle with our son," Mat's mother tells Mr. Samuels.

"Oh, trust me... I'm hoping for the other way around, I assure you." He chuckles.

We walk downstairs. My mom and Mateo's parents have all gathered for this practice.

"We have high hopes for our son," Mat's father says.

"As you should," Mr. Samuels replies. "He's exceptionally talented."

What am I even doing here? I feel like a third wheel. Or a fifth.

Mr. Samuels pats me on the back. "And Aiden wants to learn all this, too. So, it's good you're here." It's like he's reading my mind. "There's a lot we can learn from one another. You master form while you're healing."

Mateo's parents, my mom, and I sit on the floor. Mateo wears a gray sleeveless workout shirt and black shorts. Mr. Samuels carries a duffel bag and excuses himself to change. He comes out of the bathroom wearing blue shorts and a yellow T-shirt. His muscles bulge in the sleeves, and his thighs are thick and strong like tree trunks. I've never seen this side of my teacher before.

Mateo and Mr. Samuels warm up.

"So, Tanner is bigger, stronger, and more experienced," Mr. Samuels states. "What will your strategy be, Mateo?"

"I'm working on my strength to match his." Mateo holds a foot with one hand to stretch out his quad. "Aiden's helping me with that. Since I'm smaller, I'm gonna rely on speed, I think."

"That's a good idea. May I make a suggestion? Use his size against him. Let's work on techniques that use your opponent's strength and momentum against him. It gives the smaller guy the advantage."

"I need to learn those kinds of moves," I tell Mom.

"Just wait," she says. "I said you'll be surprised."

"Let's have a match. You come in with everything you've got," Mr. Samuels says. "All of your strength. I'm gonna stay very relaxed. And we'll see what happens?"

"Okay." Mat's eyebrows narrow. Like me, he's still trying to figure out our teacher. He gets into a stance, and Mr. Samuels does the same. Mat's arms tense. He curls his fingers in and cracks his knuckles. Mr. Samuels looks the opposite, more like he's floating on water. He's relaxed and smooth.

Mr. Samuels nods, giving Mateo the go-ahead to begin.

Mat lunges for a takedown. Mr. Samuels spins in a circle, and Mat stumbles to find his balance. Then Mat jumps in and grabs our teacher. He pulls him forward, and Mr. Samuels moves with the pull. He remains relaxed, and even though it's Mateo who is executing the movements, Mr. Samuels appears to be in control.

Then Mat steps in for a sweep. Mr. Samuels turns circularly again and kicks his leg out so swiftly it's a blur of light. Mateo falls hard and fast on his face. Mr. Samuels moves on top, putting him in a chokehold. Mateo taps out.

Mr. Samuels laughs. "I know choking isn't legal in your matches. But they are in my training."

"How did you do that? Take me down so easily?" Mat rubs his neck, speaking hoarsely.

"If two rocks slam against each other, what happens?"

Mateo shrugs. "They crash. They hurt each other?"

"Okay. Yes," Mr. Samuels says. "What else?"

"They stop each other," I add.

Mr. Samuels smiles at me. "Exactly. They will hurt each other and stop the momentum of one another. Now, picture a rock being thrown into a moving stream of water. What happens?"

I scratch my temple. "The water carries it away."

"Very good. If you have to fight, especially someone bigger, you want to be the water. Not the rock." Mr. Samuels faces Mateo. "Do you understand?"

"I think so," Mat answers, still rubbing his neck. His parents watch with concerned looks, but they don't interject.

"Good. Now this time, I'll be rock. You be water."

Mr. Samuels lunges in for a throw, and Mateo spins. Our teacher lands on his face, and we all laugh.

"I bet that felt good for more than one reason," Mr. Samuels says, and we laugh harder. "Nice work. Let's do it again."

They wrestle for the next hour, and my jaw keeps dropping. Mr. Samuels truly moves like water or even the wind. He's strong, but it's a continuous motion. Watching wrestlers like Tanner or Coach Krake, I have always pictured them like bulls. Or semis charging at you.

Mr. Samuels has a flow about him, and it's hypnotic.

When they take a break, I ask, "How did you learn all of that?"

He takes a drink of water. "When I was a kid, a neighbor of mine would practice karate in his front yard. I used to watch him in awe. He started teaching classes out of his basement, and I begged my parents to let me join."

"Is that karate, then? What you did with Mat?"

"Yes and no," he answers. "My karate teacher was also a black belt in judo. He made us learn how to defend ourselves when we were on or off our feet. So, I learned both karate and judo."

"What's the difference?"

"Karate is mostly strikes—punches, kicks, blocks. Judo is the Japanese way of wrestling. It literally translates into the gentle way. You see, if you strike someone, it could really hurt them. But if you use their momentum against them, defending a punch by doing a throw instead, it is considered to be a gentler defense. Throw them down, put them in a submission, and talk to them about their bad behavior." Mr. Samuels grins.

"Have you ever taught anyone before?" Mateo asks.

"Not until today."

"Would you teach me, too?" I ask. "Privately? I mean, with Mateo if he wants to?"

Mat nods, his eyes wide with excitement that match my own. "Yeah. That would be awesome."

Mr. Samuels smiles at my mother, and I have a feeling they talked about this last night. "Coach Krake won't like you training with anyone else."

"We don't have to tell him," I say.

"If it's all right with your parents, I will work with both of you. On one condition," Mr. Samuels says.

"What?" Mateo and I ask at the same time.

"No matter what, you never ever use what I teach you to hurt someone else. This is for fun. It can only be used in self-defense. Do you understand?"

"Yes," we both say. "Absolutely."

18

Everything is B.S.

A WEEK HAS passed, and finally my ribs are healed, so I can train. It's a double-edged sword. On one hand, I get to participate with Mateo and Mr. Samuels instead of only watching. On the other, I have wrestling practice after school today.

Camila has given me space, but it's too much. I haven't made up for our movie night. Her smiles appear forced. Even in class, she's daydreaming instead of talking to me. She wears long sleeves and jeans even though we've had a late fall heatwave. Something's off with her.

The moment Mat walks by my focus shifts elsewhere.

Logan no longer sits with Tisha at lunch. When I join my usual table, Logan gives me a dirty look and kisses Tisha's cheek on his way to the wrestling table.

"Sorry, babe. Gotta climb those ladders," he tells her. "You're the only girl for me, though."

Ironically, perhaps, Mateo leaves the wrestling table to join us.

It's both wonderful and awkward to have Mateo with us. To my right is my girlfriend, who is upset that we haven't been spending any time together.

To my left is the guy I'd love to make my boyfriend. It's fantasy hell. I catch myself thinking about kissing much more than punching when we train, but I wouldn't give up our practices together for anything.

"So this big match is tomorrow?" Camila asks.

"Hey, we gotta cheer on Mat."

"Guess it's better than watching a movie by myself." She speaks with a bitter tone.

Ouch. "It will be fun!" She deserves to feel angry at me, I know. But that doesn't mean I like it.

Camila sighs. "Why don't they have any girls on the wrestling team? It's just a bunch of gross boys. No better than football."

"Why don't you ask Krake to join the team?" Mateo asks.

Tisha snorts, and her iced tea shoots out her nose.

It makes us all laugh.

"Maybe I will." Camila rolls her eyes. "You might be surprised."

She stares over at Logan and the other wrestlers. What is going through her mind?

"I'm sure Krake would love that," I say. "Tell him it's about equality, and he has to allow girls on the team."

Mat and I laugh, but Camila frowns.

"Why don't we go to a movie or something instead?" she asks Tisha.

"I already promised Logan I'd go," her friend says.

"Well, I haven't even been invited," Camila snaps.

"Hey," I say. "I thought it was a given. Come with me." She turns her head away from me. "Please." Guilt strikes me, though. I must admit one perk to having her with us is that it would be nice to hold hands with her if Logan and the other douchebags start in with their homophobic crap. But really, I'll be focused one hundred percent on Mateo. If he wins, we'll celebrate! If he loses, he'll need me even more. It's not fair to Camila at all.

"Do you really want me to come?" Camila asks softly.

Didn't I *just* say that? "Of course." I try to bury the guilt I feel. I'm a better person than one who lies like this.

Or am I?

I look over at Mateo, hoping to see something on his face. Jealousy, maybe? A look that would suggest he'd rather it be the two of us? But no, I don't see anything. He leaves a half-eaten sandwich on his tray and spaces out, nervous about tomorrow.

"You'll win," I tell him.

"Huh?" He blinks several times. "Oh. Yeah, thanks. Hope so."

"You've worked so hard." We haven't told anyone that our extra training is with Mr. Samuels. We don't want it getting back to Krake or Tanner or anyone on the team. It's our secret weapon. "It has to pay off."

"Everything just makes me nervous." He takes a deep breath and pokes at his sandwich. "I'm tired of being crapped on by the team. Krake made me captain because I'm good. JV barely listens to me anymore. It's all because of Logan and Tanner and this B.S." He slams his fist on the table. "It pisses me off. Why? Because unlike everyone else, I don't pick on you?" His breath is heavy and quick, and I hate the anger in his voice.

"I'm sorry." My hand slides close to his. I don't know how to comfort him. My stomach flips, a little out of guilt and a little out of anger. It's my fault this is happening to him. But it shouldn't be my fault at the same time. I don't know how to feel. "You're one of the good guys. That's all."

He frowns. "Yeah? If this is what being a good guy gets you, then maybe—" He shakes his head. "Sorry, I'm just really nervous about tomorrow."

"I'd fight him for you if I could. Even if I'd get my ass kicked, I'd fight Tanner for you."

He looks me, and his eyes are a dark mystery. There's empathy there, but there's also anger and bitterness. Then he smiles, and everything changes. "Thanks, dude. You're a good friend."

My heart races, and I wish I could hold his hand. Of course, I can't do that, and the bell rings, anyway.

I turn around to say bye to Camila, but she's already gone. Tisha shakes her head at me. "If you weren't so busy paying attention to your *boyfriend,* maybe you'd notice that your girlfriend isn't too happy right now."

Mateo winces. *Thanks a lot, Tisha.* That's exactly what he needed to hear right now.

Everything is bull.

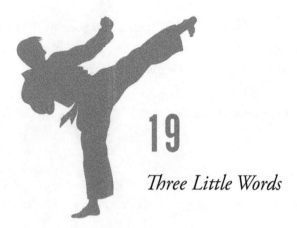

19

Three Little Words

CAMILA TEXTS THAT she will meet me at the exhibition match and that she's riding with Tisha and Logan. Ugh. Stupid Logan. Mr. Samuels picks up Mom, and I ride with them.

Mr. Samuels has continued to work on using an opponent's momentum and size to our advantage—what he calls rock versus water—and I hope it pays off for Mateo's sake. I really want to move on from just judo, too. I'd love to work on strikes and kicks, especially when I close my eyes and picture Logan's face.

When we arrive, we gather in the gymnasium. The floor is covered with black wrestling mats, and not the ones we practice on but the ones we sit on. The rolled-up ones along the edges of our wrestling room are the special mats reserved for meets. They're cleaner, crisper, and don't smell like decades worth of teen boy sweat, at least not yet. The shiny, black mats and the smell of popcorn transform the gym into some sort of carnival.

With the exception of Mateo, tonight is all about the varsity team. A large crowd shuffles in the gym. About a hundred people already sit on the bleachers. Isn't there anything good to watch on Netflix tonight?

Krake walks to the center and picks up a microphone. He's dressed up for the occasion—a red button-up shirt, black pants, and a red and black tie. He looks like Satan, so that's appropriate.

"Good evening. I'm Coach Krake, your Washington Hornets wrestling coach. Tonight is our annual kick-off to our season. We have a series of exhibition matches which will be followed by our main event. Captain versus captain." He pauses, and a round of applause echoes throughout the gym. *"May the best man win."*

The look in his eyes makes my skin feel hot. There's something not right about him, and it's more than just the fact that he's a homophobic dick.

From the entryway, Camila waves. Logan and Tisha walk behind her. They motion for me to join them. I guess it would be cooler than sitting with Mom and Mr. Samuels.

"Gonna go sit with Camila," I mutter and head down to meet them.

The bleachers groan as I hop from one section to the other. I beeline right to Camila. I reach for her hand, but she sticks both hands in her pockets. "You want a soda or something? My treat."

"What a gentleman," Logan mumbles. "Take him up on it, Mila."

Why does *he* get to call her by her nickname?

"No thanks," she replies dryly, her eyes still avoiding mine.

"Can we talk?" I whisper, hoping Logan doesn't hear. "Somewhere private for a sec?"

"You don't want to miss your wrestling, do you?" she says loudly.

My throat dries up. "Please. Just for a minute."

She rolls her eyes. "Save me a seat," she tells Tisha, and we walk out of the gym and into a hallway surrounded by trophy cases.

"What's wrong?"

"What's *wrong?*" she repeats. "Are you *that* dumb?"

"Ouch. I'm sorry. All I ever do is say I'm sorry."

"Cuz all you ever do is stupid stuff."

"I told you—we just needed to practice. Tonight's important."

"For who? Not for me. Not for you."

"Mateo's my best friend." I reach for her hand, but she crosses her arms. "That's why it's important."

She shakes her head. "Yeah. Then what am I? Huh? You sure care a lot more about him than me." Her face turns red and tears well in her eyes.

I can't reply to that.

Because it's true.

"I'm sorry." It's the only thing I can think of to tell her.

"Aiden, are you—" Camila pauses abruptly and wipes at her eyes.

"Am I what?" I ask, even though I don't want to hear the question.

"Logan says—"

"No, no, *no!*" I shout. "I *hate* him. Don't listen to him. Do you know—he's such a jerk! You have no idea." I press my arms against a trophy case.

Camila takes a step toward me. Her arm reaches toward my shoulder, then she pulls back. "You never talk to me!" she shouts. "He said you would say nasty things about him, too."

Fire burns in my throat. "What did he tell you?"

"Are you gay?"

There it is. Three little words that are my nightmare.

I hate the question. Shouldn't I get to decide when and how I tell people? But no—thanks to Logan, I'm getting asked right now. The only decision I get to make is whether to lie or tell the truth. My fingernails dig into my palms.

I take a deep breath, then put my hands on her shoulder. "I can't even touch you without you acting weird. But you ask me *that?*"

Camila winces again. She pulls at the long sleeves of her hoodie, looking away. The zipper falls down a bit, and she's wearing that same T-shirt that caught my attention before. The one with the fist in the middle. This time I almost make out the word around it. *DECK*—but then she zips up her hoody.

"It's not you. I'm just pissed." She sighs. "Look. There are rumors. Maybe you're gay, and maybe you're not. But if you're not gay, then you clearly don't like me."

"That's not true," I tell her.

"I'd rather you be gay. At least maybe there's a reason then for why you're so obsessed with Mateo and never wanna hang out with me." She sniffs and wipes at her eyes again.

What do I do? I don't want to break up with her, and I know my rationale is crappy. If she's in my corner, I've got some kind of buffer from—from the truth.

When I don't say anything, she says, "I think we should break up."

"I don't wanna break up."

"Sorry. But I do."

We stand in the hall awkwardly, and I don't know what to say.

"Let me try to be better. Please. We don't have to do this."

I reach for her hand, and she swats it away, almost violently. There's a fierceness to her, something powerful and strong. And, to be honest, scary.

"Maybe one day we can be friends. When you can be honest with me, that is. You're a liar, Aiden. I know you're a liar." She speaks with such bitterness that my chest burns with guilt.

I don't want to come out. Not yet. I'm not ready. It's such a scary thought. I don't want to say those three little words. My entire world will change with those three little words, and I don't think I'm ready to say....

I am gay.

No. Doesn't she see what I put up with already? How will coming out make that any better?

Camila stares at me for a minute. She exhales hard through her nose. "You may not like Logan, but he's honest. He says what he thinks and what he feels. He's not a liar. *You* are."

She turns and walks away.

My body shakes. I feel like I've been punched in the stomach.

It feels worse than breaking up. Somehow, I feel like I've made another enemy.

Another person to hate me.

Someone else who likes Logan.

How is that even *possible?*

I stall for several minutes before returning, pacing the halls outside the gym, trying to get a grip on my thoughts.

I'm here for Mateo, I tell myself. I'm here to cheer for him. He needs me, right? He needs someone cheering in his corner.

I go back and sit with Mom and Mr. Samuels, walking quickly, avoiding making eye contact with anyone sitting in the bleachers.

"What's wrong, honey?" Mom asks when I take a seat. I shake my head. I don't want to talk about it. I'm just gonna sit through these stupid wrestling matches and then cheer for the only other person my age in this gym who might actually care about me.

20

Captain vs. Captain

I SPACE OUT during the first few matches. Whenever I risk a glance toward Camila, Logan flashes his teeth at me like he's a vampire and crushing my self-esteem is his way of getting blood. Why would Tisha and Camila hang with him? Don't they see how awful he acts?

My head hurts, and I rub my temples. So, Camila knows about me. So what? She dumped me, and that's for the best in the long run.

But it's like *evidence!* Logan will keep spreading his stupid rumors, and they'll all say, "Even his girlfriend broke up with him. Did you know he never even made out with her? What a loser."

My insides burn. I glance over to Camila and Logan again, and Logan kisses Tisha on the cheek. She giggles. They don't have a care in the world. Doesn't he see how easy it is to be straight? He can kiss a girl in his high school gym, and no one says a word. If I kissed Mateo like that, there'd be a full crisis. The school would probably call in extra guidance counselors. There'd be a town hall because the administration wants to seem progressive and pretend to care what all parents think. The media would do a big story. Homophobic idiots would get online and post terrible comments.

I don't give a crap what the law is or how much everyone on TV supports gay pride. That's not *my* reality. And, sure, maybe some cool parents tell their kids it's okay to be gay. But what if they don't mean it?

It's okay to be gay, but don't be gay at school. Or around your grandparents. Or any other person, for that matter. Don't cause a scene. Don't talk about it.

In other words, keep it in the closet.

My palms start to bleed. I didn't realize how hard I was pressing my fingernails into my hands.

"Ladies and gentleman, if I may have your attention," Coach Krake speaks from the microphone and interrupts my thoughts. *"I want to introduce our main event. Rarely has our school ever seen two more talented athletes. First, our JV captain, Mateo Hernandez."*

Mateo walks to the center of the mat. For the first time since I arrived, I relax. A subtle smile forms on my face. There's something about his beauty—it's overpowering, and it takes me out of my dark place.

He doesn't even have to flex—his muscles radiate with strength, and he wears a look of confidence. I forget everything. I only want to see him win.

The crowd applauds, although no one more enthusiastically so than Mr. Samuels. Krake adjusts his Satan tie and glares at him.

"Mateo is a freshman, who will likely be bumped up to varsity before this year is over. His talents are exceptional, and his leadership will help develop an extraordinary junior varsity team. I saw him a couple years ago at a wrestling camp, and I made sure to take him under my wing." He looks again at Mr. Samuels, his eyes narrow and accusing. Does he know something? *"To give him the proper guidance, as best I can."*

Mateo waves at the crowd, and they applaud once more. Well, not everyone. Logan scowls, and the JV wrestlers that sit near him applaud as if this is a golf match. It pisses me off. Mat's a great leader. They should show more respect and not fall for Logan and Tanner's bull.

"Next, a man who needs no introduction to this school, your varsity captain and three-time state champion, Tanner McQueen!" The gym roars with applause, and the wrestlers and parents give a standing ovation. I stick out my tongue, not caring who sees. Mateo catches my

eye, and he covers his mouth quickly. I can't tell if I surprised him or if he's covering a laugh. It doesn't matter. I give Mateo a great big smile, and he returns it.

"Tanner has won state three years in a row, and we expect him to go all the way this year, too!" More applause fills the gym. More thoughts on how much I hate everyone fill my head.

"Today is only an exhibition match between two tremendous athletes," Krake announces. *"They represent the future of this sport and our school, and thanks to their participation, we were able to raise quite a lot of money today."*

Krake steps off the mat, and a referee enters. Tanner and Mat briefly shake hands. Tanner's upper lip curls into a snarl, and my heart pounds hard against my chest. Mat is strong, but Tanner is a boulder. It's like seeing someone the size of Bruce Lee enter the ring against Dwayne "The Rock" Johnson.

I swallow hard and turn to Mr. Samuels. "Look at them. Why did he agree to do this?"

Mr. Samuels wipes his sweaty brow. "I'm nervous, too, Aiden. Size isn't everything. Let's give him a chance."

I hope he's right. Maybe Bruce Lee could have taken down The Rock, but Bruce Lee had a lot more than a week's worth of training.

Rock versus water. It doesn't matter how big the rock is. Water will always carry it away.

Tanner reaches for Mateo, grips his arms, and shoves him off the mat. Mateo flies backward, stumbling, but catching his balance again. Tanner's showing off his strength, and I clench my fists. "C'mon, Mateo!" It's louder than I intended, and a few kids laugh at me.

But Mr. Samuels helps out. "Yeah! Let's go, Mateo!" Mom applauds, and a few others match their cheers.

Tanner and Mateo lock arms again. With each step, Tanner nearly lifts Mat off the floor. Mateo stays relaxed, though, modeling Mr. Samuels's teaching. Krake's eyes narrow, and he fidgets with his tie.

This isn't his coaching style at work, and he knows it. His nostrils flare, and I laugh with excitement.

Tanner steps inside with his right foot and pounds his knee into Mateo's stomach. That's an illegal move! The referee doesn't say anything, and Krake grins.

The strike clearly hurts, and Mateo winces. Tanner wraps his right arm around Mat's neck, spins and drives his hip hard into Mat's stomach, and then flips him violently down on the mat.

"Takedown—two points," the ref shouts.

Mateo makes a huge thud, and the audience gasps. Tanner moves in for the pin, and I hold my breath. I can't watch. My hands cover my eyes, but then the crowd gasps again.

Mateo's on his feet, and he smiles at Tanner. No one gets out of Tanner's pins.

Even Krake looks surprised, and Tanner's angrier than ever. He didn't hold him long enough to even score a point.

"Escape, one point!" the ref shouts.

I throw my hands up and laugh. "Get him, Mateo!"

21

The Winner is...

"C'MON, MATEO!" I shout again.

They lock arms, and Tanner moves hard for a sweep. He drives Mateo counterclockwise and then reaches for Mat's legs. Mat sees him coming and goes with it. He's using Tanner's strength against him, just like Mr. Samuels taught us.

Then as Tanner reaches for his legs, Mateo whirls and grabs Tanner from behind. He shoves Tanner face-down on the mat, and Tanner howls. The crowd roars with electricity! My feet stomp like crazy on the bleachers. Even Mom releases a great big, "Wooo!"

"Takedown—two points!" the ref says.

Mateo's doing it!

"He's going to win!" I shout. I can't hold back my excitement, and Mr. Samuels pats my shoulders in celebration.

Throwing my fist in the air, I glance over at Logan. His eyes are locked dead cold on the match, and his face burns red.

Tanner gets up on his knees, and Mateo locks his arms around Tanner's stomach. Tanner tries to get up, but Mateo has the advantage, and he squeezes Tanner. Tanner goes for one of Mat's legs, and Mateo shifts his weight. Then Tanner jerks the opposite way.

Crap! Tanner got out, and he faces Mateo again. A roar erupts from the crowd for the varsity captain, and my stomach flips.

"Escape!" the ref shouts and holds up a finger to indicate one point.

"Three to three," I mutter. "C'mon, Mateo!"

"Huh?" Mom asks. "How do points work?"

"You get two points per takedown. One point for an escape. I'll explain later, Mom," I say quickly, my hands locked together.

"No, there should be penalty points for Tanner," Mr. Samuels says.

I laugh and shake my head. "Not under Krake's rules."

Both boys breathe heavily and sweat rolls down Mateo's face. Tanner lunges to grab Mateo's legs for a takedown. Mateo quickly moves back, but no—Tanner was faking. He pushes forward, and he slams Mateo hard on the mat.

"Takedown!" The referee holds up two fingers.

Tanner's biceps bulge, and he gets Mateo in a lock. It's a near-fall, close to a pin position, and this time Mateo doesn't snap out of it. The referee counts the seconds. Mateo grimaces, and Tanner roars.

"He's gonna break Mateo's arm," Mr. Samuels mutters and stands. "Stop that!" he shouts.

"Five seconds," the ref says. Tanner releases Mat, and the ref holds up three fingers. It's now eight to three, Tanner.

They stand back up. Mateo can still win if he can just pin Tanner. A full pin—with both shoulders on the mat—for two seconds earns an automatic win. Otherwise, the match goes to whoever has the most points.

Tanner bites down on his mouthguard and sneers. His eyes grow wide with adrenaline. He charges at Mateo and wraps his arms around Mat's torso. With a howl, he picks Mat off the floor, spins, and slams him down.

He rolls right into a pin. *No!* Both of Mateo's shoulders hit the floor, and the referee counts.

One-second.

Two-seconds.

The ref blows his whistle. *Game over.*

"No!" I yell.

I catch Logan's eyes, and they're wide with arrogance. He laughs and puts his arm around Tisha. Camila avoids looking at me altogether.

"He did well," Mr. Samuels says.

"He lost," I reply.

"Tanner has twice the size and experience, and still Mateo scored three points. He held his ground. He should be proud."

"But you said in our training—"

"What I am teaching you is true, and it will work. But it takes time and practice. Not a week. Not even a month. You've got to give your training time," he says and pats me on the back. "Mateo did great. Three points!"

"Yeah, look at him now," I say.

Mat lowers his head. My heart sinks at his expression.

Tanner celebrates with the varsity squad off the mat. No one cheers for Mateo now.

Krake takes the mic, and I want to puke. I close my eyes and wait for him to shut the hell up so I can comfort my best friend.

"What a match! The winner—your varsity captain, Tanner!" Krake turns to Mateo. *"Well done to our JV captain, too. Not even top varsity wrestlers are able to score points against Tanner. What tremendous potential."* He looks up at the crowd in the gym. *"Here's to our best year of wrestling yet, with these two leading each of our teams!"*

I don't want to give Krake any credit, but at least he complimented Mateo. That's something.

When Krake finishes, I run down to Mat. "You were awesome, dude! Mister Samuels is so proud. Three points against Tanner!"

I hold up my fist, but Mat ignores me.

"I lost. That's all they'll remember." He gestures ambiguously.

"It's not. What matters—"

"Aiden, just leave me alone," he interrupts me. "I wouldn't be in this position if it weren't for you."

It feels like I've been punched in the gut. "What do you mean?"

He shakes his head. "Nothing. Never mind. Just leave me alone." Mateo walks away. I want to run after him, but my legs feel weak. Why would he tell me that? As if I don't feel crappy enough.

Slowly, my knees close to buckling, I stumble back to Mr. Samuels and Mom. "What's wrong, honey?" she asks.

"Mateo's upset."

"Just give him time," Mr. Samuels says. "Right now, it feels like the end of the world. He'll feel better tomorrow."

I hope he's right. But it feels like it's the end of my world, too. Why doesn't Mateo know that I only wanted to cheer him up? To help him? Instead, he crapped on me just like everyone else.

22

*Saturday
Morning Practice*

THE WORST THING about joining a sports team is losing Saturdays, I think as I get out of bed way too early for the weekend. But the best thing is that I will get to see Mat. Hopefully, he got a good night's sleep and will feel better today. He was tired, frustrated, embarrassed—that's what caused him to be mean to me, right? I don't know what I'd do if I found out Mateo is just like all the other creeps.

After last night, I'm ready for practice, anyway. If I can't punch someone in the face, I at least want to throw someone around.

Mom drives me to practice early. "What are you looking at?"

I catch myself staring at her hair. It looks too nice for this early in the morning. "Nothing," I answer. When a smile grows on her face, I turn my attention to the passenger window. The nice hair, the cheesy grin—I shudder, not wanting to think any more about it.

When she arrives at the high school, I bounce out of the car with a quick "bye" and rush into the locker room. Strong smells of bleach make my eyes water. I'm the first to arrive, except for Krake. I hear him talking in his office, and I approach hesitantly. Certainly, I don't want any one-on-one time with him. I'm just going to dress quickly and get to the wrestling room. I can't stand it when any of the guys make a scene about changing in front of me.

Krake's laughter echoes off the cheap metal lockers. It's deep and raspy, like a drunk old man. "No, no. Hell, you don't have to tell me that. You try to make these pussies into real men, and some helicopter mom complains." He laughs again. "Oh, I've got a couple real sissies on the team, too." I hold my breath during a long pause. I don't hear any other voice, so I assume Krake must be on the phone. "You're right. It's all about discipline. These students sure need it. Hell, this *country* needs it. But we do what we can with what we have. I've got a team I'm proud to make into strong men." Another pause. "It really *is* a great business idea. Count me in, for sure. Let's talk more soon. I need to get ready for practice."

Business idea? Oh, please tell me Krake isn't opening some business here. That's all we need—some crap like Krake's Bar and Grill, where drunk fools come together to watch Fox News.

Turning around, I run out of the locker room but smash right into another kid.

"Ooof!"

"Oh, hey, sorry." I adjust my practice singlet.

"It's okay." Thank goodness it was DeMarcus and not one of the other jerks. He smiles at me, those cherry-red lips revealing beautiful white teeth. "You running from something or toward something?"

The question makes me laugh a little. "Ain't it always from something with me?"

"Just wondering if there'd be any dicks to deal with in here." He runs a hand over his short, buzzed hair. His magnificent dark skin makes my stomach twirl. He's absolutely adorable. Every time I look at him, my mind feels a bit dizzy.

I lean in and whisper. "Just Coach Dick." I can smell his deodorant, and suddenly my heart races.

DeMarcus laughs. "He's the worst."

"Yeah." Besides Mateo, DeMarcus seems to be the only person who sees Krake for who he really is.

A few other wrestlers enter the locker room. I say "bye" to De-

Marcus and take off. Even though he's cool, I can't risk a bad reaction from him. If he were to laugh at something one of the other guys said or abruptly cut me off so he wouldn't be seen talking to me, my heart would break. It's best if I just run away and don't give him the chance.

I'm the first to enter the wrestling room. A few minutes later, Krake joins. He doesn't bother to look at me or say hello. He walks in the supply closet and comes out with a handful of jump ropes.

Ugh. Why do I torture myself? I could be in bed, eating Cap'N Crunch, watching *Rick and Morty*.

Then Mateo enters the wrestling room, and my pulse quickens. He's why I put up with this, at least in part. Mat's got my back, and I got his.

"Hey," I say.

He doesn't say anything back.

"How you doing?" I ask.

He shakes his head.

I walk closer to him. "You really did great last night. I'm not just saying that. It was amazing."

Mat looks over his shoulder. Krake goes in and out of the supply room and catches Mat's eye. Krake flashes him a look, something I don't understand.

"Look, Aiden," he says, still not making eye contact with me. "When we're out here, I need you to leave me alone. I can't give you special treatment." He keeps looking over his shoulder.

"I don't *want* special treatment." My skin burns at his harsh words. "I'm your friend. All I want is to be treated like one."

Finally, he makes eye contact with me, and his eyes look wet. "Out here, we can't be friends. I'm sorry."

He walks away, and my body shakes. I reach for his shoulder, and he spins around.

"Don't touch me." His face twists with anger, and it would terrify me except right now all I feel is broken.

"I don't understand." Tears well in my eyes, and I blink to hold them back.

"Don't you cry out here. Jesus, you'll just make it worse."

"Make what worse?" I choke on my words. My throat dries up, and my eyes feel hot and wet.

"Everything. Don't you get it?" Mateo asks. "They hate me because of you. I can't be the captain if they hate me."

I can't breathe. My skin feels like it's on fire. "You're not much of a captain if you can't do the right thing." Spit flies from my mouth as I talk. Wrestlers fill up the wrestling room.

"Stop it. Now," he mumbles, glaring at me.

What *happened* to him?

I march over and sit on a wrestling mat. My heart pounds against my chest. I want to leave. I want to quit. But I have to get tougher. If I want to earn the team's respect, I have to at least be able to earn Mateo's, right? Or am I just deceiving myself?

Logan and Jeff walk in shoulder-to-shoulder, and they laugh. I don't know if they're laughing at me or something random, but their laughter pisses me off regardless.

"Homo," Logan mouths at me when he walks by. Jeff laughs harder.

I try to swallow the lump in my throat, and my eyes burn with tears that roll down my face. I can't hold them back. Screw everyone here!

"Dude, you okay?" It's DeMarcus, and he sits next to me.

"No." I wipe my eyes.

"What's wrong?"

Mateo walks by, and I answer loud enough so that he can hear. "You better not talk to me. They'll all just hate you, too." Mateo doesn't even flinch. He walks right on by, and his reticence hurts more than his words.

My head throbs as I do everything I can to hold back tears.

"Aiden, what is it?" DeMarcus asks. It should feel nice to have someone care, but I'm too pissed off right now.

Krake blows his whistle. "Line up. Mateo—warm them up."

"Yes, sir."

I force the tears back and wear a stoic expression for the rest of practice. We work on takedowns, and I keep hoping that someone will knock me out. Just send me to the hospital again.

Anywhere but here.

With anyone but Mateo.

23

Cool

WHEN PRACTICE ENDS, I pace the parking lot. I texted Mom right away, and naturally she's running late. I can't wait to get my driver's license so I never have to wait to be picked up again.

That is, of course, if we can afford to buy me a car. Who am I kidding? Mom had told me we can't afford braces for my teeth, so how the heck would we ever be able to buy a car?

I run to the far end of the parking lot, the opposite side of the wrestling room entrance. More boys trickle out of school. Some have rides, and some sit on the curb and wait. They talk to each other and laugh. Watching them fills my chest with pain.

I should be able to have friends like that. Mateo's not acting any better than Logan and the rest of the jerks. DeMarcus appears to be the only decent guy left on the team, but how long until they corrupt him?

A car pulls up and honks, but it's not Mom's car. I peer inside the passenger window as the car slows down. A friendly face smiles and waves at me.

Why didn't Mom tell me she was sending Mr. Samuels to pick me up?

I open the door slowly. "Hop in, kid. It's cool, I promise. I'm not offering you candy or anything." He laughs.

"Huh?"

"Never mind. Get in." I step inside and buckle up. "I told your mom that you, me, and Mateo could do extra training today. That is if you've still got some energy left after practice?"

Practice with Mateo? What a joke. "Um, I dunno."

Mr. Samuels frowns. "Oh? Why not?"

I fidget with the seatbelt. "Have you asked Mat about it?"

"I thought I'd make it a surprise," he says. "You guys are still enjoying your training, right?"

"Oh, yeah. It's ten times better than wrestling practice. A *thousand* times better."

That makes him smile. It's true, too. Wrestling practice with Krake is like military boot camp. Mr. Samuels is fun. There's something special about his lessons, even if I don't understand everything he says when he goes on a rock versus water kind of lecture.

"So, what's going on?"

"Why don't you ask if Mateo's up for it first?"

"Very well." Mr. Samuels nods, takes out his phone, and sends a quick text. Then he puts the car in drive, and we take off. "In the meantime, how about a little lunch?"

"I'm starving." I skipped breakfast to get here as early as I could, and two-plus hours of wrestling have worn me out.

"You pick," he says.

"Um, how about KFC? The one by our place has a lunch buffet." Fried chicken is probably my favorite food ever. I could eat it all day.

Mr. Samuels pays for both of us, and we fill up our trays with chicken, mashed potatoes, mac and cheese, and biscuits. The smell of it makes my stomach growl, and I take a giant bite of a chicken leg.

"Your mother doesn't talk much about your father," Mr. Samuels says. "Do they talk at all?"

"Well, um, you know the story. At least a little, right?"

"From what you've written in your personal essays, yes. Does your mother know that you've written about them?"

I shake my head. "Don't tell her. Please. Especially now that you're, uh, dating or whatever." I take a bite of mac and cheese. "I think she'd probably want to tell you herself. In her own time. When she's ready."

"You're a bright young man, Aiden. Has your father, um, made any contact with you recently?"

I shuffle in my seat. "It's been a long time. I don't know if I even remember. Um, he called maybe a couple of years ago. He was drunk."

We sit in silence for a moment. I poke at my mashed potatoes with my fork. "I'm sure he does love you and miss you, Aiden," Mr. Samuels says. "In his own way."

"Are you close to your father?"

"My father died when I was a teenager. When I was about your age, actually."

"Oh, no. I'm so sorry."

"Thank you." He pauses, folds his hands, and puts them under his chin. "I was taking martial arts lessons at the time. My teacher became like a father to me during all that. But I understand some of your pain. Not all of it. All of our pain is unique to us. No one understands completely. But my teacher turned out to be a bad guy. He hurt me."

"Wow. What happened with your teacher?"

He sighs. "Story for another day." After a moment, he picks up a chicken thigh and takes a bite. "We better eat this food, or it'll get cold."

We enjoy the rest of our meal in silence until it's time for dessert. "It looked like you had a fight with Camila last night. You okay?"

I shrug. "We broke up."

"I'm sorry, Aiden. How do you feel?"

"I dunno. It's weird." I eat a spoonful of ice cream. "Part of me is, like, relieved. We weren't working out. But I'm sad, too."

"Relieved?" He raises his eyebrows.

Crap. I've said too much. What boy would be relieved that a hot girl dumped him?

"I dunno. That's not what I mean, I guess. Did, uh, Mat's parents ever text back?"

Mr. Samuels takes out his phone. "Oh, yeah. His father said, 'I asked Mat, and he said cool. That's about all the words I get out of him these days. We are doing lunch, but later this afternoon we are free.'" He looks at me. "You still up for that?"

Mateo has to know I'd be coming too, right? He wouldn't say "cool" if he didn't want to train with us, would he?

"I guess so." I feel full, and I push away the tray.

Cool. What's going through Mateo's head?

24

Learn How To Smash

"YOU BOYS WARM up. I need to get something out of my car," Mr. Samuels tells us. My arms tremble when I think of what Mateo will say to me. He glanced at me and nodded when we first arrived, but then he turned around and went straight downstairs without saying anything.

I stretch, and I keep my mouth shut. Mr. Samuels is sure taking his sweet time coming back. It's been the longest few minutes of my life, sitting here in complete silence with the boy who I thought was my best friend.

Mat clears his throat, and my eyes catch his. He fidgets with the bottom of his T-shirt. "Um, look, I—" He takes a deep breath. "I'm sorry about the way I talked to you. This morning." He looks away.

That's something, at least—an apology for the way he talked to me. But not for the actual words?

"Camila dumped me last night." It's a bit out of nowhere, but I want him to know that I could have used a friend.

"Oh. Shoot." He rolls his shoulders, warming them up. "I'm sorry. What happened?"

"Do you really care?"

Mateo sighs. "Look, man. I can't—don't you understand? Ever since day one, I've been losing respect from the team. The real season starts now. If I can't motivate the team, Krake will replace me. Then what?"

"Who cares?" I roll my eyes. "You told me I'd earn their respect by showing back up after embarrassing myself. Again after taking a kick to the gut. Why would you want respect from jerks like them?"

He crosses his arms. "They're the only team I have," he mumbles. "I don't have a choice."

"That's bull."

"You don't get it."

"Don't get *what?*"

"I almost beat the varsity captain, the best dude on the team." His eyes widen. "I've got a shot to be the best ever."

"At what cost?"

He shakes his head. Mr. Samuels's voice permeates from downstairs. He's talking to Mat's parents, and he'll be back down here any second.

"What I said to you this morning," Mateo continues, "I'm sorry. We *can* be friends. Here, you know? Just not—"

"Not where anyone will ever dare think you actually give a crap about an alleged homo."

He gulps, and his face turns pale. "Aiden, are you—?"

"No! Stop it, already," I lie. Tears well in my eyes. I can't control them. I hate everything about this. I hate people asking me about it, too. First Camila, and now Mateo—don't they understand that it's me who gets to decide when, where, and how to say it!

The door opens, and Mr. Samuels walks down. I wipe the tears away and turn my attention to our teacher. My jaw hits the floor at the sight of him. He wears a black martial arts uniform and wrapped around his waist is a black belt with four gold stripes.

"This is called a *gi,*" he says. "It's a traditional karate uniform. In my dojo, we earned black *gis* as advanced students. I have a white *gi* for each of you. A gift for both of you." He hands us each a small package.

"Wow," I say. "Thank you."

"Yes, thank you, sir," Mateo says.

"Will you teach us karate, too? In addition to judo?"

"If you'd like that." Mr. Samuels flashes a proud smile, and his eyes sparkle. "I want both of you boys to know that it's been a great joy working with you. I didn't know how much I missed martial arts until we started," he says.

My father's words echo in my memory. *Karate is for pussies.*

"Put on your uniforms." Mr. Samuels turns around, and I guess we're just supposed to change here.

"Do we get a belt?" Mateo asks.

"You have to earn it," Mr. Samuels replies.

"Even a white belt?" I ask.

"Yes. You have to learn and demonstrate five moves to earn your white belt. Your first block, first punch, first kick, first stance, and first smash," he says.

"What's a smash?" I ask.

"Oh, I think you'll like learning smashes." He opens his mouth and laughs. "A smash is a strike with your elbows, knees, or head."

"Sounds awesome," Mat says.

"It is," Mr. Samuels says after we're all dressed. "Let me show you. Mat—come grab me from behind like you're attempting a takedown."

Mateo wraps his arms around Mr. Samuels, and then our teacher jumps out with both feet into a wide stance, throwing both elbows into Mat's gut. Mat grunts, and Mr. Samuels throws him over his shoulder.

"Cool!" I shout.

"Yeah. You weren't on the receiving end." Mateo rubs his belly, and Mr. Samuels chuckles. "That's a trick Krake would like."

"It's called a double-elbow smash. Um, Mateo. Don't show Krake or anyone else on the team what you learn with me. Okay?"

"No problem. Krake would kill me." Mat takes Mr. Samuels's hand and gets up off the floor.

"Okay, Aiden. Your turn. Grab him, Mateo."

Mateo puts his arms around me. I put my hands over his. They're smooth but strong. For a moment, his hands open, and our fingers lace together, like we're holding hands. It only lasts for a second, and then Mateo squeezes me in preparation for the move. Still, it sends a tidal wave of chills through me. Every inch of my skin tingles.

Did he do that on purpose? Spread his fingers out wide enough for me to hold his hand?

"Like this," Mr. Samuels models the technique. I bury the questions for now, determined to learn the move. I jump out wide, bending at the knees. "This is also your first stance. It's called a horse stance." It's not a squat. It's more balanced. Mateo presses his hands harder around my waist, and my lips curl up.

I can't help but enjoy this part.

Then I toss my elbows into his stomach. His grip loosens.

"Remember that judo throw I showed you," Mr. Samuels says, and I grab Mateo's arm and flip him over.

He falls on the floor, and I can't help but laugh. "That was great."

"Now, reverse roles."

Mateo stands, and I put my arms around him.

Taking another risk, I spread out my fingers, just like he did moments ago.

His fingers interlock with mine.

He squeezes my hand. Again, it's only for a second.

But it has to mean something, right? *Maybe.* Maybe it's all in my head. But that doesn't mean it's not real, I guess.

It's not a bad way to spend a Saturday evening. Not bad at all.

25

Sleepover

WHEN OUR TRAINING concludes, Mr. Samuels presents each of us with a white belt.

"White represents a new beginning. Innocence. A clean slate," he tells us. "In the old days, *karate-ka* would receive a single white belt to hold up their pants. Like many of us, they never washed their belts. Over the course of many years, it got very dirty. Do you know what those white belts became?"

"A black belt?" I answer.

"That's right. It showed they had been training a long time. They were really just dirty belts." Mr. Samuels laughs.

"So, there's no real, like, rank system?" Mateo asks.

"Judo was the first martial art to introduce a belt system. Then when martial arts came to America, every school pretty much just made up their own thing."

"So, Americans screwed it all up?" I ask.

Mr. Samuels laughs but doesn't answer.

"Will we become black belts?" Mateo asks.

"One day at a time," Mr. Samuels answers. "If you work this hard, it would take you at least four years. So, maybe by the time you graduate high school."

"That's so long," I say.

"Just remember that all experts were once beginners."

"Can we call you *Sensei?*" Mateo asks.

Mr. Samuels laughs again. "If you'd like. *Sensei* is just the Japanese word for teacher."

"Cool. Thanks, Sensei," Mat says.

"You're welcome." He looks at the clock on the wall. "Well, I have a date with someone's mother tonight, so I should take off." He grins at me, and I shake my head and laugh. "Aiden—do you wanna come with me, or do you and Mateo have plans?"

I look at Mat. It's like what happened this morning was a hundred years ago. "Stay the night," he says. "If you want."

Slow down, heart! He'll hear your excitement!

"Yeah. That'd be cool." I try to make my voice sound deep and speak slowly.

"Call your mom first," Mr. Samuels tells me.

"I'll ask my parents, too," Mateo says.

"Yeah, okay." I get my phone and talk to Mom. She gives me permission, and it dawns on me when the call is over that she may be excited to have me out of the house for the night. Gross!

"It's cool with my parents," Mat says.

"All right. You boys have a good evening," he says. He looks just as happy as I do, and all I can think is ewww.

Then I look at Mateo. It's worth the ew. I just can't think about it too much.

"I'm hungry. You?" Mateo asks.

"Starving," I say.

"Let me see if I can get my parents to order us pizza!" He runs upstairs, and I follow him.

He talks to his parents in the living room, and I stand back, waiting in the kitchen. I look at the pictures and magnets on the fridge. There's an absolutely adorable one of Mateo in a singlet that must be at least a few years old. He's so young, but even then he's got a thicker shape to him like he was born to wrestle. Another picture captures my eye—it's Mateo, his older sister who I have yet to meet, and his parents. It's a pic from some theme park, and Mateo's father wraps his arms tightly around both of his kids. A sharp pain hits my chest.

Mateo enters the kitchen. "Okay, we got pizza coming. Wanna see my room?" he asks.

"Sure." Every time I've been here, we've only trained in his basement.

"C'mon." He motions, and I follow him up another flight of stairs. He has a big house, and when arriving in his bedroom, my jaw drops. It's huge. He has a double-sized bed, which makes me instantly envious. I still sleep on a twin. Next to his bed, a dresser showcases over a dozen trophies. On his wall, he has several posters. One is of the band The Glorious Sons, which makes my heart leap into my throat. That's one of my favorite bands ever, and Mateo and I have never once talked about it. How cool. Another poster is of Rhonda Rousey when she was in the UFC, and one is of Finn Balor from the WWE. The Finn poster nearly makes me choke. He's got both arms wrapped around the wrestling ropes. He stands outside the ropes, his back to the ring, and thrusts his crotch forward.

Wow.

"What video games do you like?" he asks.

"I'll play anything. I'm mostly into RPGs."

"Me, too!" He flashes a smile. He doesn't have any other furniture except for a giant bean bag, and I wonder where I will sleep.

"I got the newest Smash, too," he says.

"Oh, cool. Let's do that!"

He laughs with excitement and sets up the game. We change out of our karate gis, and Mateo gives me a pair of shorts and one of his T-shirts. I nearly swim in his shirt, but I take it. It smells like him—sweet and clean. I will breathe it in all night long.

We play for hours, only interrupted by his mother when she brings us pizza. Before I know it, it's after midnight, but I'm not a bit tired.

Mateo yawns, though, and I throw a pillow at him. "There's no sleeping at a sleepover," I joke.

"Man, I am sore as heck today." He stretches his arms.

"Me, too. I was at the same practice as you."

He hits me with a pillow.

I laugh and grab it. Then I stand and smack him on the head with it. He grabs another pillow from his bed and hits me back. Then I lunge at him and throw my arms around him.

"What a surprise!" I yell. "The scrawny Aiden takes down the Washington Hornets number one wrestler!"

Mateo falls back on his bed and laughs.

Then he flips me over.

26

The Happiest Boys Alive

"YOU'LL NEVER PIN me!" He flips me and puts me in a scarf hold, one arm wrapped under my head, the other gripping my body. "Let's see you get out of this."

I squirm left and right, trying to bridge my legs. Mat's too strong for me. Even with the give of his mattress, I can't shake him. I tap out, and he releases me.

"Maybe if you weren't five hundred pounds, I'd stand a chance."

He laughs and pushes me. "Five hundred pounds of pure muscle!" We roll on our backs, and I stare at the ceiling. I certainly don't want to sleep, but I wouldn't mind staying like this in his bed all night. His shoulder brushes against mine. The hairs on my arms and legs rise in excitement.

"Mat, I'm sorry that—I dunno." Shut up, mouth! Why would you even *talk* about it? My brain betrays me. "I mean, you know. I don't wanna be the reason—"

"Stop." He rolls to one side, propping himself up on his elbow. His brown eyes melt with empathy. "I'm sorry. I dunno what got into me. I was tired." His lips curve, and I want nothing more in the world than to put my mouth against his.

This is insufferable.

The very thing that got those jerks picking on me is what I want the most—I want Mateo. I want to call him my boyfriend. Is that so much to ask?

"Thanks," I mutter, breaking eye contact before my body betrays me. I stare at my own skinny arms.

Even if Mateo were gay, what in the heck makes me think he'd like me? What do I have to offer anyone? I'm a bunch of insecurities bundled into a less than mediocre body.

"You wanna sleep?" he asks.

I take a slow, deep breath. "You tired?"

"Beat."

I don't want to sleep, but I'll do whatever he wants. Especially if I can stay right here next to him all night long.

"Yeah, me, too. I can sleep."

"Cool. I just gotta go to the bathroom." He gets out of bed, and my eyes follow his every step. The shape of his butt in those shorts creates an odd tingle in my stomach.

When Mateo returns, he takes off his shirt, and I press my hand against my chest, trying to calm my beating heart.

"My turn." I hop out of bed. The bathroom's just down the hall. After I pee, I wash my hands and splash cold water on my face. *Calm down. Don't mess this up.*

I take several deep breaths and walk back to his bedroom. He's under the sheets, and he smiles when I return.

I pull at my shirt. I don't usually sleep with a shirt on, but I feel terribly shy. My body is nothing like Mat's.

"Um, I know the floor's hard. Sorry, I don't have an air mattress or anything," he says.

"I can crash on the beanbag," I tell him, sending mental vibes that he asks what I want to hear.

"Well, um, you can crash in bed. We can share it. It's a big bed."

My heart leaps into my throat, and I have to force away the smile that wants to grow on my face.

"You sure?"

"Yeah."

Carefully, I put one foot in front of the other. I want to sprint over to him, but again I have to control my emotions. My legs shake as I walk.

When I get in bed, I sit up for a second, and I swallow the lump that's formed in my throat. Taking off my shirt, I pray he doesn't get weird. He rolls to one side, looking away from me. I get under the covers. I'm not touching him, but I feel his body heat.

It is absolutely magical.

When I'm in, he reaches up and pulls a chord on the ceiling fan and light above the bed. The room darkens, and my heart beats so fast I'm certain Mateo is going to be able to hear it.

He just says, "Night."

"Goodnight." I stare at the ceiling, my eyes wide open, my pulse off the charts. I'm too afraid to move.

For a long time, I remain frozen. Then, a soft snore comes from Mateo. It's the cutest sound, not rough or loud like I've heard in movies. It's simple soft, rhythmic breathing.

My body relaxes. I match his breathing, in and out, like a weird game. Then the real mental fight begins.

Do I touch him? Not, like, in a perverted way. Just, like, accidentally? You know, my body turns and my arm finds itself wrapped around Mateo's chest?

Yes. I move a bit closer to him, rolling over slower than a sloth. My body trembles. I'm terrified I'll wake him up.

Oh, boy! What if he wakes up and gets mad? What if he kicks me out of his house in the middle of the night?

Chills erupt all throughout my body. I can't stop what I'm doing. Let him throw me out. Let him never talk to me ever again. I don't care.

I just want one moment like this. One moment like this, and I swear I could die peacefully.

An hour or three must pass by, and sleep never comes. I don't want to forget a second of how this feels, this closeness to someone I like so very much. At some point, I must pass out because I nearly have a heart attack right before the sun rises. When I wake up, my arm somehow found itself around Mateo's chest from under the blanket.

Even better, at some point his arm must have moved right over mine. I awake to my arm across his chest with his arm holding mine.

Oh. My.

It's the most amazing feeling in the world.

I wake up the happiest guy in the world.

27

Waking Up to Reality

I MUST HAVE dozed again. The room is brighter, and Mateo and I have reversed roles. I've moved over to my opposite side, and his arm rests across my chest. I hold my breath, excited and terrified. Listening closely, I no longer make out any snores. Instead, warm air glides against my neck. Every few seconds, the hairs on the back of my neck rise as Mat breathes against me.

What if he wakes up and sees this?

Well, good. Maybe it would be better than the other way around.

But what if he freaks out? He's not… not like me.

Or what if his parents walk in and see this? Would they be weird about it, or would they just see it as two kids sharing a bed? I hope for the latter. I want to soak up this moment. It could be over any second, and it's certainly possible this will never happen again.

I close my eyes and enjoy it.

Mat moves closer.

I freeze. Panic pulses through me. Then Mateo rolls the other way. His arm leaves me, and I remain paralyzed. Every few seconds, it's the same rhythmic breathing. He's still asleep.

And just like that, sadness rushes through me. Does he know any of this happened? That he slept with my arm wrapped around him?

Mat stirs, and I hold my breath. He sits up in bed, stretches, and yawns. I roll over so my back is flat on the bed, and so that he knows I'm also awake. "Hey," Mat mumbles. *"Buenos dias."*

"Morning." I don't know how long we slept, but I've never woken up more refreshed.

"I gotta run," he says.

"Huh?"

"I run every Sunday morning. Long-distance." He stretches again, and his long, muscled arms get my blood pumping. I don't want to get out of bed. "Wanna go with me?"

I hate running. "Sure. How long do you run?"

"I'm up to ten miles now."

My stomach churns. "Oh."

He laughs a little. "But after we can have a huge breakfast. It will be worth it." He punches me gently on the shoulder.

"Or you could just help me work on my pins!" I toss the blanket off and jump on him, trying to put him in a scarf hold. He laughs, but he's way too fast for me. He flips me, and his bare stomach slides on top of my head. His hands hold down my hips. It's a pin that's basically a sixty-nine position.

Oh, my goodness, someone help me.

"Man, ain't nobody got time for that," he says. "We'd be working all day."

He starts to move, but before he rolls over, I bite his stomach. He yelps, leaping off me. Panic instantly floods me—did I go too far? But Mateo laughs and rubs his belly.

"Cheap move," he tells me.

"It's a Krake move," I reply.

"Yeah," he nods. "So you wanna run with me?"

I don't want to go back to reality. I don't want to leave this bedroom. I also really don't want to run. But I guess if I had Mat's butt to stare at the entire time and breakfast after, then maybe I could survive.

After we both have a chance to use the bathroom and get dressed, we head outside. It's a beautiful fall day. Crisp, refreshing air and warm sunshine welcome us. Fall even smells nice.

We start with a moderate jog. "I don't go too fast," he tells me. "During the week, it's all high-intensity stuff. So once a week, I work on endurance. An hour or so of running."

An hour or so? I inhale a big gulp of the cool, fall air and push ahead. I'd love to be tough like Mateo, and it sure doesn't happen by sitting on my butt. I'm determined to keep up.

We're side-by-side for the first mile, but I start to feel it already by the second. "You can go ahead," I tell him. Besides, it will give me something nice to look at it.

I follow Mateo for as long as I can, but soon pain shoots through my side, and my legs cramp. "I'll meet you back at your house."

"Okay." He waves at me and keeps going. I watch him run off in the distance, wondering how he's so motivated.

I turn around and walk back. Maybe I should call Mom to pick me up instead of walking. It would be quicker.

The thought vanishes when a car drives by slowly. Loud music bursts through the lowered windows. The tires squeal on the pavement when it comes to an abrupt halt right next to me. "Hey, homo," a boy says from the passenger side. I don't recognize him, but the driver is unmistakable. It's the varsity captain Tanner.

And in the backseat, Logan rides with them.

They pull over to the side of the road and get out.

28

Run, Aiden

"WORKING THE STREETS now, eh?" Logan asks.

"Huh?" I put my hands in my pockets and look around. A lump forms in my throat, and a van driven by an old lady passes us. She doesn't even glance my way.

"Like a hooker," Logan adds, standing next to the boy I don't know.

"What do you want?" My voice shakes, and they laugh at my fear.

Tanner takes out his wallet. "Maybe I'm just a paying customer," he says. "What's the going rate for a hand-job? I bet you get, like, a whole five bucks."

"No, man," Logan says. "He likes it so much he does it for free." His green eyes burn with hate, and I'm filled with nausea.

Tanner puts his wallet in the back pocket of tight jeans. He has thick legs but still wears skinny jeans. "You're all sweaty. Had a lot of work today?"

"I was running," I say. For a moment I consider telling them that I had been running with Mateo, but I don't think that would help either of us.

"Trying to get in shape?" Logan asks. He takes a step closer to me. "You sure need it."

"Just leave me alone." I put my head down and walk away. Tanner steps in front of me. He's huge. "What do you want?"

"Aww, I think Aiden's gonna cry." Tanner puts his fists under his eyes and makes a cry-baby gesture. His head is smooth with a fresh buzz cut. His eyes shift from mocking to glaring, and it terrifies me. "What's wrong? Your boyfriend not here to stand up for you?"

"He's not my boyfriend!" I clench my fists. "Get out of my way." I try to walk around Tanner, but his jerk of a friend with the long hair grabs me from behind. He ties up both of my arms, and Logan faces me. "What the *hell* do you want?"

"We want you to quit," Logan says. "We don't want no fag on the team." Spit flies from his mouth when he talks.

"I'm not a quitter," I say, and the boy behind me tightens his grip.

"Notice he doesn't deny the fag part," Tanner adds.

"You're right," Logan says. He hits me with an uppercut right in my stomach. I gasp, and the boy behind me twists my arms hard. "Weakness has to be beaten out of you. Haven't you learned that yet? It's the only way to get tough." He punches me again in the stomach, and then the boy from behind lets me go. I fall on my knees. "Are you gonna quit the team?"

I take rapid breaths and try not to throw up. Logan grabs my shoulders and pulls me closer to him. My head is level with his crotch.

"Would you rather blow me, homo? Is that what you want? A dick in your mouth?" Logan thrusts his hips into my face and then pushes me back down.

The boy with the long hair grabs my neck, picks me back up, and puts me in a chokehold. "You gonna answer him, homo?" the boy asks. Then he reaches around, grabs my crotch, and squeezes.

I cry out in pain. Then I jump wide and throw my elbows into the jerk's ribs. He yelps and lets me go.

I stand tall even with tears in my eyes. I want to knock the terrible grin off Logan's face.

Adrenaline races through my veins. Logan's eyes grow wide, and he charges at me.

I kick him right in the groin. He grabs his crotch, yells, and falls. I take one look at Tanner and know that I'm out of luck. I turn and run. Footsteps pound the ground from behind, matching my own. I race with every bit of energy I have, but in seconds, I fall hard on the sidewalk.

Tanner jumps me from behind, tackling me. The concrete slaps my body. Tanner gets up and pulls me with him. "Why'd you have to do something like that?" he asks and smacks me in the face.

Logan and the other boy have caught up to us. Tanner holds me, and there's no smash that could get out of his powerful grip.

"You're gonna pay for that, faggot," Logan barks. "Oh, man. Are you gonna pay." He swings his foot into me, and I bend my knees together as much as I can. He hits my thighs and not my groin, thankfully. He punches me in the face. Blood flies from my mouth, and a wave of dizziness hits me. It's kind of nice, though. I can't feel the pain right now. The world around me spins and turns gray.

Then a car screeches to a halt right by us, and a man runs out of the vehicle. "Hey! Stop that right now! What are you doing?"

It's Mr. Samuels!

I blink and refocus.

"This isn't school," Tanner says bitterly. "Get in your car and turn around, old man."

"What?" Mr. Samuels runs to me. "You let him go. Now!" Mr. Samuels pulls me away from Tanner. For a second I think Tanner's going to attack our teacher.

Instead, he mumbles something I can't understand and backs up. "C'mon," he tells Logan and the other kid.

"What is *wrong* with you boys?" Mr. Samuels shouts. He's fuming, and I can feel his hot breath against my skin as I nearly pass out.

Tanner stops and turns around. He glowers with such fierceness. My body trembles.

"There *will* be consequences for this," Mr. Samuels says.

"We aren't at school. You can't give me a detention," Tanner snaps.

"You're right," Mr. Samuels says. "I have no intention of giving you a detention. I do, however, have every intention of calling the police and reporting what I just observed. Three against one."

Logan shakes, and a little smile comes to my face.

"You better think twice about that," Tanner threatens. "You call the police on us, and I'll have the entire varsity team after Aiden every single day of his life. Every. Single. Day. You got that?" The boys run back to Tanner's car. They peel out, and I can still hear their laughter over screeching tires.

"Let's get you home," Mr. Samuels says. He puts me in the back seat of his car. I close my eyes, and the world turns dark.

29

*Bruises
Coming Out*

"AIDEN, WHAT'S going on?" Mom asks.

Mr. Samuels carried me inside my house. Mom had sent him to Mateo's to pick me up. Thank goodness, or who knows how much more of a beating I'd have had to take.

Seriously, I could have been killed. Is *that* what they want?

I sit in the bathroom with my shirt off. The immediate concern is my ribs, but fortunately—if there's any kind of pro to my getting beat up—it appears that my face and my stomach took most of it. I don't tell Mom or Mr. Samuels that they hurt my groin, too. I'm too embarrassed.

Mom wants me to go to the hospital, but I've begged her to not make me go.

Tanner's threat looms over me. A hospital visit in this condition would lead to a police report. What if Tanner was serious?

"I told you," I say, adjusting the ice pack on my head, "they're bullies, but I'm fine. Just a couple scratches."

"I'm calling the school, and I'm calling their parents," Mom shouts. She examines my head again. "You could have a concussion!"

"I'm fine," I lie.

"I'll talk to Coach Krake," Mr. Samuels tells us. "Privately. He'll take it better one-on-one than if you try to get several members of the team in trouble."

"I don't care what that bull-headed idiot thinks. This stops. It stops now." Mom puts her hands on her hips and sighs loudly. "Screw some seventeen-year-old's threat! Let him come after *me*. I've got heels that will castrate him, and I'd be doing the world a favor!"

I laugh a little, but it turns into a cough.

Mom shakes her head. "We're seeing a doctor. I'm not taking any chances," she says.

Maybe I should go, but I don't want to. "You'll really talk to Krake?"

Mr. Samuels nods. "Yes. First thing tomorrow. I'll put a stop to it. I promise you that."

"I don't like promises when it comes to dealing with assholes," Mom snaps. "Trust me. I promised Aiden a lot when he was a little boy. Assholes get in the way of those promises." She runs her fingers through my hair. I still have bed-head from sleeping next to Mateo.

Mateo.

I need to call him. He'll be wondering what happened to me.

"Let's go to that urgent care at least," Mom says. "Get a check-up."

"What will we say when they ask how this happened?" I asked.

"I don't care about their threats!" She pulls at her hair.

"But *I* do! I want to be able to walk the halls and not be afraid. You don't know what it's like." I press my hands into my temples, and my eyes fill with tears. "You wanna know why they hate me so much?"

My pulse quickens. I want to tell them the truth about me. Maybe in a year or two, though. Not today. Maybe when—or *if*—I ever get a real boyfriend. But right now, my mind races. If I say it, it might distract Mom. It buys me some time, so she doesn't end up on the phone screaming at Logan's parents or at the police. If I look and feel better in an hour, then maybe she won't make me see a doctor today.

But the big thing is—oh, my stomach flips. The big thing is that once I say it, there's no going back. Who I was yesterday, I can never be again. The knowledge is irrevocable. Coming out is irrevocable.

Am I ready for this?

Maybe I should want to call the cops and get the boys arrested. But the wrestling team is big, and they will do anything Super Captain Tanner tells them to do. I'd never find peace.

Never.

"What, sweetie? Why would they hate you?" Mom blinks, and a tear runs down her cheek. She reaches for Mr. Samuels's hand and holds it.

I shuffle on the toilet seat.

"If I tell you—" Suddenly, I'm crying. The tears rush out of me. I've never been this close to saying it out loud before.

What if Mom stops loving me?

What if she would hate me?

How would I get through life without Mom's support? I don't have Dad anymore. I need someone on my side. The thoughts crush me.

I try to swallow the lump in my throat, and I wipe away my tears. My chest hurts, but I force myself to speak.

"If I tell you something, maybe something you won't—I dunno— understand. Or like. If I tell you something like that, do you promise not to hate me?" I choke on the words. More tears spring from my eyes.

Mom releases Mr. Samuels's hand and hugs me. "You listen to me, and you listen carefully. I cannot imagine any part of you that would make me not love you." She kisses me on the cheek. "And, Aiden. I can imagine a lot. Do you understand? I will love you, no matter what."

I clear my throat. "They hate me because—" I take a deep breath. My chest clenches.

I'm about to say it, and chills run through my body. But I am ready. I don't care if it's irrevocable. Who I was yesterday—that wasn't the real me. The real me is buried inside me.

I'm ready to meet the *real* me.

I want to introduce the real me to Mom.

I clear my throat. I feel the words on the tip of my tongue. I free the words.

"They hate me because I'm gay."

Once the words come out, so do more tears. Mom hugs me tighter and kisses me multiple times on the cheek, the forehead, the top of my head. "I love you, Aiden. That certainly does not and never ever could change anything I feel about you."

"Then why are you crying?" I ask.

She pulls away from me and wipes her face. "I'm crying because I hate that we live in a world where you'd think that I'd love you less— or even hate you—because of who you are. I hate that others don't understand it. I hate that others hurt you like this because of it. You are perfect, Aiden Rothe. Do you understand me? Absolutely perfect."

She hugs me again, and we both share a good, long cry.

After what feels like an eternity, she lets me go.

"I didn't want to interrupt," Mr. Samuels says, "but I agree with everything your mother said. I'll fight for you, Aiden. We'll make this right."

"Thanks," I say.

"Now, would it be all right if I hugged you, too?" he asks.

I smile and open up my arms.

30

Take a Stand

WHEN MONDAY MORNING comes, I limp out of bed. I could stay home from school today. But I need to do two important things.

First, I need to talk to Mateo. Naturally, he had texted yesterday, and I told him briefly what had happened. I wanted to be able to talk to him in person.

Nervousness pulses through me, though. Mat acted fine when it was just the two of us. He's different when it's in public. After this last beating, he won't treat me like that, will he?

I hope he's cool.

The second thing I need to do is talk to Krake. If nervousness rocked me before, this thought nearly gives me a stroke. Mr. Samuels had told me he'd talk to Krake, but before I went to bed, we had decided it would be best if we do it together.

"How are you feeling? Want breakfast?" Mom asks when I enter the kitchen. Her hair is extra disheveled for the morning like she tossed and turned all night.

"I'm really okay." I flex my skinny bicep. "Resilient, see?"

"I can see that." She takes out a carton of eggs from the fridge.

"No breakfast, though. I'm too nervous."

"You need something," Mom argues. Her blue eyes study me. All this is a lot for both of us, I'm sure. I got beat up. I came out.

Holy crap. I came out.

She puts the eggs back and stares into the fridge.

"Maybe just a Pop-Tart?"

"So nutritious." She rolls her eyes but goes to the pantry and takes out a box of brown sugar cinnamon Pop-Tarts. "Warmed up?"

"I can do that, Mom," I say and walk over to the toaster. She hands me the pastry and smiles. Then she gives me a hug. I've had a lot of hugs in the last twenty-four hours.

I was so worried everything would change if I told Mom I was gay. I guess it has changed—when she hugs me, I know she's hugging the real me. There's no guilt festering inside me, no shame. I feel light like I'm floating around the house instead of walking.

It's an incredible feeling.

Of course, I know it could have gone the other way—no hugs, no breakfast, Mom hiding behind a closed door. It's weird to feel lucky after getting my ass kicked, but I do feel lucky. I've got Mom and Mr. Samuels. Two people in my corner.

"Text me after the talk." She squeezes me again.

"Just give us a chance first. Before you call the principal or anyone's parents. Please?"

"You're lucky I'm dating a very nice teacher at your school," she replies. "Or I'd have already been at the principal's door."

"Thanks, Mom." Mr. Samuels pulls up out front. I thought he might stay the night, but that has not happened yet. Well, he might have stayed over Saturday night, but I didn't ask.

He walks up to the front door, and I run out before he can knock. He opens his mouth to say something, but I don't give him the chance. "I'll be in the car." If he wants to kiss Mom good morning, he can do it while I wait in the car, thank you very much.

He steps inside my house, and I distract myself by playing a game on my phone. At least I don't have to ride the bus.

Mr. Samuels returns, and we drive to school. "How's it going?"

"Can't I wait in your classroom while you talk to Coach?" I ask, holding my stomach.

"I won't let him bully you, Aiden. Not him or anyone on his team if I can help it." His hands squeeze the steering wheel. "Why do you think I want you to come with me and tell Krake what happened?"

I adjust my seat belt. "I know. It's about standing up for myself."

"The world can be a brutal place, as unfortunately you know too well already. These wrestlers—" He shakes his head. "I've had most of them in class, even Tanner when he was a freshman. He wasn't mean then."

"Do you think Krake made him mean?"

He sighs. "Maybe."

"But if that's the case, then what chance do we stand against Krake?"

His hands slide down to the bottom of the steering wheel. His dark knuckles turn white from the intensity of his grip. "When it comes to things like athletics, especially if you're working with the same person for years, you develop similarities to that person." He turns down the radio, which was already pretty low. "Do the kids look up to Krake?"

I shrug. "I guess so." Then I remember the one time I said something kind of negative. DeMarcus had agreed, but that other kid—Jeff—he snapped at me. We had only been training with Krake for a few days at that point.

"When you're young and motivated like you, Aiden, we want to become our heroes. And that's not always a good thing. Sometimes the people we see as heroes aren't that good."

I shake my head. "Krake isn't a nice person. Why would anyone want to train with him?"

"Why do you?"

"Oh," I mumble, suddenly feeling stupid. "Should I quit? That's what those jerks want."

"I can't answer that for you," he says. "Just be careful about what you're willing to give up in order to become who you want to be."

I don't understand what he means. All I wanted to do was find a place to belong. To get stronger so I wouldn't feel weak. And what sucks the most? The exact opposite of both those things has happened. I don't belong, but I don't want to be a quitter. Plus, I'm getting my ass kicked all the time. So much for getting stronger.

I text Mateo. *Can we meet up when you get to school?*

Mr. Samuels parks in the faculty lot, and we get out of the car. It's pretty early—no buses have shown up yet.

Mateo texts me back. *Hey. Coach called me in to talk to me. I'm in his office now. Um, yeah, we def need to talk. Can't explain over text.*

My eyes feel like they're about to pop out of my head. "Crap."

"What is it?" Mr. Samuels asks. I show him Mat's text. "Well, this will certainly be interesting. Won't it?" His voice is steady—the opposite of how I feel—but there's anger in it, too.

He holds the door open to the side entrance of the school, and we head toward Coach Krake's office.

31

Bombshell

MATEO STANDS OUTSIDE Krake's office. "I'm sorry," he mouths silently. It's early, but his thick, wavy hair is still styled. He scratches at the bit of stubble on his chin. His eyes hang on my bruises.

"Sorry for what?"

Mateo doesn't answer. He tightens his lips, and my heart pounds against my chest. He goes inside Krake's office, and we follow.

"Mr. Samuels," Krake says in a less than enthusiastic tone, "and Aiden Rothe." His eyes dig into me with hate. It's a look of contempt that I don't understand and never will. What have I done except want to be on his team? He closes his laptop and places both hands on his desk. His big arms make the laptop look like a bookmark. "To what do I owe the pleasure?"

"May we sit?" Mr. Samuels asks. Krake nods. Mr. Samuels looks at me, waiting for me to start. "Go ahead," he speaks softly.

I glance at Mateo, who stands in the corner behind Coach. What had they been discussing?

"I, uh, I don't wanna be a tattletale, you know?" I start.

"If that's true, I don't think you'd be here." Krake narrows his eyes. "Let's hear it, kid. I have a full day ahead of me."

Mr. Samuels shuffles uncomfortably in his seat, but he doesn't interject. I know this is something I'm supposed to do.

"It's about Tanner. And Logan." I clear my throat. "Really the entire varsity team, but it starts with them."

I tell him the story about yesterday morning, how they jumped me on the street, along with some other long-haired boy I don't know. Mat lowers his head while I tell the story. What would have happened if he had been with me? Would he have stood up for me?

Krake doesn't flinch, even when I show my bruises. His eyes remain focused and apathetic. He only reacts when I say that the kids called me a fag. His eyes narrow further at those words. When I finish, I say, "I don't know what to do about it. But it's not right."

Krake remains quiet, and the silence in his office is both awkward and humiliating. It doesn't make me feel stronger to say what happened. It's the opposite, rather, like I'm putting all my shame on display for everyone to see.

Mr. Samuels speaks up first. "As a coach of one of our most successful programs here, I was certain you would want to know. To protect your students. All of your students."

"What is your involvement here?" Krake asks my teacher.

"I'm a direct witness," Mr. Samuels replies. "I was driving by when it happened, and I vouch that Aiden's story is true. So, before we go to the principal or to law enforcement, we made the decision to come to you. As their coach, you have the most influence over them. Not the principal or the police, though we'll report this as necessary if proper methods aren't taken to stop this egregious behavior."

The color of Krake's face completely drains, and Mateo's jaw pops open. Hearing Mr. Samuels stand up for me is awesome. But hearing him talk to Krake like that is even better.

Krake stands and walks to his office door. It's shut, but it has a small window, and he looks out. Then he turns and faces us. His face twists into that of a dangerous animal getting cornered.

"I don't know who you think you're talking to, Lloyd." Krake's nostrils flare—his nose is huge on his face already, but the width of each nostril is almost comically wide, or it would be if I wasn't sitting here paralyzed with fear. "You wanna call the police? Have you forgotten who would answer that call? Wanna get the principal involved? Let's see how strong your tenure holds up. Don't start a fight you'll lose."

Mr. Samuels, somehow, remains perfectly calm. "One step at a time, Terry." Krake's first name is *Terry?* "We're here to resolve this appropriately with *you.*"

Krake walks over to Mateo and puts an arm around his shoulders. Mateo flinches and looks at me briefly. Shame fills his eyes. "Mat, what do you think we should do about this? As Aiden's captain, what do you recommend?"

Mateo looks down again. "This team does not have room for weakness," he says softly.

"Can you say that a little louder?" Krake asks.

Mateo looks up. Any shame or empathy in his eyes has vanished. They're dark and harsh—like Krake's. "The team doesn't have room for weakness," he repeats, louder this time. "Maybe you should quit."

Mr. Samuels grips the arms of his chair so hard that they creak as if they're about to break. He stands slowly, pushing off the chair. "Mateo, is that how you really feel?"

Mateo looks down again.

Krake takes a step forward. "The words came out of his mouth, didn't they?" He turns to me. "So, what's it gonna be?"

Why shouldn't I quit? It's not like I'm enjoying any of this. But it's the principle of the matter. I should be able to stay on the team, and Krake should put an end to the bullying.

"Are you saying that you condone the actions of your wrestlers that I have witnessed first-hand?" Mr. Samuels asks.

The office door opens, and a uniformed police officer steps inside with a cup of coffee. "Oh, sorry, Terry. I didn't know you had visitors." The officer smiles at us through yellow teeth, but it feels very phony, like this was a setup. "I was just bringing my favorite team's coach a fresh, hot cup of Joe."

Krake takes the coffee and grins at us. "Aiden and Mateo, let me introduce you to my brother-in-law, Captain Decker of our local police force." He turns to Mr. Samuels. "Of course, you two are well acquainted, aren't you?"

Color rushes to Captain Decker's face when he sees Mr. Samuels. "Well, hello, Lloyd. Been a long time, hasn't it?"

For the first time, Mr. Samuels trembles. Krake didn't scare him. But something right now bothers him. He looks like he's seen a ghost, and the white in his eyes grows wide. If I didn't know him better, I'd say that was fear.

"Yes, Sensei. It certainly has," Mr. Samuels replies, his voice shaking slightly as he speaks.

Woah. Did he just call the police captain Sensei?

32

A New Challenge

"I DON'T THINK I've seen you since you graduated high school," Decker says. "It's a small world, eh? I married a beautiful woman, Krake's sister. Did you know that? How are you, my old student?" He strikes me immediately as disingenuous.

Mr. Samuels's arms tremble. I've never seen him afraid. Decker is tall and lean, more like a basketball player than a cop. Muscles rip through his uniform. He hands Krake a cup of coffee with his long arms. I bet he has a hell of a punch with arms like that.

"I continue to enjoy the martial arts," Mr. Samuels says calmly.

"I'm sure you do," Decker says. "The safety of a dojo is a nice place to hide behind. I have real-life fights every day with criminals."

"You certainly have a lot of great experience, Captain," Krake says, emphasizing the title. Mr. Samuels takes a step toward the door and motions for me to follow. My heart sinks. It looks like we lost this battle.

At the door, my teacher turns around. He looks like he wants to speak, but no words come out of his mouth.

Krake continues to do all the talking. "You see, Lloyd. The police are my family. My team is a family. What do you have? You don't have anything. Even your old teacher rejected you. Get out and don't come back."

Krake waves him away.

Mr. Samuels puts his arm around me. My eyes dart to Mateo, searching for any reaction from him, but he keeps his head down. We leave without saying anything else.

"What are we gonna do?" I ask when we return to Mr. Samuels's classroom. Krake doesn't care that I was hurt, and his freaking brother-in-law not only controls the local police but also happens to have been my teacher's teacher. This is *crazy!*

On top of everything, Mateo's harsh words were the worst part of all this for me. Krake made him say those words, right?

"What about the principal?" I ask.

Mr. Samuels shakes his head. "The principal is as pro-wrestling as anyone here. Krake's winning streaks, the championships—they bring a lot of positive press, not to mention financial gain, to this school."

Taking a seat, I put my head on my desk. "Ugh." We have nothing here. Krake's got the law enforcement and the school on his side.

"Wait," I sit up straight with what I hope is a great idea. "Coach has this support because he wins. What if he loses?"

"How do you suggest making that happen?" Mr. Samuels sits behind his desk and rubs his forehead. "Do you want to switch schools, join their team, and take down the Hornets?"

His words suck the air out of my chest. "Well, no. I mean, even if I could switch schools, I'm not good enough to beat anyone."

Mr. Samuels stands. "Do you want to quit the team?" He walks to the center of the classroom like he's preparing a lecture.

"I don't wanna be a quitter, but what choice do I have now?"

"What if you quit to join something else?" Mr. Samuels asks, moving right in front of my desk, his hands pressed against his hips.

"Like, um, what?"

"What if the wrestling team does lose? Maybe not a big title or even a local match. What if they lose at something else that takes away their pride?" Mr. Samuels's eyes glow. "Something like a mixed martial arts challenge. We could host an event for charity. Or, heck, give all the money to the boosters to make the sports people happy."

"Mixed martial arts? Who would be fighting them?" My pulse races so hard I feel it everywhere in my body. I have a terrible feeling that I know the answer.

Mr. Samuels stops in the center of the room. He faces me, and his lips curl into a grin.

I shake my head. "Are you nuts? You're out of your mind!"

"Not tomorrow. Not next week. After the state tournament. Let's say the Hornets take first again. They'll ride back into the city on a bus, and there will be a parade of people cheering for them. Then we propose a match, a celebratory exhibition. My students against Krake's. Mateo versus Tanner." He opens his mouth and laughs. "Aiden versus Logan."

"You're crazy!" I reply. But I can't deny the adrenaline rushing through me at the idea. What if I could stand up to Logan? What if I could win? Maybe he'd leave me alone forever. "What if Krake says no?"

"Let me worry about that." Mr. Samuels laughs. "I'll make him an offer he can't refuse. He can bring his brother-in-law, too."

"What happened between you and, uh, your Sensei?"

"It's a story for another time," he replies. I don't press him on the issue. It's not the first time he's avoided talking about his own training.

"What if Mateo doesn't want to do it?"

"It's his choice, of course," Mr. Samuels says. "Maybe you'll just have to fight Tanner, instead."

I roll my eyes. "Oh, now, you've *really* lost your mind." He tilts his head back and chuckles. "I'm glad you find all this funny. You're legit crazy, you know that? No disrespect, sir."

He continues laughing. "If we wait till after state, we have three months to train. You'll need to practice every day. Are you up for that?"

Am I up for that? This is moving too fast. Yesterday I got my ass kicked. Today, we were supposed to try to stop that from happening ever again. Now, if we do this, I could get my ass kicked publicly in front of the entire school.

I take a deep breath. Or—maybe, just maybe—my lips stretch into a smile, the first one since meeting with Krake. Yeah, that's a thought.

Maybe, just maybe, I could get what I wanted all along. I could get stronger without taking all the crap daily in wrestling practice. And maybe, I could be the one doing the ass-kicking this time.

"Um, well—" I think about this carefully. My life could change forever with a simple yes. "Are you up for teaching all that?"

He flashes a wide smile. "You and any other kid at this school who is tired of being picked on. Anyone who is tired of people who can get away with anything just because they bring home some cheap plastic trophy. We'll make this bigger than you and me, kid. We'll open it up to everyone. We'll start the Washington Hornets Martial Arts Club. We'll practice at the same time as the wrestlers. That gives you an excuse to leave the team."

"What about Mat?"

"Mat, you, and I will still have private lessons. We'll need that if we're really going to challenge the wrestling team."

"Do you really think we can win?"

He sits on the edge of his desk. "Honestly, Aiden, this shouldn't be about winning. It needs to be about standing up for yourself. Showing others you aren't afraid to face them in a fair match. Karate isn't about fighting. It's self-defense. But you've reached a point where it's necessary to change the rules for your own sake."

"That sounds like a long way of saying no."

He smiles gently. "Okay. Well played." He takes a deep breath. "Yes, I think we can win."

My eyes light up. I want to win. I don't want to be the kid—especially the gay kid—who gets picked on all the time. It's about time we flip the script.

"When can we start?" I ask.

33

A New Student

WE DON'T WASTE any time. Mr. Samuels visits the principal, and I wish I could have heard what was said behind those closed doors. I picture the principal questioning a martial arts program—what if a kid gets hurt? What if someone learns how to punch too well and slugs someone in the hallway?

During fourth hour, our school reads announcements. Today I hang on every word. First, there are announcements about the football awards and banquet. Barf. The girl reading them over the public address system announces this month's library book club selection, some teen Halloween read called *Rabbit in Red*. Who wants to read a horror book about rabbits? Sounds dumb. Then she announces a bake sale to support the cheerleaders, then the first wrestling meet—really *BARF!*—but just before she gets to today's lunch, which is always the last thing read and really the only thing most people pay attention to, she reads what I want to hear!

"Attention all students—Washington High is proud to announce a new club! Learn the awesome art of traditional karate starting this afternoon. Meet in Mr. Samuels's room 208 after school today for an informational gathering. The club is completely free. You will learn self-defense, improve fitness, and meet new friends."

I nearly scream! We did it. Just like that, we have the Washington

Martial Arts Club. The rest of the school day drags by as I stare at the clocks in each room, willing them to go faster. Finally, when the eighth hour bell rings, I race to room 208, my favorite place in this big stupid high school.

I'm the first to arrive. "Do you think anyone will join us?"

He shrugs. "Things like this start slowly. One or two students at first, maybe. Everyone's busy."

"Yeah." I stare at the door. "So, you know I should be in wrestling practice. It feels weird not going. Thank you."

"For what?"

"For everything, honestly." I look away, a little embarrassed at how happy I feel. "But for giving me an excuse to not be there. And for, you know—" I shrug and then speak softly. "For, uh, yesterday. Understanding and all."

My cheeks burn, and I release an awkward, nervous laugh.

He walks over to my desk. "I'm proud of who you are. Proud of your strength, Aiden."

He smiles at me, and the first new student walks through his door. My jaw drops to the floor. No—really? *She's* interested in karate?

"Good afternoon, Tisha," Mr. Samuels greets her. "Thanks for joining us."

Her lips only slightly curl up, and she nods. She takes a seat right next to me.

What is Logan's girlfriend doing here? Is she going to be like some kind of spy? She'll tell him everything we're doing! What the hell!

"Logan and I, uh, we broke up," she whispers to me, shattering my theory.

"Oh, I'm—" What do I say? I'm not sorry. "What happened?"

She looks around the room, still empty. Mr. Samuels moves back to his desk and glances up at the door occasionally. I follow his gaze, and the hall appears empty. Maybe it will just be Tisha and me. My mind wanders to Mateo. I haven't talked to him since the announcement. He'll see I'm not at practice and put two and two together of course. I hope he'll join us when practice ends.

"You can't tell anyone," Tisha mumbles, interrupting my thoughts.

"Okay."

"He, uh, well it's been going on for the last week or so. I should have ended it sooner. He keeps trying to make me do things." She rubs her forehead.

"Oh, crap, Tisha. I'm sorry. Are you okay?"

She nods. "We broke up this weekend. He came to my house on Sunday, gloating about what he did to you." She looks up and studies my face. My bruises linger. "He's not a very good person."

"No, he's not," I say firmly.

"Sunday, he—when I said no, he squeezed my arm so hard I thought he was gonna break it." She rolls up her sleeve, and her bicep is black and blue.

"Oh, no, I'm so sorry." Anger pulses through my veins. How could he do that to her? Tears well in her soft brown eyes. The black and blue look so out of place on her tan skin. She's a beautiful girl and sweet, too. How could anyone hurt her?

"I don't know what I'm even doing here." She looks around the still empty classroom. "I haven't told Camila. I haven't told *anyone*. I didn't even wanna come to school today. Just going through the motions, I guess. I heard this announcement, and then lunch happened."

"What happened at lunch?"

She shakes her head. "It's not true. Whatever you hear that I supposedly did is *not* true."

"Did to Logan?"

She nods. "He lies. But that doesn't stop the entire wrestling team from believing him."

"I'm so sorry. Logan's a total jerk."

She smiles a little at that. "Yeah. So, karate?"

"Trust me," I say. "It's so much cooler than you ever would have thought. Mr. Samuels is the best. And, um, if Logan or anyone ever grabs you like that again, you'll know what to do."

"That's kind of why I'm here. He scared me yesterday. The announcement today—just kinda sounded like I was supposed to be here. You know?"

I nod.

A couple of other kids walk into the room and sit in the back row. It brings a smile to Mr. Samuels's face.

Tisha leans in and whispers in my ear again. "I'm sorry for everything Logan did to you. His lies about calling you gay. And all the stupid stuff. It's not right."

I lock eye contact with her, and my heart jumps into my throat. It beats so hard I could fall out of my chair. "Just so you know, and I've only told my Mom and Mr. Samuels this. No one else." I swallow hard. "He wasn't lying. It doesn't make him any less of a jerk. But what he said wasn't a lie."

Tisha smiles at me and reaches for my hand. She squeezes it gently.

It feels good to tell her that, but something in me says I need to say the specific words—that to not state it directly is weak, and that's not who I want to be.

"I'm gay," I whisper to her. "And I want to kick Logan's ass."

"Can I help you? I want to see how far my foot can go up it."

I laugh hard, and it's contagious.

It feels fantastic to be honest—and to have a friend again.

34

Bad Pics

OUR FIRST WEEK of martial arts practices went well. We ended the week with nine students altogether. Not even one-fifth of the wrestling team, but it was a good start. Turns out that there were other kids looking for a place to fit in. The new karate kids all like Mr. Samuels, too. They started calling him Mr. S, a sign of affection for only the most likable teachers here.

Unfortunately, Mateo has not joined us, and he hasn't spoken to me at all this week. When I tried to make eye contact with him, he turned the other way. When I texted him about getting together with me and Mr. Samuels for an evening private session, Mat texted back that he was too tired.

At least he texted back, I guess.

I replayed his "I'm sorry" repeatedly in my memory. The Mateo who stood by Krake wasn't the Mat I knew. He did that to make Coach happy, to retain his place as captain. Right?

Each night, I had hoped that we'd get together for private training. Now, it was Friday, and there's nothing more I wanted than an invite to stay over again. Anything to let me know he's still my friend.

At lunch, I sit with Tisha and Camila. It's a strange turn of events. I sit next to Tisha instead of my ex-girlfriend. Logan sits with the wrestling goons on the other side of the commons. Most depressing, Mateo joins them. It hurts to see him sit with the very people who hurt us, especially without any explanation.

Camila plays with her food, dipping a French fry in ketchup but never eating it. I have no doubt that Tisha told her what I said and that Camila knows for certain now that I'm gay. Tisha's her best friend, after all. Camila hasn't looked me in the eye since I sat down. She wears her dark hair pulled back. I stare at the freckles on her nose, but her eyes won't meet mine.

"Ugh," Tisha mumbles and slams her fist on the table, distracting me from my thoughts.

"What's wrong?" Camila asks.

Tisha hands Camila her phone. "Oh, wow," Camila says. She glances over at Logan and the other wrestling jerks.

"What is it?" I ask. Camila hands me the phone without making eye contact. It's a picture that Logan edited and shared to a private group, but of course nothing on social media is ever really private. The picture shows Tisha with a penis drawn next to her face and text that reads, *Gives good head.*

"He's such a freakin' jerk." I don't look at Logan, though. I watch Mateo open his phone. I have no idea who all received the picture, but it's obvious that Mateo sees it right now. He gasps. The rest of the boys at the table laugh like lunatics. He puts his phone away, removes his hand, and forces a smile. It's not genuine. But he still smiles for the sake of his laughing, idiotic teammates, and that pisses me off.

His brown eyes flash over at me. He looks like he wants to send me a message, and I wish I could read his mind.

You don't belong with them, Mat. Get up. Leave. Sit with us.

He doesn't move, though. It's why all of this hurts even more. How can he be sitting with them? He's stronger than every single kid at that table. Doesn't he see that he could make things better if he really wanted to?

"Can I use your phone?" I ask Tisha.

If Mat won't do anything, *I* will.

"What for?" She raises her dark eyebrows.

"Wanna get back at him? You can approve it first. But let's get back at that dick."

She hands me her phone. Camila finally makes eye contact with me—it's an inquisitive *WTF-are-you-doing* look. I ignore her. Not even her cute dimples can change my mind on this one.

I screenshot the image Logan sent. Then I open a photo editor. I do my own quick art work. I may not be Picasso, but it gets the job done.

When I show the pic to Tisha, she bursts out laughing so hard she snorts. She holds a hand against her chest. When she can finally speak, she says, "OMG. Yes. Send it back to all of them."

Camila grabs my arm and looks at the picture. "You can't do this," she says without a trace of a smile on her face.

"Why not?" Tisha asks.

Camila leans in and whispers, "Won't everyone think what Logan said you did is true?"

Tisha crosses her arms. When she shakes her head, her long, braided hair bounces on her shoulders. "They already do! Nothing I say matters."

"People believe what they wanna believe," I add, speaking firmly but softly.

Camila's eyes narrow. "Sometimes what they hear is true," she retorts. "Even if it comes from someone else."

Nausea rises in my throat. I want to tell everyone the truth, but it's not that easy. It's one person at a time right now. Maybe if Camila didn't look at me with such hostility, then I'd talk to her.

Why don't people understand that the gay thing is about me and not about them?

I ignore her for now. "Ready to send?" I ask Tisha. Tisha sends my artwork to the group chat, which apparently is half of everyone sitting here in the commons.

Their phones vibrate, and their jaws drop when they look at my revised work.

I circled the penis that Logan drew next to Tisha's face and wrote "normal-sized penis." Below that, I drew the tiniest little penis I could and wrote, *Logan's dick* next to it.

He stares at his phone, and the color of his face instantly matches that of his hair. He gets up, presses his hands on his table, and glares at Tisha. He marches over to us.

"Bitch," he calls her.

I rise. "I'm the one who drew it, dude. So if you're gonna hate on someone, hate on me. Oh, wait. You already do that." I step back ever so slightly. It's a fighting stance Mr. Samuels taught me, barely noticeable to anyone else.

"You're dead, homo," Logan snaps and swings his fist at me.

35

Threesome

LOGAN'S FIST FLIES toward my head. I step to the side, and his punch misses my face.

But it does smack hard into something else—Mr. Samuels's hand.

His large, dark palm catches Logan's fist. It looks like a baseball glove holding a golf ball.

Blood rushes to Logan's face, and the kids in the commons all "ooh" at the scene. Mr. Samuels locks eye contact with Logan. "You're coming with me, young man." Then he glances at me. "You, too."

Mr. Samuels pulls Logan forward, still gripping the fist that had attempted to hit me. We march out of the commons, but we're not heading toward the principal's office. Instead, Mr. S takes a sharp turn towards Coach Krake's office.

Without knocking, we barge inside. Krake's got a mouthful of a taco, and he coughs when we enter. Little pieces of meat and lettuce fly from his mouth.

"What's going on here?" Krake asks.

"Your student attempted to hit my student," Mr. S snaps.

Krake rolls his eyes. "And your student can't stand up for himself?"

Mr. Samuels releases Logan's fist. Logan swings his arm violently back to his side and steps over to Coach Krake. "Aiden quit wrestling. It's time your wrestlers grow up."

Krake laughs. "What is it you're doing now, kid, a knitting club?"

Mr. Samuels doesn't flinch. "I have a proposal for you."

Instantly, heat spreads through my muscles. Mr. Samuels is going to challenge Krake already?

"An exhibition challenge," Mr. S tells him.

Yep, my stomach drops to my feet. We haven't even been training but a week.

"A fundraiser," Mr. S continues. "Just like your earlier event between Mateo and Tanner. Except, this time, we'll have a friendly martial arts versus wrestling match. MMA style. You can keep the proceeds. You in?"

Krake snickers. "We have much more important things to attend to." He wipes his lips with his sleeve but misses a brown spot, hot sauce perhaps, on the side of his lips. "Even if it would only take us seconds to do, I'm not wasting time on your silly idea."

Mr. Samuels's lips curl into a grin. "Scared you'll lose?"

My pulse races so quickly I'm certain I'll have a heart attack.

Krake wipes more taco food off his shirt and stands. "Why do you want this? What's in it for you?"

After a deep breath, Mr. Samuels says, "Your boys clearly like to fight. Let's save that energy for a special match. Then maybe we can have some peace inside and out of these halls."

Krake takes time to consider, and I wipe away a few beads of sweat that have formed on my forehead.

"No," Krake answers. "There's nothing in this for me." The way he speaks—something's not quite right. It's a poker face with words that don't exactly match. There's something else Krake's thinking about, I'm sure. What does he know that we don't?

Mr. Samuels laughs. "Why do you think I came here like this right now? Today? One hundred plus witnesses just saw Logan attack another student. It's on the school's security camera." Mr. S smiles bigger, his big white teeth shining brightly. "No authority will be able to turn a blind eye to that. Not once the media gets ahold of it, regardless of relation." Mr. Samuels places his hands on his hip. "Do you understand me?"

Krake scowls at him. "You want Logan versus Aiden? What else?"

"Yes, and we'll work out the other details as my club grows," Mr. Samuels replies.

"After my season," Krake says. "I won't waste time on this during the season."

"Or risk an injury," Mr. Samuels adds, lifting his eyebrows tauntingly. "I understand."

Logan moves closer to his coach. "I'd happily fight him, Coach."

"And we insist on peace between now and the fight," Mr. Samuels demands. "Save all that energy and tension for the event. It will make it more interesting."

Krake places his hands on his desk. "Very well. But I have one condition. One change." Once again, my stomach drops. Mr. Samuels came in here thinking he had the upper hand, but I'm certain that somehow Coach Krake was prepared for this.

"Go on," Mr. S says.

"Not Logan versus Aiden," Krake tells us. "Aiden versus *Mateo.*"

The words make me want to throw up. I don't know if I could face Logan, let alone Mateo. There's no way! And what would be the point of that? It would be over in seconds.

Mr. Samuels turns to me, and my face pales with panic. I shake my head. Mr. Samuels nods and considers the question.

"Make it tournament style. Logan versus Aiden. The winner takes on Mateo," Mr. S suggests.

"When Logan wins, what purpose would that serve me?" Krake says. "Logan and Mateo wrestle all the time in practice."

Mr. S shrugs. "Different rules. Different style. The audience will eat it up. You'll get more money for your program, and you'll get to extend your season even longer. Everyone wins."

Krake studies us. I'm glad to stand up to Krake and not get beat up for a while if the team sticks to this rule. Part of me wants to fight Logan—to kick his ass. But part of me is scared, too. He's stronger than me. I mean, who isn't? What if I lose in front of everyone?

And now—what if I win? This is the threesome I definitely wouldn't want. I don't want to fight Mateo. Is that the trick Krake had up his sleeve? Somehow, I think there's more. Something he's not revealing. The smile on Krake's face says everything. He's not surprised by this.

I guess I could let Mateo win, if I had to face him. Not "let" him win—of course, he'd win no matter what. We could plan something in advance. I just tell him to pin me right away, and I'll submit.

Yeah, I think, and a smile finally grows on my face. Maybe I could kick Logan's ass with Mr. Samuels's training. Maybe it will feel good to have the homophobe submit. And then Mateo and I will play the ultimate joke on the team.

We won't put on any show for anyone. The show will be over. *"Krake Sucks"* will be the end credits.

Krake extends a hand. "You've got yourself a match." He speaks with such confidence that goosebumps rip across my body.

36

Still Friends?

I AVOID TEXTING Mateo until Saturday afternoon. I had stayed up all night Friday watching one random movie after another, obsessively checking my phone. I wanted more than anything for him to message me, but I force myself to be patient.

So, this is how it is. He spends his week wrestling, and he's too busy or tired for anything else. Right?

That's why today I have hope. Maybe we can train tonight. Maybe I can spend the night again.

Karate tonight? I text. *Just you, me, and Mr. S.*

He should be home by now, able to see his phone and reply. A few minutes go by and nothing. I keep checking the text over and over, and it takes about four minutes and thirty seconds for it to be marked *"read,"* not that I'm counting or obsessed or anything.

I stare at my phone. Bubbles appear, and my pulse immediately quickens, but then nothing. What does that mean? That he started typing and deleted it?

An hour passes, and my heart feels like it's beating in my throat. Maybe he typed something and forgot to hit send?

So I send another text. *What do you think?*

It gets read immediately, but then nothing. I pace my room and toss my phone on my bed. What did I do? Why the hell is he ignoring me? I throw myself on my bed next and groan. I don't know what else to do.

Then my phone dings, and I dive for it.

Hey. Sorry. Out with my parents. Yeah, that would be cool. Same time? Mateo texts back.

I jump off my bed and cheer. Yay! At least we're still friends! I know the pressure of the wrestling team must get to him. He has to sit and hang with them, even if they're a bunch of creeps. Maybe we can at least have weekends to chill if nothing else. That's better than nothing.

The day creeps by slower now that I'm extra pumped. When the time comes, Mr. Samuels drives me to Mat's place. We pull into the driveway, and I may have hopped out before the car completely stopped.

Mat answers the door, wearing a tight white T-shirt and gray shorts. I wave at him like an idiot. He laughs and motions for us to come inside.

"So, what will we have you two do when you fight at our MMA exhibition?" Mr. S asks.

Mateo and I haven't even had a chance to talk about it. "Um, can't we fake it? He can throw me and put me in a submission right away. We don't really have to fight, right?"

Mr. Samuels smiles. "I'm proud of you. That's what I was hoping you'd say."

"Coach is real crazy about the whole thing," Mateo says. "He doesn't just wanna win. He wants to hurt you." He crosses his arms. "And anyone else you have fight. Why are you doing this?"

We go downstairs. Mr. Samuels sits on the floor and gestures for us to join. "Let me ask another question first." He looks at me. "Do you want to do this, Aiden?"

"I'm tired of being seen as weak. I want to stand up for myself. I want to fight for myself. Even if that means, you know, literally fight."

Mr. Samuels's eyes widen with passion like he's about to begin a classroom lecture, and he turns to Mateo. "I'm tired of things going overlooked in this school, and I'm tired of bullies. They come in all forms and at all ages," he says. I've never seen Mr. Samuels as anyone but basically a ninja the size of a truck, and I can't imagine him facing bullies. But he has, right? There are stories he hasn't shared with me about his Sensei, Captain Decker, Krake's very own brother-in-law.

And he wasn't always strong, either. It's weird to see people and understand that they weren't always that exact person. Maybe I could be like him someday.

"There's a time to turn the other cheek." He stands, gets in a fighting stance, and motions for us to join him. "Then there's a time to fight for what's right. You ready to do that?"

"I am," I say, standing to join him. I put my hands in a guarding position and face my teacher.

"We'll fake the fight," Mateo says. "I'm in. When you beat Logan, I'll be there for you. We'll send the school a message. Somehow." He jumps into a fighting stance, too.

"Won't you take heat from the team?" I ask. The picture of him sitting at lunch with those jerks fills my throat with bile.

"Let me focus on the season. If I win first in state and prove to everyone what I can do, then anything goes after that. Kay?" he asks.

His eyes reveal regret and empathy. I don't think he wants to be the person he is when he's around the team. Maybe he will change. Or maybe I'm completely misreading him. I sure hope not.

"Okay," I say.

"Good." Mr. Samuels nods. "Let's train." We begin with some sparring, and then Mr. S gives us a lesson.

"There are two ways to defend against an opponent. The first is to open them. Like this." He motions for me to punch him, and when I do, he blocks my arms by pushing them away from my body. "This allows for direct attacks, but it also makes it more likely you'll be grabbed. That's what a wrestler would want. So let me show the second way to defend. Instead of opening, we close. Closing your opponent works like this."

When I punch this time, he blocks by tossing my arm inside and against my body. "When you're tangled up, you can't grab the other person. This is when you strike on the outside—temples, ribs, back of knee. Or grab the leg like so." After he demonstrates, he signals for me and Mateo to practice.

He throws a gentle punch at me, and I close him off. We do this over and over again, until we can do it without having to think about it.

Mat whispers in my ear when I step closer. "Wanna stay over tonight?" His warm breath makes the hair on the back of my neck rise.

"You want me to?" I ask, speaking softly, afraid he'll hear my rapidly beating heart.

He gives me a subtle smile. "Yeah."

"Cool," I say, studying him closely, trying to figure out who Mateo Hernandez really is.

37

The Next Sleepover

MATEO'S PARENTS ORDER us pizza and wings. Mom tells me no running and that she'll pick me up first thing in the morning.

We eat a few slices and a couple of wings with Mateo's parents. They're really nice, and they don't ask me anything about wrestling, which I like. The wings go fast, and I laugh at barbecue sauce staining the corner of Mat's lips. He wipes his face, and we take the rest of the pizza to Mat's bedroom. We sprawl out on his bed and browse Netflix.

"I'm exhausted," he says, taking another slice.

"How was wrestling practice?"

"Terrible. Lots of endurance training." He sighs. "That's one thing I think you'll want to add, you know."

"Endurance?"

"That kind of training, yeah. The techniques Mr. Samuels is showing us are great, but you gotta add your physical workouts," he says. He runs a hand through his hair. It's not perfectly styled as usual. It's soft, and it bounces messily off his head.

I could think of a few physical workouts I'd like to have with him. Wow, I can't believe I even thought that. My face burns, and I look away. "Yeah, good idea."

"What about this one?" It's a picture of Will Smith and some alien or something.

"Looks cool," I reply, and Mateo plays the movie. "Do you actually like any of them? The wrestling dudes?"

"There a few nice guys. DeMarcus, for one. You worked with him."

"Yeah, he was nice." And cute. Adorable, really. That smile and those dark muscles—wow, what's wrong with me? I try to shake away the thoughts.

"Other than that, no," Mateo says. "They're jerks."

"So why—no, never mind."

He pauses the movie. "It's okay. You can ask."

"Why hang out with them?"

He sits up. "I thought I could, you know, like motivate them no matter what I did. But the only way I can do that is to be a part of them." He frowns. "Besides, it's also how I hope to keep them off your ass."

"You're doing this for *me?*"

He shrugs and looks away. "What happened last weekend—them hurting you like that? It pisses me off. I went to Coach Monday morning to talk to him one on one. Did you know that? He didn't call me in or anything. I went to him."

"Really?"

"Yeah," he continues. "I was gonna tell him he had to do something about this. But they got to him first." He clears his throat, and his voice softens. "He told me if I wanted to stay as captain and everything, that I had to tell you to get off the team and to"—he makes air quotes—"form a better relationship with the rest of the team."

"Oh. Crap."

"Yeah."

"Why didn't you tell me?"

"I *am* telling you," he says.

I meant like earlier than today, but I don't say it. There's a spark in his eye, and I can tell he cares about me. He likes me. No, not like the way I'd want him to, I suppose, but it's still a really cool feeling.

He resumes the movie, and I think about telling him my truth.

After all, I told Tisha. Everyone thinks it's the truth anyway, so it's not like I'm surprising anyone.

No, it's too risky to say anything. Tisha was easy. If she was going to judge me, oh, well. We weren't that close then, not really. But if Mateo were to judge me—I'd lose my best friend.

I try to turn my brain off and watch the movie.

We finish it, and Mateo yawns. It's not even midnight. I know practice was super early, but he doesn't want to sleep yet, does he?

"Got any Mountain Dew?" I ask, thinking of what could wake him up.

"You okay if I throw on another movie, and we fall asleep whenever? I'm beat, man."

"Yeah. Cool," I try to say casually.

It takes forever to find another movie. Probably as long as watching an entire movie. We keep browsing, and it's my fault because I'm not really thinking too hard about what to watch.

I'm thinking about Mateo taking his shirt off and my shoulder brushing against his under the blankets.

We settle on a late-night comedy that has sex in the title. Mateo laughs when he sees it, and we watch it. It's pretty stupid, but at some scenes, Mateo laughs so hard he snorts. It makes me laugh even harder.

Then the laughs turn into snores. I look over and smile at him. I turn the volume down, and after several more minutes, I whisper in his ear. "Mat? You awake?"

His only response is a soft snore, and that's exactly what I was hoping to hear.

Under the blankets, I put my arm around his chest and snuggle.

I don't want to close my eyes. I breathe slowly and dream of a day when every night is like this. My arm around a boy I love in my bedroom, where no one else can judge me. Just me and a happy life.

I dream while still awake, wishing the night would never end.

Sleep comes too quickly.

38

Sunday Funday

WHEN I WAKE up, the bed is empty. I hear a shower running, and it must be Mateo. I'm in the middle of the bed, and panic runs through me. Did Mat wake up with my arms around him?

I bounce over to my side and pull the sheet up to my chin. I decide to wait for Mat to return before getting out of bed. If he sees me on the opposite side, as far away from him as possible, then he'll know I was only tossing and turning. Right?

A few minutes later the shower turns off. A drawer opens and closes. Water runs from the sink. I steady my breathing, trying to hear everything from outside the bedroom. A door creaks open, and footsteps approach. Mateo's door shuts. I stay like this for a minute longer, hoping Mat will see me and think I'm asleep.

Then I roll over, and I throw the sheet over my head at what I see.

Mateo drops his towel. He opens a dresser drawer and takes out clean underwear. I shouldn't be watching, and I roll back over to my side of the bed.

Under the sheets, I smile. What a nice—

"You awake?" Mateo asks.

I cough and roll back over at the speed of a turtle. "Barely."

I'm nervous and excited to look at him. When my eyes open, he's wearing shorts now but still no shirt. What I wouldn't give to have muscles like that. Or to have muscles like that to touch. Either way would be cool.

"Mom's making breakfast. I'm skipping my run today," he says. "Wanna eat?"

"Heck, yeah."

He smiles and takes a clean T-shirt out of the dresser.

I'm still wearing the shorts from yesterday. I pick up the shirt I tossed on the floor and put it on. Then I follow Mateo downstairs.

The smell of crisp bacon fills the air, and my stomach growls. "Good morning, kids," Mrs. Hernandez greets us. "Hungry?"

"Always," Mat answers, and I laugh. We *do* eat a lot.

His mom fills up our plates with scrambled eggs and bacon. Then she puts a pile of pancakes in the center of the table. If that's not enough, a minute later the oven timer buzzes. She removes a plate full of freshly baked cinnamon rolls from the oven.

"This is awesome," I tell them.

"Thank you, Aiden. How did you sleep?" she asks.

"Never better," I say. "I mean—you know, all the training and stuff sure makes me tired."

"How is training?" Mr. Hernandez asks, entering the kitchen. He pours a cup of coffee.

"Great. Mr. Samuels is awesome," I answer.

"Now, you be careful, son," Mr. Hernandez tells Mateo. "I've been thinking a lot about this. When you get into the core of the season, it's better to listen to just one coach. Too many cooks in the kitchen, as they say, could be a problem."

"It's never been a problem in *this* kitchen," his mom mumbles with a smile.

Mr. Hernandez kisses her on the cheek. "Thank you, honey. This looks delicious."

"You're welcome. I enjoy feeding my boys," she says.

I like his parents. They have fun with each other, and they're nice to us. My gaze lingers upon the picture on Mat's fridge—two parents, Mateo, and an older sister. I've never seen Mateo's sister, and he's never mentioned her.

Mr. Hernandez puts an arm around his wife and kisses her again. I can't remember the last time I ever saw my parents like that. Even when Dad was living with us, I don't know if I ever saw my parents happily interact with each other.

"Something wrong?" Mateo asks.

"Huh? What?"

"Your face looked weird," he whispers with a smile. "But then again it always looks weird."

"Oh. No, nothing. Sorry. This is great." I take a pancake and pour syrup over it.

His parents take their breakfast into the other room.

"You wanna, like, catch a movie or something today?" Mateo asks.

"Yeah. Sure, man." Then my stomach hurts at a bad thought.

"You got that look again. What is it?"

"What if we run into someone?" I whisper.

He frowns. He doesn't answer right away, which bothers me a little. He should be able to shout out, "Screw them!" But he doesn't. "Oh, yeah. I didn't think about that."

I take a deep breath. This isn't fair. We can't even be like normal friends because of the stupid wrestling team.

"You know what?" he asks after a minute. "Forget them. It's one thing that I have to put up with their crap at school. I'm sorry about that, you know? I don't wanna be that guy. Just till the season's over. I take the team to state and prove myself. You kick Logan's ass and prove yourself. Then we do what we want. Whenever we want." He hits the table with his fist. "So, on the weekends, we'll do whatever we want."

"Okay. Cool." I try not to smile too big. I'm screaming with excitement on the inside but forcing my face to play it cool.

"So, what do you wanna see?"

As long as I sit next to you, it doesn't matter. Of course, I don't say that. "What's playing?"

39

A Superhero

WE CHOOSE THE latest Marvel movie. Once inside, we buy one large popcorn and one large soda. Splitting the cost, we figure we can make the most of it with free refills. On purpose, I get only one straw for the drink. Mat doesn't notice or doesn't say anything. I certainly don't mind sharing.

The movie rocks but sitting so close to Mateo distracts me—in a good way. The shorts he wears sit above his knee. Hair already grows thick on his legs. In comparison, my legs look like a little girl's—hairless, shiny, pale. The seats are close to one another. With my heart beating hard against my chest, I knock his leg gently with my knee. Just a quick touch. Mat doesn't flinch. A little bit later, I do it again.

Our hands hit each other when we both reach for popcorn at the same time. He holds the bucket on his lap. He smiles at me when our hands first touch. Then he pretends to hog the popcorn. I elbow him playfully on the shoulder, and he laughs.

When I take a drink from our soda, I wonder what it would be like to kiss him.

I look down at his athletic, masculine legs. Instead of tapping my knee against his, I take a deep breath and go for something different. I move my leg slowly and place it right next to his. Our legs touch, and butterflies dance in my stomach. I don't take it away this time. I leave it there.

Risking a glance, I turn to Mateo. He's concentrating on the movie. I don't think he even knows what I did. If he does, he doesn't seem to mind. I leave my leg against his, enjoying the warmth.

When the movie ends, we stay through the credits for the final scene. I don't want the movie to ever end, and I'm lucky that it is a Marvel movie with multiple end-scenes. There's something about the dark, cool theater and the escape from reality—for two hours, I lived in that fantasy, too. And not just on the screen. In my mind, I sat next to my boyfriend on a cool date.

That date's about to end, though. Then the weekend will be over. I'll be back at school, dealing with homophobic bullies. Mat will avoid me all week, keeping up his image as a tough wrestling captain. I hate the thought of it all. At least I get to train with Mr. S. I don't know what I'd do without that distraction to get me through the week.

"That was awesome!" Mat cheers when the post-credit scene concludes. "Do you think that means—"

"She'll be in the next movie, yeah! I can't wait!"

"Marvel gets better with every movie. Don't know how they do it," he says.

We stand and stretch. I look around the theater. We didn't see any Washington High students when we arrived, but some people entered the movie late. I don't recognize any of them, thankfully. Did we get lucky and avoid our classmates? Just once, it would be nice to not run into any of the stupid wrestlers.

Don't jinx it now, I tell myself. We use the restroom, then head outside. The sun is warm and blinding after being in the theater for so long.

"What now?" Mat asks.

I don't want the day to end, but I have no idea.

"Um…." I scratch my head. "How about the park? We could walk around a bit."

"That sounds nice," he says.

The closest park is a few blocks away, and we walk toward it. Mateo's arm brushes against mine.

"Quit trying to hold my hand," he jokes.

I smile but I don't laugh. I know he's only joking, but it would be amazing to hold his hand.

When we get to the park, we hop on the swings.

"I haven't done this in like forever," I say.

"Me, neither. It feels nice," Mat replies.

We kick our legs, and the crisp, fall air whips at our face.

"I love and hate Sundays," I tell him.

"Huh?"

"I mean—this is awesome. But I dread tomorrow. I don't wanna go back to not talking with you."

"I know," he says. "I don't wanna go back to that, either."

Then don't! I want to scream at him, but I choose not to say anything. I also don't want to ruin this nice day.

We swing higher. "Wanna leap off?" I ask. "Did you ever do that as a kid?"

"Hell, yeah," he says. "Let's see who can get farthest!"

"On three," I tell him. "One." I kick a little higher. "Two." We swing hard. "Three." We leap.

We both yell, and we fly far away from the swing. The swing set is over sand, so we're not worried about a hard landing. Still, it's far, and when we land, we tumble and roll forward.

I fall into him. We both lay on the sand on our backs. Laughing, he presses up on his elbows. I stare at his beautiful face. What would happen if I kissed him right now? If he were a girl, there'd be nothing to it. I'd reach for her and kiss her. She'd either reject me, or she'd kiss me back.

It's not the same with Mat. If he rejects me, I lose my best friend. I swallow hard.

Mat looks at me, his eyes a liquid-dark mystery. Does he feel anything for me, besides friendship?

"Mat, I want to tell you something—" What is my mouth doing? *No, shut up! I can't risk it. I can't tell him how I feel or who I am.*

Can I?

He nods, almost like he knows. The smile remains on his face. It gives me courage. "What is it?"

You're so beautiful and I think I'm in love with you. My heart goes crazy when I'm around you.

I want to say that. I want to say all that and more.

I take a deep breath.

He's patient, and I'm quiet.

I open my mouth. My throat feels dry, and my heart beats like a machine gun.

"Mateo, I want to tell you that—"

The squeal of tires on the parking lot pavement interrupts me mid-sentence. I was just about to say it, too! My heart panics. If it's Tanner or Logan, I swear I'll kill them.

But it's not Tanner or Logan.

It's a police car. The cop car shines its light on us.

The car door screeches as it opens and then it slams hard.

Stepping out, Captain Decker approaches. "Well, well, well. Look what we have here."

40

Breaking the Law

"I HEARD ABOUT you," Captain Decker barks. He adjusts his belt, and sunlight hits his gun. Decker walks toward us, spitting on the ground. It looks like chewing tobacco, which would explain his gross yellow teeth. "Terry told me all about you."

Freakin' Coach Terry Krake and his brother-in-law, the police captain, not to mention my teacher's former teacher.

Mateo stands, brushing dirt and sand off his shorts.

Decker glares at me. "Aiden, right?"

I nod.

"My student's your teacher, I hear."

I gulp.

"Lloyd was my best student." Decker spits again and looks around the empty park. "He had a punch that could knock out the biggest guy in the world.".

"What happened between you two?" I ask, not knowing where the courage to speak comes from. I can't help my curiosity, even if there's a part of me that worries we may end up as two dead bodies in Decker's trunk.

Decker smirks. "He didn't like what I required for him to earn his black belt promotion."

"What did you require?" I ask.

"Something he was unable to fulfill." He marches closer. He stinks of coffee and tobacco. "You know, I've been a cop in this town longer than you've been alive."

So, you're old? Way to brag.

"We used to get real cowboys on the force. Proud, strong citizens willing to do whatever it takes to make a safe community. The police force has changed so much." Decker shakes his head. "Diversity training. B.S. like that."

My arms tremble. I cross them, trying to steady myself.

"I like the boys who want to be cowboys. They're real men. You have any idea what a real man is like?" Decker asks. He turns, locks eye contact with Mateo. "Krake's a real man. He sees your potential. You'll go far with him. But he'll sure be disappointed to know who you've been hanging out with."

Sweat trickles down Mateo's forehead.

"I've seen what becomes of kids like you," he continues, glaring at me. "You turn people. Manipulate them. You're the kind that likes being a bitch in prison."

I don't understand what he's saying. Manipulate people? It's hard enough just trying to be me.

"Boys have a lot of hormones. It can be confusing. And it's easy to make things feel good." Decker reaches into his pocket, taking out an aluminum container of tobacco chew. He puts some in his mouth. It looks repulsive. "Do you know what I'm saying, Mateo?"

Mateo doesn't answer, and my stomach flips.

"People like Aiden," Decker says, making a gesture with a limp wrist, "might try to make you feel things you've never felt before. It will feel good, too, boy. That's how they trick you."

"You're disgusting." I throw my hand over my mouth, incredulous of the words that came out.

"What did you say, boy?" He towers over me.

I gulp. "We're just friends. What you're saying—it's not normal."

"You're right about that." Decker laughs. "It's far from normal. Not how the Lord makes people." He looks down at the ground. "Oh, no, would you look at that? Oh, look at all that litter."

I look at the ground, but there's nothing there.

"There's a hefty fine for littering in the parks." Decker laughs again. "I don't make the law. I just enforce it."

"There's no litter here," Mateo says, speaking up.

"Are you saying that the captain of the police force is lying?" Decker asks.

Mateo shakes his head.

"That's what I thought." Decker takes out a small notebook and pen. "I'm afraid I'll have to write you both up for littering. Hefty fines for littering."

My face burns, and my entire body tingles.

"What made you such a jerk?" I snap.

Mat's eyes widen, and he grabs my arm. "Don't!"

Decker tilts his head back and laughs. "Oh, I'll be keeping my eyes on you, kid. *Both* of you. Krake won't be happy you're back to associating with this pussy. Not one bit." He spits out some of the tobacco chew. It makes me want to puke.

He tears out two citations and thrusts them at us. "Thanks for helping keep our parks clean, girls. Now go home before you make me really angry."

We take the tickets, and we sprint out of the park. Breathing hard, we slow down after several blocks.

"What a jerk."

"You just made it worse," Mateo says.

"What?"

"I mean it. You called him disgusting and then a jerk. What did you expect he'd do?"

"Mat—I, uh, I dunno." My shoulders feel like they weigh a hundred pounds.

"Maybe we shouldn't hang out for a while." He looks away.

Tears well in my eyes. "It's not enough I'm harassed at school by jerks like Logan, you know? Then picked on by adults, too. Krake and Decker. They're jerks, and I won't take it. I'm tired of it!"

Mateo doesn't look at me or respond.

"And if that's not enough, all this crap—then there's *you.*" Finally, he looks at me. Tears run down my face, but I don't care. "All this bull, and I might lose my best friend, too? You're my best friend, Mat." I wipe my face. "You know, I, uh, you know that you're the only—" I choke up. I don't know what I mean to say.

"Only what?"

"You're the only one who really helps me get through all this. Don't be like them. Please, don't be like them!"

"I'm sorry," Mat says, his face softening. "I know it's so much harder for you. It's just hard for me, too, when it gets like this." He puts an arm around my shoulder.

His touch makes more tears come out. I can't help it. I don't want to seem so weak around Mat, but I'm holding so much in I feel like I'm going to burst.

Then he hugs me. Not a bro hug. A *real* hug. He holds me tight, and I cry on his chest. We're in the middle of some road, and I don't care who sees it either. I need my best friend. Now more than ever.

He holds me and whispers in my ear. "You're my best friend, too."

I don't ever want to let go.

41

A Surprise Visitor

THE WALK BACK to Mat's is silent except for the occasional sound of a car that passes by. Holding my breath, I glance at each driver's face, praying it's not a cop or a wrestler. I text Mom to pick me up, and she's parked in Mateo's driveway when we arrive.

He doesn't say good-bye to me, not really. He waves and gives me a bro-nod. I'd prefer another hug, but there's an awkwardness in the air. A lot happened in the past hour, including two teenage boys hugging and saying that they were each other's best friend. Now's the time when we need to go blow stuff up or something.

But I just want to hug him.

When I sit in the passenger seat of Mom's car, I close my eyes and picture our hug. His strong arms wrapped around me with affection. It was pure, awesome friendship. Sure, I'd like to have more than that. No matter what Mat does for the stupid wrestling team, at least I know that he likes me. That I am his real friend.

His *best* friend.

I have to tell Mom about the ticket I got for littering, but I can't decide if I am going to tell her the truth. I could lie and say that I got what I deserved. I'd get grounded, though. All next weekend at the very least. I can't go that long without seeing Mat.

"So, how was your night?" Mom asks.

I gulp. If I tell her the truth, Mom will start World War Three with the local police force. I'd get to see Mateo, but only because Decker will find a way to put us behind bars.

"Fine."

"Just fine? What did you boys do?"

"We watched some movies."

"How was it?" she asks.

"Awesome," Maybe I don't need to say anything about the ticket. I'll save up money and pay it off without telling anyone.

"What's with the smile?" Mom asks.

I didn't realize I was smiling. I guess I've made my decision not to say anything. "Nothing. Just was, uh, thinking about a joke in one of the movies."

"Can I ask you something, Aiden?" Mom's hands move to the ten and two positions on the steering wheel. It must be a serious question.

"Okay," I mumble, fidgeting with the seat belt.

"Is Mateo your boyfriend?"

My jaw drops. "What? No! He's just a friend."

"Okay. I was just asking." Her hands drop to the bottom of the steering wheel. "It's just—well, will you tell me if you have a boyfriend?"

"Mom!" I pull the seatbelt tight against my chest, wishing I could just disappear.

"Honey, I support you. Fully. I want to be a part of your life. That's all...." Her voice trails off, and she shuffles through several radio stations. "Well, it's not *all*. You know, I need to figure out the rules about boys spending the night with each other, if those two boys are more than friends. Like if Mateo's your boyfriend—"

"Mom, please," I cut her off. "We're just friends."

Best friends, though.

"All right." She smiles, satisfied and relieved, I hope. I haven't even told Mateo that I'm gay. Will he still be my best friend? Can a gay boy be best friends with a straight boy? I sure hope so.

When we turn into our driveway, someone's standing at our door. She turns around and waves. It's Tisha.

"Were you expecting company?" Mom asks.

I shake my head. "I don't know what she's doing here."

I get out of the car, and Mom pulls into the garage.

"Hi," Tisha says. She wipes at her red eyes. Had she been crying? "What's wrong?"

"Can we hang?"

"Of course." I lead her inside my house. "Mom, Tisha and I are gonna hang out for a bit, okay?"

"I'm making dinner soon," she shouts from the kitchen, while we head upstairs. "Tisha is welcome, too."

"Thank you," Tisha says.

"Did something happen?" I ask, opening my bedroom door. I do a quick scan—the bed isn't made, a few piles of clothes are scattered on the floor, but I don't smell anything bad. It will have to do.

Tisha sits down on my bed. Her hair hangs low below her shoulders, straightened today, not braided. It's beautiful and thick. Logan was lucky to have such a sweet girl. Why would he treat her like crap?

"I got in a fight with Camila. And it's my fault," Tisha says.

"Oh." I sit down next to her. "What was the fight about?"

"You."

"What?"

"Yeah."

I scratch my head. "What about me?"

"I told her we need to try and be better friends. The three of us."

"And?"

"She said she didn't want to be friends with liars."

"She's talking about me? About me being gay?"

"I guess. I tried to tell her that coming out about your sexuality is different. It's not lying. It's...." She scratches her arm. "I don't know what it is exactly because I haven't experienced it." She stands and walks around my room, looking at some of my posters. "Who is this?"

"Oh." I laugh. "I just got that and hung it up. It's Austin Theory. He's a WWE guy."

"Wow. With guys like that… I'd never get a wink of sleep if I had that on my wall."

I laugh awkwardly, and my cheeks burn.

"I imagine you don't sleep much when you look at it, either, though, right?" She laughs, but then she blushes and puts a hand over her mouth. "Was that—uh… okay to say?"

Panic rises in me, not at the question but at my bedsheets. She's not wrong. Oh, boy, I hope there are no stains. I see a "dirty" sock tossed on the floor. I have to start making a better effort to do my own laundry. Can't have Mom finding socks like that.

"This is kinda how Camila and I got in a fight," Tisha continues. "She doesn't understand. Not that I do, either, but I told her we need to be better friends. You've got a great heart, Aiden. So does Camila. She's just hurting."

"This is all new to me, too. I like the humor. It's, uh, nice to be real, you know? I mean, it's honest, but we can joke about it. Cuz that's what friends do."

A warmth fills my chest. Tisha is the first one to joke with me about my sexuality in a way that isn't layered with hate. It's an odd feeling, but one I kind of like.

"Anyway, I pissed off Camila because I told her she was a bad friend, and I want to make it right. You're both good people. I like you both. There's no reason why we shouldn't all be friends. Will you help me?"

It would be nice to have more friends with whom I can be one-hundred percent honest.

"Yeah. I did lie to her, though, you know." I get off the bed and kick my dirty sock into the corner of the room, under some other clothes. "I really do owe her an apology for that. But you're right. It's... well, complicated."

"Good. And maybe she can take karate with us. She might enjoy punching you."

"Who doesn't?"

We make a plan to head to Camila's, but I ask Tisha to wait for me downstairs for a second.

I gather all my dirty laundry and head to the washing machine. Mom catches me and gives me an inquisitive look.

"Just trying to help out," I say, too quickly. "It's time I started doing my own laundry, don't you think?"

She nods and a smile forms on her face.

It's a weird time to think about my father, but I do. I don't know if Mom totally understands all the changes my body's been going through. She's probably just happy that I'm taking more responsibility, right?

But a dad... a dad would know something else has been going on when his teenage son suddenly gets the urge to do his own laundry. I bet most dads flash a subtle, knowing smile. Some may even tease. Or maybe decide it's time for "the talk."

It's another experience I will never have.

42

Am I Obvious?

"SO, WHAT MADE you interested in Logan? You know, in the first place?" I ask Tisha, while we walk to Camila's. Camila lives in a nice subdivision about two miles from my house, but it's only a thirty-minute walk. The cool wind whips at my face and messes up my hair. The temperature's dropped significantly since this afternoon. That's what fall feels like here. It can be summer during the day, but it turns to winter at night.

Tisha shakes her head and laughs. "Do you ever look back at a decision you made and ask yourself, W.T.F, girl?"

"I guess so. Maybe not yet, but I probably will. With Mat, I mean."

"Logan was just so, like, complimentary. And super confident," she adds. "It felt good. That's really all. Once I got to know him, well you know who he really is."

"Yeah." I huff. "A dirtbag."

"Douchebag."

"Bag of slimy poop."

"Douchebag of diarrhea." She elbows me playfully, and we laugh. "So, what do you mean you think you might have W.T.F. moments with Mat?"

"I haven't told him the truth about me."

"I didn't know," she says, her face twitching.

"What's that look?" I ask.

"Nothing," she says.

"No, that look means something."

She stops walking and crosses her arms. "I just, um, you want me to be honest with you, Aiden?"

"Definitely."

"Mateo knows," she tells me.

My jaw drops. "What?" I can literally feel my pulse in my neck. I think I'm going to have a stroke right on the sidewalk. Mateo knows?!?

"I mean, he has to know, don't you think?" she asks.

"What do you mean? Did you tell him?" I ask, my words come out like rapid-fire, matching my high pulse.

"No," she answers calmly. "Of course not."

I take a deep breath. Thank goodness.

"But, you know, all the rumors and stuff. And, don't take this the wrong way, but you're a bit, uh, I don't know how to describe it," she continues. "Effeminate?"

"You're saying I act like a girl?"

"First of all," she says and shoves me, "there's nothing wrong with that. And I don't mean you act like a girl. It's just, like, the way you walk and stuff sometimes."

"What's wrong with the way I walk?" Now my face feels like it's on fire. These emotions can't be good for my body.

"Your hips move differently than most boys. More like the way girls walk." She sighs. "You said you wanted me to be honest. I'm sorry."

Tears burn in my eyes. Never once have I thought that I acted like a girl. I don't get it. I'm just *me*. I'm not trying to be anyone else. I don't think about how I walk or talk. I just *do*. And come to find out that I've been sending gay vibes all along without even knowing it?

"Oh, Aiden, I didn't mean to upset you," Tisha says.

I wipe at my eyes, pissed at everything.

"Talk to me," she says soothingly.

"It's just…." More tears come out. "I've known who I was for a long time. Maybe I didn't understand sex and stuff as a little kid, but even then, I knew something was different." Tisha puts her arm around me. "Hell, I even liked dolls more than toy trucks. My dad caught me playing with my action figures one day. They weren't fighting, you see. They were, uh… oh, this is so stupid."

"You can tell me anything."

"They were Power Rangers. But they weren't fighting," I continue. I don't know why I'm telling her the story, or why I'm suddenly remembering it. "They were hosting a talk show. I think the topic was best friends. They were talking about friendship."

"That's so cute," Tisha says.

"Yeah. Not to my dad. He took the toys away. He told me I can have them back when I play like a real boy." I search my pocket for a tissue, but I don't have anything. My nose is running, and I feel gross. "I'm saying that even then I knew I was different. And I bet he knew, too."

Was that why he left us? No… that can't be the reason. He was a violent drunk, and Mom got rid of him.

"Look at you now, Aiden." She punches me on the bicep. "Now, you're becoming a real-life Power Ranger."

I roll my eyes but release a small laugh. "The irony. Anyway," I say, trying not to think about my father. "So, finally, I get the tiniest bit of courage to tell the truth. I've told you, Mom, Mr. Samuels. And now you're telling me that it's all a big joke. That because of the way I walk or something, people already suspect? Like the secret that has been eating me up is really that easy to see?"

"Oh, Aiden. I'm sorry," Tisha says. "I didn't think."

"No, it's not your fault," I say. A girl walking a dog stares at us. Tisha lets go of me, and we keep walking. "I do wanna know that stuff. I want to know what people think of me, but I don't want to know at the same time. You know?"

She smiles gently, and we walk in silence for a few blocks. It helps to dry out my eyes. I breathe in the cool air.

"You really think Mateo knows?" I ask after a bit.

"Maybe. Maybe not. What some find obvious, others may be oblivious to. I don't know Mat like you do."

"You think I'm obvious?" I ask.

"I didn't mean it like that. Honestly. I just mean—why am I so bad at this?" Tisha asks.

I take a deep breath. "You're not bad at it. I'm just not good at hearing it."

Tisha reaches for my hand. "The more I get to know you, Aiden, the more I like you." She squeezes my hand and holds it while we walk. "Anyone else is going to feel the same way."

"Unless they're homophobic jerks."

She laughs. "Unfortunately, that's true."

We walk in silence for a few more blocks. I wish I could stop thinking about all this crap. If Mateo thinks I'm gay, so what? He's been hanging out with me, and he told me I'm his best friend. I shouldn't have anything to worry about.

Unless he thinks I'm straight.

My throat tightens.

It's a strange irony. I didn't like the idea that he may suspect I'm gay. But if he thinks I'm straight, then our friendship is based on a lie.

And that means it could all fall apart.

I squeeze Tisha's hand. "Whatcha thinking about?" she asks.

No, we've talked enough about that for today. I have to tell my brain to shut up.

I force a smile instead. "I think we make a cute couple. Don't you?"

She laughs.

"Wanna be my girlfriend?"

"Shut up, Aiden."

"You know, the more I get to know you, the more I like you,

too," I tell her. She laughs again, and we continue to walk hand-in-hand to Camila's.

43

Camila's Bruises

WE DON'T GET the chance to knock on Camila's door. When we reach the driveway, the door swings open, and Camila runs out. She wipes tears from her face and nearly trips on the curved sidewalk that connects with the driveway.

Her mouth pops open when she sees us. Her eyes dart to our hands, still locked together, and her face turns beet red.

"Oh, don't tell me—" Camila starts.

Tisha lets go of my hand. "Cam, what's wrong? What happened?" Her question interrupts whatever accusation Camila was about to make. Tisha reaches for a hug. Camila's shoulders relax, and tears roll down her freckled face.

"My step monster," she cries.

I knew Camila lived with her father and stepmother and that her relationship with her stepmom wasn't good. But I don't know much more. I wasn't the best boyfriend when it came to listening.

"Honey, what's this?" Tisha asks, pulling away. She points to Camila's shoulder.

"She dug her nails into me," Camila answers. "She grabbed me by the shoulders as hard as she could, and then she cut me with her nails."

"Jesus," I say.

Camila looks at me like she had forgotten I was here. "Can we get away from here? Like now?" she asks. Tisha takes her hand, and we run away until the house is out of sight.

"Tell me everything," Tisha says.

The girls walk in front of me, and I hang back a bit, still close enough to hear. "What are you guys doing, anyway?"

"Aiden wants to make things right," Tisha answers before I can say anything. "And so do I. Between the three of us. But first, are you okay?"

We walk slowly. "We had another fight. She's pushed me before, but she's never grabbed me like this."

"Where was your dad?" Tisha asks.

"He had to go to the"—Camila makes air quotes—"office."

"Oh," Tisha says.

"I know he's cheating on her, and she takes it out on me," Camila continues. She pulls the hood of her sweatshirt over her dark hair.

"You have to tell him," I say.

Tisha and Camila stop walking and turn to look at me.

"If I do that, she'll make things worse. He doesn't want to stand up to her. That's why he's spending his time with someone else. He can't stand to be around her anymore."

"Then why doesn't he leave her?" I ask.

"He doesn't talk to me about these things," Camila says. "But he won't. My real mother left him years ago. If anyone leaves, it will be my step monster. I can only hope she does."

"Do you think she will?" I ask.

"Nope. Dad makes all the money," Camila replies, pulling on the strings of her black hoodie. The hood has now swallowed her face. She looks like a lollipop.

"Oh," I mumble.

"You stay at my house tonight," Tisha tells her.

"I—I got a place. But thanks."

"Where are you going?" Tisha asks.

Camila shakes her head and doesn't answer. Tisha doesn't press the issue, and we head toward her house.

"So, I wanted to apologize for earlier. About the fight you and I had," she tells Camila.

"It's fine," Camila mutters. Her tone says otherwise. Tisha looks back at me, eyes wide. I guess it's my turn to speak.

"I wanted to talk with you, too," I say, putting my hands in my pockets. "I want to be friends with you. Friends are honest with each other. I think you told me that." I smile a little. The sun begins to set, and the sky fills with beautiful colors of purple, pink, and orange.

Staring at the sky, I try to think of the right words to say.

"I thought having you as my girlfriend was the coolest thing ever," I continue. "Because you're like the nicest person I knew. But I'm a total idiot." I clear my throat. "As you know, I'm, uh, not straight."

Camila smirks. Tisha stares at me. I sigh. It's not enough to say what I'm not. I have to say who I am.

"I'm gay," I say. Tisha smiles, but Camila wears a poker face.

"I know," Camila says. "Why was it so hard to say?"

"Did you ever have to tell anyone you were straight?" I ask.

"Of course not," she says.

"See, straight is, you know, a given. You don't have to come out. When you're something other than the given, it's harder to say. I don't wanna be abnormal, you know," I tell them.

"You're not abnormal," Tisha snaps. "Not at all. It's other people who make you feel that way."

"Are you talking about me?" Camila asks. She frowns, revealing those deep dimples.

"No, sorry." Tisha reaches for Camila's hand, but she thrusts her hands into her pockets. "That's not what I meant."

Camila turns to me. "I'm sorry, too. If I didn't understand everything you were going through. If I still don't." Her words seem nice, but again there's something about her tone that I don't understand.

"I'd like to be friends. For all of us to be friends," I say.

"Yay!" Tisha cheers. "Trust me, there are plenty of jerks out there. We gotta stick together. So, you wanna take karate with us?"

Camila releases an awkward laugh.

"I'm serious. It's fun," Tisha tells her.

Camila rubs her shoulder—the opposite one that her mother hurt.

"What happened to that shoulder? Is that a bruise, too?" I ask, looking closer.

Camila tugs at her hoodie. She doesn't answer my question. Did her stepmother hurt her more than she's letting on?

"Couldn't hurt to learn a few basic things," I add since she's not answering. "You know, to protect yourself. Plus, it will be a chance for us to all hang."

"There is something I've been meaning to tell you," Camila says. "It's just, uh, a bit awkward."

Another secret. What could it be this time? Camila dating Mateo? I shudder at the thought.

"What is it?" Tisha asks.

Camila opens her mouth, but no words come out. "I dunno. I promised I wouldn't say. I shouldn't have hinted at anything."

"Well now you have to tell us, or I'll die not knowing. You can't start something and not say it," Tisha says.

"I promised, you guys. But I'll, um, I'll ask if it's okay for me to say. It's not about any of our friends or anything," she says, catching my eye. "Just give me some time. I'll tell you."

"I'll hold you to that, girl," Tisha says.

We walk to Tisha's house, and a warmth fills me even though the evening air is getting cool. I don't know if things are okay between us, but I am hoping they are better, even if there are still secrets between us.

Camila's phone goes off, and she looks at it.

I'm still walking a bit behind her, so I can see what she sees. It's a text message.

It makes my stomach drop.

It's a text from Mateo.

But she just said her secret had nothing to do with our friends. So, why is Mateo texting my ex-girlfriend?

44

Training

"WHEN I SAY go, step out into your best horse stance, execute your double elbow smash, and *kiai*. Ready?" Mr. Samuels stands in the center of the study hall room at Washington High, which transforms into our dojo at the end of the school day. We push the tables to the side, sweep up essays that will never be turned in, and line up. "Go!"

Twelve students jump into horse stance and yell.

"Show me your blocks. Palm block to start, when I count." Mr. S takes a front stance opposite of me. My legs don't shake. I've been training for this, longer than the eleven students to my left.

"Ichi." When he counts, Mr. S throws a corkscrew punch at my chin. I block it. *"Ni."* He punches again, and once more, even though his fist is large and his punch is fast, I brush it away easily. He nods with a proud smile, then moves to the student on my left, Tisha.

Tisha's stance is low, and her legs firm. "Now, show me high block. *San!"* Mr. S punches at Tisha's nose. A strong high block knocks it away.

We continue through all the blocks he has taught us so far. My legs begin to shake, but I refuse to relax my stance.

"You may stand," he says. "And move into front stance." Some students groan. Our break doesn't last long.

"I want to see all your punches. Show me your rising punch on my count." He holds out a target for us to hit. *"Ichi. Ni. San."* We strike with each count. We demonstrate uppercut, vertical, corkscrew, back fist, and hook punches, too.

"Now, show me kicks!"

With each count, we hit the target Mr. S holds in front of us. We demonstrate front, side, round, and back kick.

"Back to horse stance, as low as you can, while I meditate for a moment," he instructs.

Several minutes pass, and my legs wobble. I try to raise up a few inches to ease the pain in my muscles.

Mr. S locks eye contact and shakes his head. I lower back down. He points a finger at me and lowers it further. Somehow, I find the strength to squat an inch deeper.

He grins as sadistically as I've ever seen him. "Stay like that."

Then he sits on a plastic chair we had pushed aside. He takes out his phone.

Unbelievable! It looks like he's texting.

Tisha shifts in her stance. Mr. Samuels's eyes dart up. He moves his head side to side, and Tisha moves back down, deeper in her stance than before.

"I can't take much more," she whispers.

"Me, neither."

"Why is he torturing us?" Heather, a student next to Tisha, asks.

"No clue," Tisha replies.

"Quiet. Get lower," Mr. Samuels commands.

It's a darker side of him we haven't seen much of, not mean like Coach Krake, but not fun like his usual self.

Tony, a boy next to Heather, falls down.

Mr. Samuels stands.

"What do we do when we fall?" he asks Tony.

Tony rubs his legs. "We rise."

"Are you strong enough to get back up?" Mr. S asks.

"Yes, sir," Tony says. Tony's a little chunky. I guess thicker is a nicer way to say it. He works hard, though, ever since he joined. He has long, messy hair that sits below his ears. He's got a great smile and an infectious laugh—he's one of many awesome new additions to our club. He rubs the back of his legs. "Sorry, sir." Mr. Samuels approaches, offering his hand. Tony takes it, Mr. S pulls him up, and Tony gets back in horse stance.

"No need to be sorry." Mr. Samuels walks toward us. "Fall seven times, rise eight. That's an important teaching in martial arts and life. Not only that, but when you can, you help your brothers and sisters up. We will all fall. That is life. So, extend a hand. That is the truest sign of strength. Do you all understand?"

"Hai," we answer in unison.

"Very good. I want everyone to go one inch deeper. For one more minute. Go!" The twelve of us collectively groan, but we push ourselves. "Thirty seconds. Ten seconds." We grit our teeth. "Okay. Relax."

Amanda and Jason, two students on the opposite end of our line, collapse. "What do you do?" Mr. Samuels looks at us.

Tisha and I are the first to react. We run—or rather, limp quickly—over to them. We extend our arms and help them up.

"One line," Mr. Samuels says.

We reform our line, and he walks in front of us. "Yes. Fall seven times. Rise eight." He pauses in the center of the room. "Today was a test. I am happy to say that you all passed."

Tisha and I look at each other and smile in surprise. Mr. S walks to the back of the room and grabs a box. Then he moves in front of me.

"Congratulations, Aiden. Today, you become a yellow belt in karate. Yellow is the color of the rising sun. The day is just beginning. As the sun rises, the color will deepen, giving life to all living creatures on Earth. But all life begins with the rising sun." He takes a yellow belt and pops it open. A small thread that held it together floats in the air. "Catch it for good luck."

"Oh." I search for it quickly.

"There!" Tisha points.

The thread is behind Mr. S somehow, and I dive for it, snagging it right before it hits the floor.

"Excellent. That is a sign of good things to come," he tells me.

I hope he's right.

Mr. Samuels ties the belt around my waist. "Upon promotion, the teacher is the first to put the belt on the student. It is a symbol of the passing of knowledge. But now it is your responsibility to continue to learn and seek new knowledge. As your knowledge grows, the color of the belt you wear will darken. Congratulations."

The students applaud, and Mr. Samuels repeats this process for each of us.

It's pretty cool. We're all yellow belts.

I can't wait to tell Mateo.

A much less happy thought replaces that one, though. I still don't know why he texted Camila or what her secret is. Is something going on between the two of them?

45

Self-Defense

AFTER THE YELLOW belt test, we use the public restrooms to change, avoiding the wrestlers. I try to not let my karate belt fall in the toilet.

A custodian who hates his job mutters something outside the bathroom stall for us to hurry up so he can lock up the restrooms.

"You did great, you know. At the test," Tony says, changing in the stall next to me.

"Thanks."

"I mean it. I don't know how we got so lucky to get promoted, too. You're like twice as good as us," he adds. Then he laughs—it's that cute, infectious laugh, one I wish I had. Every time I hear it, I can't help but smile no matter what my mood is.

I like the new karate kids. I haven't told them about my private lessons with Mr. S and Mateo, but clearly the lessons have paid off. It feels good to be good at something.

"Arigato," I say. We end our martial arts classes by thanking Mr. Samuels in Japanese. I like the word.

"Don't touch the mustache," Tony replies, laughing some more. That's how we remember to say "you're welcome" in Japanese, which is pronounced *dōitashimashite.*

Tony and the other boys leave the bathroom. I sit down on the shut toilet and take out my phone. Is Mateo done with practice? I take a pic of my yellow belt and send it to him. Hopefully this weekend Mr. S can promote him, too.

I also really need to ask Mateo a question. Why did he text Camila? I wanted to ask her, but we had just made up as friends, at least I think we did. Something's off with her. Of course, if my stepmother abused me, I suppose something would be off with me, too. But she's keeping some other secret from us, something she promised she wouldn't tell anyone.

What if Mateo wants to go out with her?

My stomach turns. Isn't there a rule about friends dating ex-girlfriends? He'd ask me first, wouldn't he?

Oh, I hope that's not why he's texting her. I don't think I could handle him dating Camila. I don't know if I can handle him dating any girl.

That's something I'll have to face, at some point. I shake the thought away and read Mateo's reply on my phone.

Congrats! Jealous! You suck!!! Hahaha j/k that's awesome dude!

I smile. It feels good that he's happy for me. I could get used to all these feelings.

How was practice? I text back.

It sucked balls. I'm so tired.

Get your mind out of the gutter, Aiden. Don't even consider writing about balls.

Sorry, I write back. *I can't wait till the weekend.*

A warmth fills my chest. No amount of tickets or harassment or even getting beat up could take away the joy I feel when I hang with Mateo. I hate how long we have to wait.

Me too. Can you stay over again on Sat?

I jump up in the bathroom stall, my elbow hitting the side. I'm too excited to feel any pain. Hell yes, I can stay the night! But I text a simple, *yeah cool.*

He sends a smiley face back to me. My entire body tingles. I zip up my gym bag and exit the bathroom stall.

I look in the mirror and flex. It's not much, but there's a little muscle in my bicep. It's progress. If I keep this up—laughter erupts from behind me. My stomach drops at the interruption.

"Long time no see." It's Jeff, another freshman on the wrestling team. Jeff had partnered with DeMarcus and me on my second day of practice. When DeMarcus and I said something negative about Krake, Jeff immediately defended Coach.

"Hey," I mumble and walk toward the exit.

He blocks me. His sea-blue eyes glare at me. A vein pulses in the pale skin of his neck.

"What do you want?" I ask, feeling my heart race.

"Just doing what needs to be done," he replies and shoves me hard against the wall.

"You guys are supposed to leave me alone."

He runs his hand through his short, dark hair and smirks at me. "Tanner and Coach had a nice talk with the JV team. Coach told us to leave you alone. That we're gonna do some expo at the end of the season?" Jeff laughs, and I hate him for it. "You must love getting your ass kicked."

"You'll see what your stupid wrestling—"

Jeff punches me in the stomach, and I gasp.

"Don't insult us, coward!" Jeff snarls. "Yeah, we were instructed to leave you alone. In public, that is. But, uh, well…." He looks around, and the bathroom is empty besides the two of us. "Tanner gave us a different challenge, you'll be happy to know. If we hurt you privately, with no witnesses, he's promised us—"

I shove him back. "Leave me alone," I demand. Where the hell is that custodian now? There's never an adult when I need one. Tony and the other boys couldn't have gone far, right?

Jeff's the same height as me, but he tries to stand taller. "You think you can take me? I've seen you wrestle. You couldn't wrestle a little girl." He leaps at me.

I step to the side and push him against the wall. He throws his hands up to stop his face from smashing into it. He spins around, and his eyes grow wide.

He throws a punch at my head. I use a palm block and swipe away his attack easily. He grabs my arm, but I apply an armbar that bends him over. I yell and toss a knee into his ribs. Jeff gasps, and then I shove him against the wall.

"I said leave me alone!" He's down on one knee, looking at me with pain and surprise in his eyes. I don't want to feel good about hurting someone, but my lips curl up. "If you force me to defend myself, I will. Tell your stupid team that."

Jeff rubs his side.

I swallow hard. Then I extend my arm and offer to help him up. "It doesn't have to be like this."

His eyes narrow.

He slaps away my arm and stands up.

"Don't touch me, faggot," he says and runs out of the restroom.

46

Dinner for Champions

THE FIRST THING I think about when I leave school is Mateo. I want to tell him about Jeff for a number of reasons. I begin to type, but then I delete it. No, there's nothing Mat can do.

Except comfort me.

And celebrate with me!

I defended myself. For the first time in my life, I'm not the victim. A surge of confidence races through my veins.

Mr. Samuels's lessons work.

I also decide not to text Mateo because I don't want every conversation to be about "who picked on Aiden today," especially because the insults stem from my sexuality. Can't I just be picked on for thinking football is stupid or not knowing a single name of any major league baseball player?

Instead of texting Mat, I message Tisha and Camila.

You free tonight? Dinner? I have a story to tell you!

Camila is the first to reply. *I'm intrigued. Okay.*

While I wait for Tisha, I call Mom.

"I'm in the parking lot, honey," Mom answers. Oh, yeah, she's picking me up today. Where is my head?

"Um, I'm on my way out. Just had a quick question. Can, um, I have a friend or two over for dinner?"

"It's a school night," Mom replies. *"But okay. As long as it's not too late. I was just gonna get us fast food tonight, though."*

"That's fine. They'll pitch in," I say.

"All right. Love you."

"Love you, too, Mom. Be right out."

When I end the call, a new text from Tisha arrives. It says, *What's for dinner?* She included a knife and fork emoji with a smiley face.

Mom says fast food. I'm thinking Taco Bell.

More like Taco Hell, Camila replies.

Girl, get out of here. Get me a Mexican pizza please, Tisha says.

Mexican poop you mean, Camila writes.

LOL I will get plenty to share. Come over in a half-hour, I text.

I run to the parking lot and hop in Mom's car. When we get to Taco Bell, I lean over her and shout an order. I get one of the taco twelve packs to share and one Mexican pizza for Tisha.

"Make that two packs," Mom adds. "I'm hungry, too."

On the drive back home, Mom asks, "You seem awfully excited tonight. Good day?"

She doesn't know the half of it. Of course, I can't tell her I got into a fight. She'd flip. I don't even think I can tell Mr. Samuels about that. Even though it was for self-defense, he'd be furious at the wrestling team.

Stupid Tanner promised them something, though. What was it? I didn't let Jeff finish his sentence. "If we hurt you privately, with no witnesses, he promised us—" Jeff had said. But my temper got the best of me, and I didn't want to hear anymore.

Does Mateo know about this? No, Tanner may be a dumb ass, but he is probably smart enough to not involve Mat.

Probably.

Jeff can't be the only one Tanner promised something to. I rub my arms as goosebumps pop up at the thought. Logan would be all too happy to start a fight with me again.

"Hello? Are you there, Aiden?" Mom asks with a smile. "You're drifting. What's going on?"

"Oh, nothing. Yeah, just a good practice. I'm really liking karate."

"I guess so." Mom laughs gently. "Today was a big day, wasn't it?"

"Huh?" Oh, duh! Naturally, Mr. Samuels would have told Mom that he was testing us. "Oh, yeah! I'm a yellow belt!"

Mom smiles. "Congratulations, honey! I'm so proud of you. Lloyd talks about you and the club all the time. He's very proud of you, too."

More chills run down my arms but for different reasons. It seems like it's been a long time since anyone other than my mother has been proud of me.

I wonder what my father would think. I wish he could have seen me defend myself against Jeff. Maybe he wouldn't think karate is for pussies if he saw what it could do.

"Thanks, Mom."

She glances at me with those analytical mother eyes. "Hmm. Now what are you thinking?"

"I don't know," I lie.

Mom sighs. "You can tell me—"

"Anything, I know. I guess, uh, it's just, no, never mind."

Mom doesn't say anything. She lets me gather my thoughts. I think she knows me too well.

I pull on the seat belt and look out the window. "I kinda wonder why someone like Mr. S, who has only known me for this school year, would care so much. I mean, you know, when Dad doesn't care at all."

"Oh, Aiden. I haven't seen your father in years. Yet he still angers me because his absence hurts you."

"It's not like I want him around. I know he sucks. It still kinda hurts, though. Is that weird?"

"No, honey. Not at all."

"Why did you ever marry him?"

She takes a deep breath. "Your father had a way of making me feel like… like the sun. Like I was the center of the universe. At least when we were young. Love can be confusing. He was my sun, too. In the sense that he blinded me to everything else. I didn't see his weaknesses before we got married. Or, maybe, I chose to ignore them." She clears her throat. "I regret nothing, though. You came from that relationship, and you're the best kid I could ever have asked for."

I gaze out the window. He's out there somewhere, my father. Does he have a new wife? New children?

Mom pulls into the driveway. Camila and Tisha hang out in my front yard and wave.

"I like them," Mom says. "Tisha looks happy. It's good to see you kids happy."

"Yeah," I say, jumping out of the car to tell my friends about my after-school altercation and ignoring the fact that Mom didn't say the same about happiness in regards to Camila. She wears a smile, too, but it looks forced. What's going on with her?

Tacos might help. Tacos make everyone happy.

47

Secret Texts

THE GIRLS SCREAM when I tell them what happened.

"That's incredible!" Tisha says. "I'm glad someone is giving those creeps what they deserve."

"Aren't they supposed to leave you alone?" Camila asks.

I nod, and we spread out on my bedroom floor, surrounded by a sea of tacos. Mom gave us an entire roll of paper towels and a stern warning to not mess up my room any more than it already was.

Camila's eyes float to my Austin Theory poster.

I blush. "Tanner's promised them something, I guess."

"Show me how you did it," Tisha says. We stand, and I put her in an armbar just like I did to Jeff. "That's the self-defense move we had to learn for yellow belt."

"Try it on me." Camila jumps up.

"You could join us after school, you know," Tisha suggests.

"I still have my dignity," Camila jokes. There's some truth to it, though. We've already been labeled as the school nerds. We are the "wannabe athletes," the place the losers who can't do any real sport go. It pisses me off, and it makes me want to show the entire school what we can do.

"Okay, grab my arm," I tell Camila. "It goes like this." I step in, bending her arm so that she almost hits herself in the face with her own elbow. Then I spin in a half-circle. As I move, I straighten her arm, putting pressure near her elbow. It forces her to bend over. "Then I kneed him in the stomach. Like this." I demonstrate gently.

"Now do it faster," Camila says.

Looking at her inquisitively, I shrug. "Okay. Why not?" She grabs my arm. I perform the move, but this time, she flips out of it. She literally does a front flip, wraps her legs around my head, and slams me on the carpet. The whole house shakes. Mom's going to lose her mind!

"What the hell, Camila? How'd you do that?" I ask. Tisha's mouth opens wide with surprise, too.

"I took gymnastics when I was a little girl. When you walked through it slowly, I had this idea as to how I could flip right over you. Just wanted to see if I still had it." She laughs awkwardly.

"Girl, you gotta join the club!" Tisha shouts.

"What's going on up there?" Mom yells.

"Sorry, Mom, won't happen again!" Turning back to Camila, I add, "Tisha's right. You gotta join us."

"I can't," Camila says.

"Why not?" Tisha asks.

She shakes her head, and I can tell she doesn't want to talk about it. I wish I knew what was going on with her. Is her stepmother still hurting her? Controlling her, perhaps, so that Camila can't do stuff she wants to do?

"So, what about your secret?" Tisha asks. "You ever gonna tell us?"

"Yes. But not tonight. I can't break my promise. I asked, but it didn't go over so well. It's not a big deal, guys. Really." Her face says otherwise, though. I can tell Tisha wants to push the issue, but she holds back. We're all friends again, and she wants to keep it that way. Me, too.

Tisha drops it for now, too. "I'm proud of you, but I'm worried," she says to me. "Jeff never should have attacked you. What if he tries again, but this time he brings the rest of the team?"

"I'll train harder in practice. I'll be ready."

"Don't get too cocky," Tisha cautions.

I laugh. No one has ever said that to me before.

"I need to wash my hands," Camila says. "Thanks for the tacos, Aiden." She leaves my room to use our bathroom. On the floor, her phone lights up.

Tisha lays down and stretches out. "Too much food," she says, rubbing her belly.

Like a sloth, I creep across the floor toward Camila's phone. Tisha groans from overeating. I listen for Camila, and the bathroom door opens and shuts. She's inside it, and then I reach quickly for the phone like it's a Willy Wonka golden ticket.

I can't open it. Camila has a code. But it lights up again to show me her most recent notifications.

She received a text.

And it's from Mateo.

Again.

The text reads, *What are you doing Friday night?*

My heart sinks. This can't be happening! Is he asking her out? Water runs from the bathroom faucet. Every sound and sensation feels magnified.

"What are you doing?" Tisha asks. She looks right at me, and I drop Camila's phone on the carpet.

"Nothing," I mumble.

"Why are you looking at her phone?"

My face feels like it's on fire.

"I, uh, I saw a text from Mateo. To Camila."

Tisha sits up. Her eyes soften. She slides closer to me and whispers. "You and Mat? Are you—"

"We're nothing," I answer. "He's not, you know, like me. Do you think he likes Camila? Has she told you anything?"

Tisha glances at my bedroom door, shaking her head. "She hasn't said anything. You could just ask her. Say you saw the text—that it lit up and caught your eye. Not that you checked it like some creep."

"I don't think I wanna know the answer." I cross my arms. The bathroom door opens and closes. Camila returns.

"What are you two talking about?" she asks.

"Karate stuff," Tisha answers. "Oh, your phone went off. Got a text from Mateo." My heart drops into my stomach. Tisha doesn't look at me when she talks. She wears a poker face. "What's going on with you two?"

Camila blushes, and I squeeze my fists. She doesn't have to answer. I know that blush. I know what causes it.

And at this moment, I hate both her and Mateo.

"It's not what you think," Camila says to Tisha.

What does she think Tisha thinks? Now, I'm confused.

"What is it then?" I ask. "Is this what you've been keeping from us? Some secrets between you and Mateo?" My mouth betrays me, and my voice shakes. I want to be good friends and tell each other the truth. But I'm screaming on the inside!

"No, it's not that. Well, actually, it's, uh, kinda weird," Camila says.

"Weird how?" Tisha asks.

"He's been texting me about Aiden," Camila replies.

"Woah, really? He's texting about me?"

48

Love Hurts

"I'M NOT SUPPOSED to tell you," Camila says. "I shouldn't have said anything."

"Not supposed to tell me what?"

"Look, you guys." Camila bites her lip. "We're just, uh, like friends again. I don't wanna keep things from you. I also don't wanna break a promise. What do I do?"

"Another promise? I can't take any more secrets, Mila!" My mind searches for answers, but there's one thing I want her to say more than anything else. Is it possible Mateo asked her if—

If *what?*

I scratch my neck. What do I want him to ask?

Do you think Aiden would be my boyfriend?

That's the question I want Mateo to ask. I gulp and stare at Camila, wishing I could read minds.

Tisha shakes her head at me. "No, she can't. It sucks, Aiden. But you have to understand. If you asked Camila to keep something private, you wouldn't want her to tell anyone, would you?"

I groan and throw myself on the floor. "No," I mumble, defeated, my arms spreading out. "Of course not." I dig my fingernails into my carpet and then roll over, frustrated. "But if it's about me, don't I deserve to know?"

Camila and Tisha exchange a look. I'm convinced girls can communicate telepathically, and it drives me nuts.

"I'm in love with him," I shout. I jump off the floor and throw myself on my bed, face first, and bury my head under my pillows. I can't believe I said that, especially with my ex-girlfriend right here in my room! I scream into a pillow, and then I kick at my mattress several times. Why the hell did I just say *that* out loud?

A hand massages my back, and I turn over. Tisha stands over me.

"I'm sorry," I say, turning face over in bed. "You probably don't wanna hear that. But I can't keep it in anymore. It's driving me crazy."

"It's okay." Camila gives me a half-smile. "I don't have any hopes of us getting back together or anything, Aiden."

"Do you know what it feels like?" I ask. "I hang with him every weekend. It's the absolute best and worst! He's my best friend. But I want to be more. It's not fair. Like, if he were a girl, there'd be some kind of possibility, right? Even if like one percent? But he's a dude. He's straight. It's zero percent, and it's killing me."

Camila looks away, and Tisha puts an arm around my shoulders.

"Then all week at school, he ignores me. All because of the stupid wrestling team. I hate them!"

"I'm sorry," Tisha says. "Have you said anything to him?"

I shake my head. "What if he rejects me? Will we still be able to be friends? Or… what if he hates me for who I am?

"All these possibilities hurt," Tisha says. "I get that. Geez, dude, you're a freshman. *Freshman!* Don't you think you'll have a hundred heartaches before you even graduate? Look at you and Camila!"

I feel like I've been punched in the gut. "I'm sorry," I say to Camila. "I'm sorry if I made you feel at all like this."

"Don't be too full of yourself," she says and elbows me in the ribs. "I liked you. I wasn't in love with you."

"I'm in love with Mat," I repeat. "And it hurts. Like a truck has run me over."

"That's why they say love hurts, I guess," Tisha says.

Tisha and I sit in silence on my bed, while Camila walks around the room. She rubs the back of her neck.

"So, can you tell me anything about his texts?" I ask. "I mean, like, does it have anything to do with this? Or if it's nothing, you could just say that, and I can tell my brain to shut the hell up."

She exchanges another look with Tisha. Does Tisha know something about this I don't?

"You planning on hanging out with him on Saturday?" Camila asks. I nod.

"He wants to go out with me on Friday. To be honest, I don't know how he feels about you. If I knew that he liked you or that he obviously didn't like you like that, I'd tell you. Okay?" Camila asks. "I would do that at least, to try and help. He asked me some random things about you. And now he wants to go out with me on Friday. I think the best thing you can do is ask him about that when you see him Saturday. All right?"

Does Mateo like Camila, then? Again, maybe he's just making sure I wouldn't be weird about it, and then he's going to ask my ex-girlfriend out. I hate that possibility.

"It's going to be a long week," I mutter.

"But hey," Tisha says. "We're yellow belts, and you kicked ass. Let's not forget the good stuff. We've got training all week. After what you did to Jeff, you better work twice as hard."

"Yeah. I have a bad feeling that next time something happens, it's not going to be one on one," I say.

We sit in silence for a bit. Camila avoids eye contact with me. Can I trust her? She's keeping multiple secrets from us now.

My stomach hurts. I wish it were only all the tacos that caused the stomachache, but there's something else I feel, too. Something even worse than my feelings and frustrations about Mateo.

It's fear. Raw, crippling fear that I've not really felt before. I think about what Tanner and Logan did to me—jumping me on the street. Grabbing my crotch and hurting me. I picture Captain Decker spitting on the ground, his eyes filled with hate, warning Mateo that I have some kind of agenda to turn him and all that bull.

I fear that this isn't a game. That my little victory with Jeff is nothing, and that something far worse is going to happen. That no friendly competition is going to settle this.

Genuine hate runs in their veins, and it's being fueled by the people in charge, the people they look up to. These people—the wrestlers, Krake, the police captain—something's wrong with them. Someone could end up really hurt.

Or even dead.

That's my real fear.

I've read the stories, and they're no laughing matter. People have been killed for being like me.

I try to swallow the lump in my throat, but it's too big. I pray that my training is enough to protect me.

49

Throats, Balls, and Showers

I DON'T KNOW how I would have gotten through the week if not for karate. I threw myself into my practices, and I trained more at home, reviewing each technique repeatedly.

So much for playing "Talk Show" with Power Rangers now, huh, Dad?

Mr. Samuels had a favorite Bruce Lee quote he told our club. "I don't fear the man who knows one thousand kicks. I fear the man who has practiced one kick one thousand times." So, that's what I did. Well, not one thousand. I practiced every technique until I couldn't move my body.

Every single night.

Then I practiced *kata*.

"Kata is our textbook," Mr. S told us. "It's a pattern of moves we memorize. We visualize attackers, and we demonstrate each technique as if we are defending ourselves for real. Within each pattern are dozens of secrets. They're not visible to the naked eye. I will show you some of the secrets in time. For now, you must search for them yourself."

The first *kata* we learned is called *Wansu*. It translates into "strong-arm form." The strong-arm teaches the most powerful punch anyone can do.

I've been practicing that like crazy, too. At the end of *Wansu*, there's also a kick-ass throw. You get into a sick stance called "tiger number one," then you grab your opponent's throat and balls. No joke. Then you squeeze their throat with one hand, their balls with the other, scoop them up, and toss them over your head.

It's the coolest thing I've learned.

I picture Logan charging in at me. I step into tiger number one, then grab Logan exactly as the form instructs. I squeeze harder than ever. He yelps. Maybe I castrate him with my power, doing the world a favor. I throw him hard onto the ground, then strike his face for good measure.

Someone help us if he ever has kids. The thought makes me wonder what Logan's father is like—is Logan a reflection of his dad?

Covered in sweat and out of breath, I lie on my floor.

Karate is for pussies, my father had once told me.

I think of the Bruce Lee quote. I get up and practice my moves until I can no longer stand.

WHEN I WAKE up on Saturday morning, every muscle hurts. Camila and Mateo—for whatever reason—went out last night. I practiced twice as hard all Friday night to keep from thinking about them. My music screamed through my headphones. I'll probably suffer from hearing loss.

Crawling out of bed, I take some time to stretch. My knees pop, and I crack my neck.

Pacing my room, I picture what my conversation with Mateo will be like today. I guess I could start by telling him directly that I am gay. I could see how he reacts. As long as we're still friends, that's all that matters. I can bury my feelings if I have to. If Mat's my best friend, then I want the same kind of honesty with him that I have with the girls.

Guys are weird, though. It's all about image. Our lives are based too much on what others think about us. Maybe girls have the problem, too. I don't know. But with Mateo, it's all about the wrestling team and respect. Will Mateo accept me still as a friend?

My truth could make things worse.

My stomach rumbles. I walk to the bathroom and turn the shower on to get the water hot. I need a nice, long shower.

Stepping in, I tilt my head back and let the water soak my face. It runs over my body, and I turn the heat up until it steams.

What did Camila and Mateo talk about? Are they dating? It's killing me not knowing.

Hot water races down my back. Placing my hands against the shower walls, I stand still, the water massaging my back.

My mind races. I want to be stronger. I am getting stronger physically. It's not just about how hard I can hit, though. It's also about mental strength. I want friendships based on honesty. I want the kind of friends to whom I tell all my secrets, fantasies, and crushes.

I don't want to hide who I am. That's weakness, isn't it?

Or maybe it's a different type of self-defense? I have to protect myself from teenage jerks. From terrible coaches and inappropriate cops, too. If anyone thinks coming out is easy, they're crazy. Or they're straight. This isn't like confessing a guilty pleasure, like secretly loving Justin Bieber's music or something.

This is an irrevocable part of one's identity. In some places in the world, it's illegal. Some places it's even punishable by death. How crazy is that? That would be like….

Like being punished because of the color of one's skin. It's just who I am! Except, unlike skin color—for better or for worse—it's not necessarily obvious. At least not to everyone.

Groaning, I turn and splash water on my face. Maybe I don't know anything. That's the scariest part of everything sometimes. I get an idea of what it means to be strong or to be a good friend or to be real and honest and all that—but I don't know much. I've only been out for a short time and only to a few people.

Of course, I'll never learn more if I don't put myself out there. Why is life so complicated?

I take a deep breath, inhaling the steam.

What about your fantasies?

The question comes from somewhere deep in my mind, but it makes my lips curl. It's a very pleasant distraction from where my mind was going. There's a lot of good to admitting to yourself what you really like.

I picture Mateo in nothing but his boxers.

And let's be honest—if I'm going to hang out with Mateo tonight, I should have a clear, focused mind.

Right?

I take a long shower, hoping the hot water will wash away my fears and frustrations.

50

Be Yourself

MOM DRIVES ME to Mateo's Saturday night. The car's vibration and the hypnotic view of the road sooth my nerves.

"You okay, Aiden?" Mom asks. "You look pale."

"Yeah, I'm fine." My voice squeaks when I talk.

"Do you wanna talk about it?"

"Talk about what?"

"How you feel about Mateo."

My stomach drops. As if it could feel any funkier. "Uh... what do you mean?"

"I know you said he wasn't your boyfriend." Mom clears her throat. "But do you like him like that?"

It's like she can see right through me. I like it and find it terrible all at the same time.

"I think I'm in love with him." I can't believe I said that out loud to my mom! My mouth continues to betray me.

"Oh." Mom adjusts her grip on the steering wheel. "That serious?"

"I know what you're gonna say. I'm too young to be in love or something. Or I don't know what love is." I sigh. "And maybe I don't. I mean, I love you. But this is a different kind of love. Something I've never felt before."

"I wasn't gonna say any of that, Aiden." Her lips twitch, though. Is she smiling at this? "No one can tell you how you feel. That's a mistake many adults make. Only you know how you feel." She turns down the radio. "Do you think he feels the same way about you?"

"No," I answer immediately. "I don't think he's like me at all."

"Oh." Maybe it's my imagination, but her voice sounds relieved. Then again, she is dropping me off to spend the night with him. "I'm sorry, honey."

"It's fine. It's just, well, I wanna be honest with him. I wanna tell him the truth. I haven't told him that I'm, you know." Why is it still weird for me to say the words out loud?

Mom takes a deep breath. "One of the hardest parts of being a parent is wanting to protect your child from all harm," she says. "That includes emotional harm. When you're young—no, at any age really—there's nothing worse than loving someone who doesn't return the feeling."

I shuffle in my seat. "How do I, uh, not feel this way? I mean, what do I do when I know for sure that he doesn't like me back?"

"Oh, honey." Mom puts her hand on my knee. "Then you find a boy who does."

"Can I still be friends with Mat?"

"I hope so," she says. "I think it's hard to love someone so much and just be friends with them. But it's also a shame to love someone and not have them be in your life. You've got a great big heart, kid. If your heart beats for Mateo, then there's something very good and very special in him. I wouldn't want to lose him as a friend."

"He's the best," I say. "I wanna tell him everything. But I don't know if I should."

"I'm gonna keep my phone on me all night, volume up. You call me anytime. Just slip into the bathroom and text even. Okay?"

"Okay." I cross my arms and stare at the houses we pass.

Mom pulls into Mateo's driveway. Before I can unbuckle my seat belt, she leans over and hugs me. "I love you."

"I love you, too."

She kisses me on the cheek. "Be yourself. You deserve to be loved, kid."

"What if he doesn't love me back?"

Mom shakes her head. "Love is funny. You can't help that you love him. So, remember that he may not be able to help who he loves. He may like girls and that's not a rejection of you. That's just who he is."

"Kay," I mutter.

"Cheer up. He's your best friend. Go have some fun. Not too much fun!"

"I wish." A smile forms on my face.

"Aiden—"

"Mom, I haven't even kissed a boy. When I have my first kiss, I'll tell you, and we can have the talk. Okay?"

She returns the smile. "I love you so much." She hugs me again. "I'm rooting for you. Call me or text me. I'll be thinking about you all night."

"I will. Thanks, Mom." I step out of the car and wave as I shut the door. She blows me kisses, and I laugh. I don't know what I'd do without her.

She watches me walk up to Mateo's front door. I ring the bell, and his dad answers. He waves at Mom, who gestures back and then pulls out of the driveway.

I step inside and take a deep breath.

Be yourself. You deserve to be loved.

51

Telling the Truth

"WHAT DO YOU wanna do first?" Mateo asks.

Let's wrestle. I don't say what I think. My stomach flips like I'm on a carnival ride, and dizziness makes me stumble. "Uh, what do you wanna do?"

"Hmm." Mateo jumps on his bed. "Video games?"

"Cool." I sit next to him on his bed. Mat hops off to get the controllers and returns. We're close enough that our legs almost touch. There are so many things I want to say, but my mouth dries up.

He turns on the system and hands me a controller. I don't even know what I'm doing or what game I'm playing.

"Crap!" Mat shouts. Did his character die? Is it my fault? Then he laughs, and I laugh, too, even though I don't know what's funny. I mash buttons together, but my mind drifts. So do my eyes. Mat's shorts ride up his legs, and the muscles in his thighs flex with even the slightest movement.

I clear my throat and force my eyes to focus on the game. We both die, but I can't say I'm sad.

"How's karate been?" he asks, tossing his controller to the side.

"Lots to catch you up on." I say.

Lots to tell you. Where do I start?

"Can you show me the moves?"

"Yeah. Sure." I jump off the bed. "We're learning the coolest thing ever. It's called *kata.*"

"What's that?"

"Mister S says it's like our textbook. But it's not boring like a textbook. It's really cool."

"Show me."

I demonstrate the form. It's far from perfect, but Mat's mouth drops open when I step into tiger stance at the end.

"What was that?" he asks when I finish. "This part." He tries to mimic the tiger stance, and I laugh.

"Here. It's a horse stance. Your make your fists like this." I bend my fingers back and extend my palm. "It's a tiger claw. Then you put one hand high. One hand low." I touch his arms, and butterflies rush through my belly. "Bend your elbows more."

"Awesome," he says.

"Yeah. It's my favorite stance."

"What is the move you do after?"

"You're defending against a charge. Like someone is trying to tackle you." I crouch like how I imagine football players do before they race down the field. "You stop the charge by striking the throat and the balls." Mateo laughs again. All the laughter is infectious, but it's cool, too. I'm teaching him something for once, and—all laughs aside—I can tell he loves it. My hands morph into the tiger fists, and I pretend to hit him. He fakes an injury and bends over. "Then you scoop 'em up, like this."

I reach an arm in between Mat's legs. A tidal wave of chills rips through my body. My right arm squeezes his thigh. My left grips his arm, high up, near his shoulder. Standing up, I scoop him right off the ground.

"Oof," Mat grunts.

Even though he's heavier than me, I have no problem picking him up when I use the right stance.

I spin. Mateo yelps, and I toss him on the floor. Stumbling, I lose my balance and fall on top of him.

He breaks into laughter so hard he snorts. I roll, placing the back of my head on his stomach. With each laugh he releases, his abs make my head bounce. I don't want to move. I don't want the moment to end.

Does this mean something? Is it just simple friendship?

No, it's not simple. Far from simple. It's a best friendship. The best I've ever had.

Am I willing to lose that? If I open my mouth and say the words I want, it risks everything.

"That's a sweet move," he says.

"The coolest. I wish you could do the karate club with us."

"When wrestling is over, I will."

"Yeah?"

"Yeah."

I swallow the myriad of emotions in my throat. My head remains still. Mat doesn't move, either. He doesn't tell me to move. It's a perfect moment.

My mouth opens. I have to say something. Closing my eyes, I rehearse the words in my mind. Mateo, I have to tell you something. Will you promise to still be friends with me, no matter what?

His hands touch my shoulders. I hold my breath. Is he—?

He pushes me off him and chuckles. I know he meant no harm. Still, something hurts terribly, and it's not the carpet burn on my knees.

My perfect moment is gone, and my desire to tell the truth slips away with it. I force a smile and look up at Mat.

He grins back at me. Why does he have to have such a perfect smile? Part of his thick, dark hair stands up in back, and my heart melts.

"Now what?" he asks.

What was he thinking while I was on top of him? Anything?

"I dunno," I answer.

"You hungry?"

"Always."

He laughs. "How about Chinese? Maybe my parents will order delivery. I could kill for crab rangoon right about now."

"Sounds good."

He stands up and walks to the door. Before he opens it, he turns around. "You okay?"

My eyes widen, but I nod.

"Okay. You just, uh, look weird." He cracks a smile. "Weirder than usual, I mean."

"There *is* something I wanna tell you," I say. The blood rushes from my face. Words have a way of coming out of my mouth without my permission, it seems.

"Yeah?" His hand grips the doorknob, but he lets it go.

What were the words I had rehearsed earlier? I can't remember now. "We can get food first," I mumble.

"No, dude. It's cool." He sits down on the floor next to me. "What's up?"

Coming out to Mom was hard. Coming out to Tisha and Camila wasn't exactly easy, but it wasn't as complicated. This is ten times harder. A *hundred* times harder. My arms shake, and beads of sweat develop on my forehead.

What I'm about to say—it could make me lose my best friend. But there are possibilities, too. Dreams of holding Mat's hand. Having a boyfriend. I breathe hard and fast.

"There's something—I dunno, weighing on me," I start. "Something I wanna tell you. Because you're my best friend."

He smiles at the words but remains silent. Those dark eyes flash with kindness.

I look away and play with the carpet. "I think you kinda know, anyway. But it's hard to say."

Twisting my neck, I risk a glance at him. His warm eyes blink, but his face remains stoic. What is he thinking? Can I do this?

"You know the stupid rumors and everything?" Of *course* he does. I shake my head. I sound stupid to myself. "I, uh, well—they're true."

52

Mat Reacts

MAT DOESN'T SAY a word. Every second of his silence chills the blood flowing in my veins. I rub my cold arms. Did I just lose my best friend?

I catch his eyes and hold contact. This feels like a stupid game of chicken. I don't want to be the first person to speak. I said what I wanted—no, needed—to say. It's his turn to open his mouth and tell me it's okay. That's all I need to hear.

It's okay. Is that so hard? Sure, in the minutes and days before this moment, I had dreamed of a dozen possibilities. Maybe he'd be my first boyfriend. Maybe he'd hold my hand and be my first kiss. My eyes dart to the indentation on my side of the bed. Will I ever get to share that spot again now that he knows who I am?

I'd forget all of those fantasies if only he'd say those simple, little words—it's okay.

He lifts his left hand. He places it on the side of his face. He scratches the little stubble that never seems to grow on his chin. What is he thinking?

I can't take the silence anymore.

"Are we still friends?"

"How long have you known?" I hate that he doesn't answer my question, but at least he speaks.

I shrug. "Forever, I guess."

"Even like as a little kid?"

"No. Kinda. Not really." I scratch my chest. "It's hard to explain. I think I always knew something about me was different. I didn't always like all the things boys usually like, I guess. But I couldn't exactly place it till, you know, puberty." I release an awkward laugh. Mat doesn't laugh, though.

"So, you've known since we met? That first day you got a—uh, you know?"

That stupid boner in that stupid singlet. That one thing that started all the negative attention. I wish I could go back to that day—and do what?

I don't know.

I nod at Mat's question.

He moves over to his bed and sits. Looking at the side of the bed I've slept on, he runs a hand over the sheet.

"So, you lied to me." His brown eyes narrow, and his face frowns.

My chest throbs with pain.

"No, Mat. It's not that simple." I rub my forehead and think of what to say. "You've seen how cruel Logan and the team are. And that was based on a rumor! They didn't even know for sure. Imagine—I dunno—how much worse it could be?"

Silence fills the air. Did I ask the wrong question? Mat's had it hard because of me, too. Crap. I move closer, standing over him, while he sits on his bed. He runs a hand through his hair. I scratch my shoulder.

Mateo shakes his head. "I can't imagine how difficult this has all been." He speaks softly like he's telling me a secret.

My eyes feel wet. *Please* don't cry!

"It's been really hard. I told Mom not that long ago. She was the first. I wanted to tell you from the very beginning."

He looks up at me as if my words surprise him. "Yeah?"

"Of course. You're my best friend." I try to clear my dry throat. "The scariest part of all this is that, you know, you wouldn't be my friend anymore. That's why I waited so long. I was scared." I pause. My lips tremble, and my legs shake. "I'm scared right now. Terrified, really."

Mat looks down at his sheets. He tugs at them nervously. "You think I wouldn't be friends with you because you're gay?"

"You already ignore me at school." I wipe my nose. "All cuz of those jerks. Can you be friends with me even if they all know it's totally true?"

The color washes away from his face, and my heart sinks more. Maybe he hadn't thought of that, and my dumb self brought it up. Stupid, Aiden! *Stupid!*

"It's not your fault," he says. "Not your fault they're a bunch of dicks. Not your fault you're gay. They make it sound like a bad thing or a choice or something. I don't know how anyone today doesn't get that it's just a way people are. Like people are born black, brown, or white, people are born gay or straight. It is what it is."

My arms lighten. I fill with hope, and my heart pumps with joy. He gets it. That's it exactly!

"Yeah, like what year is it? We're smarter than the jerks who lived a hundred years ago. At least I thought we were." He cracks a smile finally, and I return it. Slowly, I sit next to him on the bed. He moves over a little, making room for me.

"Are we still friends?"

"Course," he says.

I hug him. I can't help it. I pretty much jump on top of him and hug him. I feel his arms around me, too. They're not tight like mine, but he hugs me back. That's the it's okay I needed.

When I let go, I move back slowly, my face inches from his. My heart pounds like a drum. One barrier down—I've told him the truth about me. We're still friends.

But there's still another truth.

My stomach flips upside down, as I hold contact with his beautiful brown eyes.

Like my words so many times before, my mouth betrays me.

I lean in.

I press my lips against his.

His warm lips set my face on fire. It's the best feeling I've ever had.

I move my lips against his, and I swear his mouth presses back against mine.

But then I feel instant pain in my chest, and I fly off his bed.

His two strong hands push into my chest with all his strength. I hit the floor with a terrible thud.

"What the... *no,* Aiden!"

I can't breathe. What did I do? What's happening?

"What is *wrong* with you?" His face burns a deep red.

"I, uh, I dunno," I mumble. Tears well in my eyes, and my stomach feels sick.

"No!" he yells again. "You can't just do that! Get out of my room! Get out of my *house!*"

The words hurt more than anything I've ever felt. I have no power to stop the tears. They roll down my face.

"I'm sorry," I cry. "I'm sorry!"

He shakes his head. "You can't do that! That's not okay!"

"I'm sorry, Mat!"

He marches toward me. I stand on shaky legs.

"Get out!" he shouts.

More tears roll down my face. I reach for him, and he swats my arm away. "Please, Mat!"

"Out!"

"I'm your best friend!"

"*Was.* "

I reach for him again, and he pushes me hard. I fall on the floor. I look up, and anger mixes with my tears. I want to punch him. I clench my fist. I bounce off the floor and swing at his face. He dodges and hits me hard in the stomach. I buckle over, and tears soak my face.

"I said out!" He opens his bedroom door and pushes me into the hall. "Don't ever talk to me again. *Ever!*"

I crawl out of his house. His parents stare at me like zombies from the kitchen. They don't say a word to me or ask if I'm okay.

Once I'm outside, I call Mom.

I have no words to say. I sob into the phone. I can't form a single audible thought. All I do is cry, but Mom gets the message.

"Oh, baby. Oh, no. I'm on my way," she says.

I put down the phone and bawl outside of Mateo's house.

53

The Worst Pain

"WHAT HAPPENED, HONEY?" Mom asks when I get in the car. I can't talk. My muscles feel rubbery like I have no bones for support, and I can't stop crying.

I don't answer. I raise my arm, pointing and waving at the road. Mom gets the message. She puts the car in drive and heads home.

It's not that I don't want to talk to her. I just can't talk at all. My chest and throat hurt with each sob like I'm tearing apart vocal cords and my little pec muscles. Mom doesn't push. She puts a hand on the back of my neck and gently massages me. I lean against the window and want to die.

When we get home, I struggle to open the door. Mom races around the side of the car, opens my door, and pulls me close, hugging me hard.

"You listen to me, Aiden. Heartbreak sucks. It's the absolute worst pain. And this is coming from someone who went through labor to have you." Her hug tightens as she speaks into my ear. "I love you so much. So, so much. You are my world. Someday, someone else will see how incredible you are. They will fall in love with you. And on that wonderful day, you will look back at this moment and…." She pauses and kisses me on the cheek. "You'll look back and understand that sometimes you have to live through pain to find joy. It's not fair, and it's not easy. But you will find joy. I know right now you're hurting, but you will, son. I promise you." She kisses me again on the cheek. "I love you."

"I love you, too," I mutter. "I just wanna go to bed."

"I'll be here all night if you wanna talk, okay? I'm here for you."

I walk upstairs to my bedroom. But I don't have any desire to sleep. I'm putting my sadness and my anger into one thing and one thing only—I'll train until I pass out.

Kicking off my shoes, I grab my earbuds. I play the angriest music I can stream. My feet come together. I bow.

Then I perform *Wansu*. I run through the kata not one time but a dozen times. I lose count. Maybe I do it a hundred times. Sweat flies from my brow, and the music pulses through my ears.

At one point, the door cracks open, and I know Mom is checking on me. Let her see me—I don't care. It's better than getting caught crying myself to sleep.

I don't want to cry anymore.

I keep running through the form over and over again. My muscles cramp, but I push through the pain.

I soak it up, taking sadistic pleasure in every muscle spasm.

When I step into tiger stance, I picture Mateo. I taught him this stance. I picked him up, spun him around, and tossed him on the ground. I rested my head on top of him. He laughed.

Then I told the truth, and the truth was not the problem. The problem was *me*. I pushed it too far. I just had to kiss him.

I picture him shoving me away and hitting me. I hit the lowest, strongest tiger stance I can. Visualizing Mateo, I strike him with the tiger fists—one in the throat and one in the groin. I grab him and toss him on the floor, finishing the series with a strike to the face.

Lying down, I take some time to stretch out my sore legs. This stupid exhibition match between karate and wrestling will be here before I know it.

I'll fight Logan, and if I win, I follow that up with a fight against Mateo. Mateo and I were going to fool everyone. He would have given a metaphorical, or who knows—maybe a literal—middle finger to the wrestling squad and Coach Krake.

But now?

Now, I'll have to fight Mateo for real.

No fake match.

That stupid kiss shattered several realities. Long gone is any chance I have of being Mat's boyfriend. It's all too obvious that he's not gay like me at all—I can still feel his hands against my chest and hear the harshness of his voice when he yelled "out!"

Gone is my best friend, the one who hugged me after we got ticketed by the police captain.

Gone is any play fight. It will be a real fight. Mateo will want to get back at me for that kiss, for betraying his trust. He'll do whatever his stupid coach wants, and his stupid coach wants him to hurt me.

Assuming I can even beat the red-headed, homophobic Logan so that I advance enough to face Mateo, that is.

I clench my fists.

I will *beat* Logan.

After a few minutes of stretching, I stand back up, ready to practice some more.

I will practice every night until my legs fall off to make sure I can beat Logan.

I want to stand in the middle of a ring and face Mateo one-on-one.

I want to show Mateo that I am not some weak loser that needs his help. I will show him that I can stand up for myself.

I will show him that I am tough enough to win, even against him.

Even if it kills me to do so.

54

*Sunday with
Mr. Samuels*

A KNOCK ON my bedroom door wakes me up. I must have fallen asleep on the floor. I arch my stiff back, trying to work out the soreness.

"Come in."

The door opens slowly, and Mr. Samuels enters. His heavy eyes look around my room.

"Can we talk?"

I sit up to the sound of more popping in my joints.

"Do you mind telling me what happened last night?"

"I practiced. A lot."

His lips tighten. "Between you and Mateo, I mean."

I sigh. The first lesson we ever learned was that karate is for self-defense only. If I tell him the truth, will he see what happened as a violation?

The truth has already gotten me into too much trouble.

"Nothing."

"You're not obligated to tell me, Aiden. But do *not* lie to me." The sternness in his voice makes me tremble.

I try to swallow the knot in my throat. "I need something to drink. Please."

"I'll get you something. Then, you tell me the truth or tell me nothing at all."

When he leaves, I push myself off the floor and sit on my bed. Mr. Samuels returns with a Gatorade. I twist off the cap and swallow the entire beverage.

"Better?"

I rub my throat. Jeez. Did I not hydrate at all last night? "Can I have another?"

My question makes Sensei smile, and he gets me one more drink. I take a few big gulps but save half of it.

"Now, what happened?"

"Mateo and I got in a fight."

"Why?"

"It's my fault," I tell him. "I told him the truth."

He crosses his arms, and his face twists. "Did he hurt you because you're gay?"

I shake my head. "He hurt me because I tried to kiss him."

His face turns from anger to empathy. His arms drop by his side. "Is that all?"

My eyes widen. "All? He never wants to see me again!"

"Aiden, boys can be sensitive about sexuality." He sits next to me on the bed. "It's like, I think some boys counter affection with fighting. I bet Mateo will forget all about last night."

A warm feeling pulses through my veins. "Really? You really think so?" Here I just trained for a night like I was John Wick, with zero thoughts of hope and happiness. In one breath, Mr. Samuels gives me back some hope, just an ounce, but it's enough to not feel so deflated.

"You like him. You reacted in a way to show that. It's a compliment," he says. "Of course, if he doesn't like you in that way, you can't do things like that. And you must always get consent first. You are smart enough to know that. But overall, I think he will forgive you." He flashes me a smile and puts an arm around my shoulder.

"I dunno," I mumble. "He was pretty mad. He kicked me out."

"What would you do if you were hanging out with Tisha and she kissed you?"

"Ew. She's my friend, but not like that. That would be so weird. I'd—oh." I take a deep breath. "I see what you're doing."

He releases a little chuckle and squeezes my shoulder with his strong hand. "I'm sure you wouldn't hurt her or throw her out. I don't understand all the dynamics here. It's complicated." Mr. Samuels's eyes look around my room. He ignores my WWE poster, and his eyes lock on my yellow belt, proudly placed on the top of my dresser. "Let's go there together. Today. A private session with me and the two of you. Okay?"

Can we really bounce back from this? In just one visit? No matter what, Mateo has great respect for Mr. Samuels, too. Maybe with his influence, Mat and I can at least be friends again. I'll apologize, and I'll force myself to stop thinking about Mateo like I do. I'll get over the crush, somehow. Just as long as we can be friends, that's all I'd need. I find myself smiling slightly for the first time in what feels like forever.

"How many times did you practice your *kata* last night?"

"At least a hundred times." I rub my legs. "Maybe more. I don't know how much practice I can do today."

"That's all right. We'll focus on other lessons. Do you know why the form you practice begins and ends with a block?"

I hadn't thought about that. Our form begins with a block, which makes sense. But why does it end with a block, too? "Because karate is about self-defense?"

"Yes. There is no first strike in karate. Every form you learn will always begin with a block because it is about self-defense. But why would it end with a block?"

I shrug.

"It further symbolizes the defensive nature of karate. It goes to show that if you can stop a fight with a block and only a block, then there is no need to follow it up with a strike." He pats me on the back. "Do you understand?"

"I think so," I tell him.

"Good. Let's call Mateo."

I swallow that lump in my throat, and I say a quick prayer, hoping for the best.

If you can stop a fight with a block and only a block, then there is no need to follow it up with a strike.

55

A New Battle

MR. SAMUELS TRIES calling Mat's parents, but they don't answer. He tries Mateo directly. Mat doesn't pick up.

"Will you—?"

I shake my head before he can ask the question. I can't call or text Mat. No, sir.

Mr. Samuels sends a couple of texts. His big fingers type fast on his phone. "I told them we're on our way. I guess we'll just stop by."

My stomach drops. "Do you think that's a good idea?"

"Why not?" He folds his arms. "They'll see the message. If they don't want us to come, someone will call us back before we get there."

Oh, I hope he's right. I swallow hard. Grabbing my gi and duffel bag, I follow Mr. S out of my room.

Mom waits for us in the kitchen. She reaches for Mr. Samuels's hand. He takes it and kisses her on the cheek. It's still weird to see my teacher and Mom together, but in comparison to the other crap that's happening in my life—well, it's nothing. I'll take someone else's happiness over the other garbage life has tossed my way, that's for sure.

Mom whispers in Mr. S's ear, but I can hear. "You sure about this?"

He nods. "I won't let anything happen." He flashes a smile my way. "Karate taught me many things. One of which—when there's conflict, you look your opponent in the eye, and you bow. Why do we bow in martial arts, Aiden?"

Why is he always teaching me a lesson? "Because of respect."

"Yes. We respect each other, even our opponents," he says. "We also aren't afraid to face conflict head-on. But before you throw a punch, you bow. If you can face your fears and give them respect at the same time, what comes next isn't a strike at all. What comes next is forgiveness."

Forgiveness. But this isn't like I spilled a soda in Mat's room. I broke the rules of our friendship with that kiss.

"Call me," Mom tells him as we walk out of the house. "I love you."

"I love you, too." We both say it. Mr. Samuels chuckles and slaps me playfully on the back. It's weird to hear another man say that to my mother. But if he's going to be with her, I guess he better love her.

We get in the car and drive toward Mat's house. Was it really just last night that Mom took this same route to drop me off? We had such a good night until I ruined it.

"You have a very special mother," Mr. Samuels says.

"I know."

"That's the first time I told her that I love her."

"Really?"

"Yeah. The funny thing is—I think she was just saying those words to you, not me." His fingers tap rapidly on the steering wheel. Is Mr. Samuels nervous? Huh. I guess I didn't picture a strong adult—a super black belt at that—getting nervous.

"She loves you. I can tell," I say.

"You think so?" The tone in his voice has shifted. It's like he's a kid on the playground asking about another girl. Maybe some things never change.

"I know so. She's been so different, so... happy since she's been with you. She comes home from work less stressed. She wakes up happier. She makes me bigger meals. It's been good."

"I'm a very lucky man to have met someone like your mother. And to have met you. I want you to know that you both mean a lot to me."

"Thanks." I shuffle in my seat, a little embarrassed.

"I don't have my own kids, you know. And I don't know if I ever will. I also know you don't really have a father. That sucks, Aiden. You're such a great kid. Any man would be lucky to call you his son. I take such pride in you as my student. I can't imagine why anyone wouldn't feel the same way."

My cheeks burn, but it feels as nice as it is uncomfortable.

"What I'm saying is—maybe we can help each other fill the gaps in our lives. I get to spend time with you, and you spend some time with me. Okay?"

"Okay."

We turn on Mateo's street, and another emotional wave hits me. Is there any chance that I still have my best friend?

Fear forms a lump in my throat. There are two cars parked in Mateo's driveway. One is a police car that I recognize all too well.

Mr. Samuels's eyes narrow. He knows that car, too. But he doesn't slow down or turn around. He keeps driving forward.

My arms tremble.

I can barely open the door when we park.

We walk to the front door, and it opens before we reach it.

"Well, well, well. My old student and his new student," Captain Decker says with a chuckle, stepping outside. His yellow teeth make me sick, and he presses his long, gangly arms against his hips.

Behind him stands Coach Krake, wearing his usual Hornets polo. The shirt looks stretched out against his thick chest. Krake steps outside, and Mateo follows.

Mateo doesn't avoid my eye contact or look away. There's no discreet whisper of "I'm sorry."

He glares at me. His brown eyes darken, and I don't even recognize him with that intensity in his eyes.

I mouth the words I had hoped to hear. "I'm sorry." Krake and Decker stare at Mr. Samuels. "I'm sorry," I mouth again.

Mateo slowly shakes his head side to side. His eyes narrow, and his cheeks redden.

"I came to chat with Mateo about this stupid exhibition you want to have after our season," Krake says. "We have a new challenge for you."

"Oh? What's that?" Mr. Samuels speaks each word firmly. He steps in front of me, not backing down. I wonder what would happen if both Krake and Decker attacked him. Krake is built like a truck, and Decker is my teacher's teacher. That means he has more experience and more knowledge, right?

I place a hand over my beating heart, which is apparently trying to escape my body.

Decker hands Mr. Samuels a flyer.

"Washington's First Annual Mixed Martial Arts Challenge. Open to all high school students. March first. Grand prize five-thousand-dollar college scholarship fund," Mr. Samuels reads.

"We had an epiphany," Krake says. "I coach my top athletes wrestling. Captain Decker will teach them mixed martial arts in the offseason. Doesn't that sound like the perfect collaboration? Two top teachers, two strong perspectives. One perfect athlete."

I want to scream. *Hell no, it doesn't!* That's the *opposite* of perfect! It sounds like hell.

My legs shake, and I try to dig my shoes into the concrete.

"So, I'm gonna tell my wrestlers that they have this to look forward to after our season. Real MMA training. And, of course, a chance to compete with Aiden and the rest of your students on the first of March. Five grand scholarship—no one will want to lose out on that." Krake crosses his arms and laughs.

"And if you don't enter," Decker adds, glaring at me and Mr. S, "then, um, the wrestlers can do whatever they want, whenever they want. Do you understand what I'm saying? Hell, they don't have to worry about the law looking the other way. They may just have the law right by their side, helping them."

"Why are you doing this?" Mr. Samuels asks. The white of his eyes pulses with anger.

"I've missed teaching," Decker says. "I didn't realize how much I had until recently. I picked up a few students. Been working with them privately. I want to teach again and see if I can get it right this time."

"These kids—they don't need to fight," Mr. Samuels argues.

"But you wanted this. You wanted the exhibition," Krake says loudly, a mocking tone in his voice. He takes a step closer to us. Any closer and Krake and Samuels would be nose to nose. "We're just making it a lot more interesting, not to mention worth a lot more. You get everything you wanted. And imagine if Aiden wins—he'll get five thousand bucks."

"Mateo, what do you want, son?" Mr. Samuels asks. "Do you want to train with them? Or do you want to train with us?"

Mat's eyes haven't left mine this entire time until Mr. S asks him the question. Mat breathes hard through his nose.

I study those eyes, hoping he's hiding something. My best friend has to be in there somewhere. Could one kiss turn him into this person? I don't understand. No, something worse has happened. Something has poisoned Mateo.

He speaks, his voice stern and deep. It's a voice I don't recognize. "I'm taking the five grand prize. I'm taking everything I can get for my future. That means I train with the best of the best." Krake flashes an arrogant smile, steps back, and puts an arm around Mateo's shoulders.

I think I'm going to throw up.

56

Must See Status

MR. SAMUELS AND I ride back to my house in silence at first. Krake and Decker have somehow manipulated my best friend into turning against me. I'm convinced of that—Mateo is not a homophobic jerk like the rest, and this is about much more than a kiss.

On top of all that, I now have to fight in a real tournament.

If I lose, I'll be ridiculed. They'll make fun of my karate. They'll mock everything Mr. Samuels has done for me.

If I win, I have to fight my best friend, the love of my life.

Mr. Samuels sighs as if he's reading my mind. What is he thinking? He has to face his own Sensei. He has to train me in just a few months to fight someone who is years ahead of me in physical ability.

"Um, so, Captain Decker said he had already been training people," I say, breaking the silence. My voice sounds weird in the car. There's no radio, only the sound of the car's fans pushing out soft warmth. "Who do you think he's training?"

"Some of the wrestlers, probably. Giving it a practice run before telling us." His voice is quick and short. "Or to get a head start on us."

Some of the wrestlers? Crap, like Logan and Jeff? Not only will they have Krake's wrestling, but they'll now also know Decker's mixed martial arts, too? They'll know as much as me, if not more. How will I ever stand a chance against them?

We park in the driveway and exit the car. Mom opens the door before we can knock.

"What happened?"

Mr. Samuels frowns.

"That bad?"

"I'll be in my room," I mumble. "For the rest of the year."

"Aiden," Mr. Samuels calls. I turn around. "There's a lot to process. First, you have to decide if you want to do this. There's no need to fight. We can find an alternative."

I lean against the wall and take a deep breath. "I don't wanna be afraid anymore. I'll face them—Logan, the entire team, even...." I gulp. "Even Mateo. Will you train me? Harder than ever? I don't care if I lose. I just don't wanna be afraid, you know?"

He puts his hand on my shoulder. "You are so much stronger than the boy whose essays I read when school started. You may not be able to see it. Change happens slowly. But you are stronger than you realize. If you want to compete, I will give you one hundred and ten percent. But you will need to match that. Okay?"

"Excuse me," Mom interrupts. "Do I get a say in this? And can someone please explain what's going on?"

"Mister S can tell you," I say. "Sensei?" I step away from the wall. I put my feet together and my hands at my side. I bow. *"Domo arigato."*

He returns the bow. "Rest tonight. You have a lot to digest, and we need your focus. We start tomorrow at six in the morning. We train before and after school now. Every day until March."

"Yes, Sensei."

Mom puts her hands on her hips. "Why does it look like you two are preparing for war?"

I look at Mom. "Because we are."

I go to my room, but I don't rest. I take out my phone and call Tisha. I tell her everything.

"Can girls enter this tournament? Because I will so be there," she says.

"It said open to all high school students."

"Knowing those sexist jerks, they may try to keep me out. But that's not happening. I'm entering this with you, Aiden. You and I are gonna kick some major ass."

"I wish I had your confidence."

"What time are you practicing tomorrow?"

"Six."

"In the morning?"

I laugh, just a little. "Yep."

"I'm gonna meet you. If that's cool with you. I don't wanna, like, crash your training. But I'm serious. I'll buzz my hair and stick socks in my shorts if I have to."

"I'd like that. I mean, not you, um, buzzing your head or pretending to have balls. But training with me."

She laughs. *"I'm there."*

"What's so funny?"

"I was just thinking—if Mister Samuels is training you that early, is he gonna spend the night at your house?"

My face burns. "I hadn't thought about that."

"He's probably already hooked up with your mom."

"Stop! Don't say that." I sigh into the phone. "It doesn't matter. He's cool, and he really likes her. But there are still some things I don't wanna think about."

"I know." Tisha laughs. *"I was just trying to take your mind off other things. And it worked, didn't it?"*

"It did. Thanks, I guess."

"We gotta tell Camila. Hang on. Let's get her on this call, too."

Sitting up in bed, I look out the window. The sun begins to set. The sky fills with a beautiful purple and orange. Sometimes it doesn't make sense to me how the world can be so gorgeous and ugly at the same time. I guess it's not really the world that's ugly. It's people.

What made Krake the way he is? Or Decker? Or Logan—*especially*

Logan? He's just a kid. How can a kid my age already have so much poison in his veins?

And what about Mateo? Who's the real Mat? There's a Mat that I worked out with, watched movies with, even cuddled with. Is that the real Mat? Or is the Mat I saw today, like the one who avoids me at school, the one who wouldn't hang out with me except in private where no one could see, the one with the dark, insulting, hateful eyes—is that the *real* Mat?

"Um, Aiden?" Tisha asks.

"Yeah?"

"Um, can you put me on speaker and check your socials?"

"Okay."

"I don't know if you'll want to see this, but I think, I mean I guess, I dunno." She clears her throat. *"I think you have to."*

"What are you trying to say, Tish?"

"Just go to Camila's stories."

It's the first thing that pops up on my feed as if my socials somehow knew this would be the most interesting thing for me to view.

Camila has changed her relationship status.

"What the hell?" I ask. Nausea rises in my throat.

Camila's socials say that she's in a relationship... with *Mateo.*

57

Continuous Fighting

MY ALARM BUZZES way too early. With eyes half-closed, I fumble my phone, dropping it on the floor. Why the hell did I ever choose an alarm that sounds like a siren? It's the worst sound ever. I need to change it to like a WWE entrance song, something that will pump me up first thing in the morning. Rolling my legs out of bed, I drop on the floor to turn it off.

Then my bedroom door opens.

"Mornings are for endurance. Nights are for techniques," Mr. Samuels greets me. His face remains calm and focused. I stretch and yawn, barely able to find my balance in my bedroom.

"Endurance?" I cough, grabbing a T-shirt and shorts.

"Follow me," he says. I get dressed quickly, and we leave my room, heading downstairs. It's dark and quiet. The familiar rooms of my house look different this early, almost like they belong to someone else.

He opens the basement door. I don't go in the basement except to grab laundry. What are we doing down here?

"Morning, sunshine!" It's Tisha. What the heck is Tisha doing in my dirty basement?

"It's not much, not yet, anyway," Mr. S tells me. "Tisha came over early to help. Your mother and I came up with the idea. A little basement dojo."

I walk by the washer and dryer, and to the left is an empty room. Mom had just used it for storage—a place to toss boxes of Dad's crap that for whatever reason she had decided to keep. The room has been emptied and cleaned. I step on the floor, and it's lined with colorful puzzle pieces of foam. There's a punching bag in the corner and a handful of striking targets.

"Wow," I mumble. Hairs rise on the back of my neck. It's only a tiny dojo, but it feels like seeing Disney World for the first time. I face my teacher, put my feet together, and bow. "Thank you, sir."

"It's my pleasure, Aiden. You two get geared up. As I said, mornings are for endurance."

"Geared up?"

Mr. Samuels moves to the dryer. On top of the dryer sits a box, and he reaches inside it. He takes out two more pieces of equipment—body protectors. It's a pad that wraps around the stomach and chest.

"Are you wearing one?" Tisha asks Mr. Samuels.

He smiles. "No. This is to protect *you.*"

"Protect us from what?" Tisha asks.

"From each other." His smile grows. "And also from me."

It takes us a few minutes to figure the equipment out, but we manage. "Now what?"

"Line up. We'll rotate. Aiden against me. Aiden against Tisha. Tisha against me. And so on. Two-minute continuous fighting. No breaks. If you're not hitting me or each other, you're doing something wrong. Aiden, you're up first. Face me." I gulp. I've never sparred Mr. Samuels. He's demonstrated techniques plenty, but we've never been in a one-on-one situation. "Bow."

I do.

"Fighting positions," he says, stepping back, putting his hands up.

I mimic his stance.

"Begin."

I take a deep breath, but before I can blink, my teacher is in my face. He throws a punch at my stomach, and I bounce back. He whips a kick at my face, controlled but smacking me nonetheless.

"I would be doing you a disservice if I held back, Aiden," he shouts at me. "Defend yourself. Now!"

He throws a sidekick, and I spin to the side. I lunge in, striking a reverse punch to his ribs.

"Good. More!" he calls.

He kicks me in the stomach with a round house, but I block it. I dive in for another reverse punch, but he hasn't set his foot down. It smacks me in the head again with another round kick.

"One hand by your head, one by your heart," he instructs. I don't know how he's talking. I can barely breathe.

"Two minutes!" Tisha yells. I collapse on the basement floor.

"No breaks yet," Mr. Samuels tells me. "Tisha, you and Aiden are up next."

"Oh, so *you* get a break," I say.

"I'm the teacher, Aiden. And clearly, you need a little more practice than I do." He grins. It's tough training, as hard as anything I had ever experienced with Coach Krake. It's different, though, too. Hard but encouraging.

I stand.

"Ready to get your ass kicked?" Tisha asks.

"Language," Mr. S tells her, but his lips curl mischievously.

We bow and step back into fighting positions. Mr. Samuels yells, "Begin!"

Tisha comes at me with a series of quick punches. She gets me several times in the stomach and ribs. I'm against the wall, and I look at Mr. Samuels for advice.

"Any wrestler would have grabbed you and had you on the ground by now. What do you do?" he asks.

I jump to the side, placing a roundhouse in Tisha's stomach. It connects, and she groans. Tisha spins and charges at me with a ridge hand. I perform a jump front snap kick, the ball of my foot targeting her chin. She dives low and executes a roundhouse at my leg. It connects with the back of my standing leg, and I fall hard on the ground.

"Time is *not* up. Keep going!" Mr. S calls.

I try to perform a kip-up like they do in the movies. I fall hard on my back, knocking the wind out of myself.

"Time," Mr. S calls.

Thank goodness.

Mr. S faces Tisha next. We rotate back and forth like this for an hour. I'm drenched from head to toe, and I haven't even had breakfast yet.

"Line up," Mr. S says. Tisha and I stand next to each other. "We will train like this every morning. Tonight, we work on technique and form. I'm proud of both of you. We can do this."

I hope he's right. It's only one day of practice, but I feel better already. Of course, the wrestling team is training, too.

We've got only a few months to prepare. Is it enough time to face them? To face—I rub my arms, suddenly cold at the thought of his name—Mateo?

"Now, go shower. Please. You both smell," he says, chuckling on his way out.

We don't have a lot of time to shower and eat before school, but there's one other thing that's been on my mind since last night.

"Did you ever talk to Camila?" I ask Tisha.

She nods. "Yep. It's no joke. We had a big conversation. I've got a lot to tell you."

"She and, uh, Mateo are what—dating?"

"I'm sorry, Aiden. Yeah, they're official. I guess that's what Mat had been texting her about all along. He likes her."

I shake my head. I don't believe it!

"So it had nothing to do with me at all? Was that a lie? And what about her other secret?" I kick at the basement floor, and Tisha shrugs awkwardly. "Did you tell her what happened? Everything else?"

She lowers her head, sweat still dripping from her hair. "Yeah. And I hate to say this, but it gets worse."

"What? How can any of this get worse?"

58

School Day Confrontation

"TISHA, YOUR MOTHER is here," Mom calls from upstairs. "You guys don't have a lot of time to get ready."

"I'll talk to you at school," she says. "It can wait till then. Meet you at lunch, okay?"

She doesn't give me the chance to reply. She runs upstairs. I check my phone. Shoot, we really do have to rush. I hop up the stairs and jump in the shower. It's a quick one, and the hot water doesn't provide any comfort.

My ex-best friend is dating my ex-girlfriend. And it gets worse than that?

I get dressed and grab a Pop-Tart. I ride with Mr. Samuels. A week ago, I'd have felt weird going to school with him. Certainly, other kids would see us riding together and tease me about his relationship with Mom. Today, I'd beg for that to be my only worry.

First period, even with Mr. Samuels, is the worst. Camila sits next to Mateo. I stay as far away as possible, but I can't not watch them. I try to persuade myself to ignore them, but it's impossible. She brushes his arm, and he laughs. He laughs! It makes me want to puke.

Mr. Samuels asks them to be quiet, and they glare at him. It's pure disrespect. They challenge him, but Mr. S chooses his battles wisely. For the most part, he succeeds in ignoring them.

Mateo looks at me only one time during class.

His dark eyes narrow. I used to find so much warmth in his eyes. Now, it's liquid-hate washing through his eyes, and I don't understand it.

What could have changed so quickly? He was going to accept me for who I was—I know it! He was nice when I told him the truth, wasn't he? Then I had to kiss him. Stupid, stupid Aiden!

The first-hour bell rings—thank goodness! Mateo and Camila hold hands when they walk out of the room. When he whispers in her ear, she laughs. Those dimples that I used to find so cute make me sick now. I thought she was my friend, too. How could she do this, especially after the conversation we had in my bedroom?

She not only knows that I loved him. She knows that, and she doesn't care. My insides are crumbling, and I wish I could go home and go back to bed.

Mateo and Camila ignore me on the way out of class, and that's fine. One more second of seeing them and I might put my fist through the wall and projectile vomit in the hole.

I need to talk to Tisha more than ever, but there are still three classes to go.

I watch the second hand on the old-fashioned clocks that some-how missed twenty-first century technology tick by in each classroom. Each class feels like a day. It takes forever, but finally the lunch bell rings. I don't bother with food, even though I'm starving. The Pop-Tart did little to refuel my body after the intense morning workout.

"So, what could be worse?" I ask Tisha as soon as I see her. Her hair is pulled back, and she frowns.

"I saw some pictures that Camila posted. I took screenshots to show you. Look." Tisha starts to hand me her phone but pauses. "I, uh—crap, Aiden. I feel like I'm just the bearer of bad news. I know this morning was enough to think about. Before you look at this, um, how are you feeling?"

Her eyes wash with empathy. At least someone cares.

"I feel like crap." My face turns hot, and suddenly my eyes feel wet. "How can they do this?"

Tisha puts her arm around my shoulder. "I dunno. Maybe they weren't very good friends, after all. Maybe they were hiding other things from us all along. That's what's worse. That's what I want to show you."

She hands me her phone, and I look at the screenshots.

My jaw hits the floor.

I swipe through each photo, confused and incredulous. Camila wears shorts and a T-shirt that reads Decker's MMA. She poses in a fighting stance.

She stands next to Mr. Decker, who wears an all-black martial arts uniform, with what I assume used to be a black belt around his waist. It's gray now and holds on by threads.

How long has Camila been training?

That's when it hits me. I've seen that shirt on her before! She had it mostly covered by a hoodie, but I remember the fist and the letters *ECK*. How long ago was that?

"When we invited her to join our club," Tisha starts, "that's when she told us she had a secret. Remember? Keep scrolling. It gets worse."

Camila and Decker pose in fighting stances.

Then there's one with Mateo and Decker. Then there's the three of them—Camila, Mat, and Decker all in one picture.

I grip the lunch table with my free hand. Dizziness hits me. This is so much more than someone going behind your back. This is an utter betrayal. I didn't think it was possible to feel anything more painful than what I felt when Mateo kicked me out of his house. Right now, though, this—this may be worse.

He wasn't who he said he was. And for all the crap Camila gave me about being honest, this is what she was doing all along!

"When was this taken?" I ask.

"Look at her hair," Tisha says.

"What about it?"

"You're not very observant for a gay guy."

"I don't find that funny right now." I frown. "What is it?"

"It's longer there. She got her hair cut a couple of weeks ago. Before we even invited her to join our martial arts club, before she had that fight with her stepmother."

"Oh, no," I say. "So that means—"

"It means they've all been training together longer than we thought. It means they've been planning this all along, I think. They're several steps ahead of us."

"Decker said he started training people privately. Did you ask her about this, too, when you talked with her?" I ask.

"Yes, but she wouldn't tell me much. She said she started looking for self-defense classes after one of the big fights she had with her stepmother. She found a place for private lessons. Thought that would be perfect, as she wanted to keep it private. Apparently, Decker made her vow as part of her training to not tell anyone what she was doing. That was the promise she couldn't break."

"Holy crap." I stare at the pictures, and bile rises in my throat.

Tisha groans. "Looks like I have an opponent for this tournament." Tisha gets up and walks over to their table.

"What are you doing?"

She turns her head. "Getting some answers."

Tisha taps Camila on the shoulder. I race over.

"Hey, girl," Camila says.

"Hey." Tisha gestures wildly. "So, you're just sitting over here now?"

"Yes," Camila says. She eats a spoonful of yogurt. Mateo puts his arm around her shoulder.

Tisha taps her harder, digging her finger into Camila's flesh.

Camila puts her arms on the table and pushes herself up. Then she steps out from the bench, facing Tisha.

"What?" Camila asks.

"We were your friends," Tisha says. "I don't understand."

"*Were,*" Camila says. "My ex-boyfriend lied to me." She turns toward the wrestling team but locks eye contact with Logan. "Everything you thought about him is true, in case you were ever wondering. Gay as a rainbow."

My entire body burns with anger and embarrassment.

Logan tilts his head back and laughs.

But that's not the worst of it.

Mateo laughs, too. His amusement breaks my heart. Tears threaten my eyes, and I bite my tongue, praying not to cry. How can he be so cruel?

"What happened to you?" Tisha asks Camila. The question echoes in my mind, and I wonder the same thing about Mat.

Camila scowls and takes Mat's hand. "First, Aiden lies to me. I give him my heart and my time, and he lies to me! What you don't know is that Mateo comforted me. Mat has been here for me, but I couldn't tell you, could I?" She glares at me. "Because you're in love with him!"

The wrestling team breaks into laughter. My stomach plunges, and my heart aches more than ever. I want to scream, but I hold my breath, praying not to break down and cry in front of everyone. Mateo flinches at Camila's statement, just for a second, and then his eyes turn cold again.

"It wasn't enough to hurt me. You had to try and take the next boy I liked, too, didn't you?" She wipes at her eyes.

"Camila, I'm—"

"Shut up! I don't need you guys. I have new friends. I told my teacher, Sensei Decker, about everything, too! You know what he said? That you used me!" She glares right at me. "He said you never wanted to be my friend. He said you used me as your beard. He told me if a person can do that, then they have evil in their heart. You're not my friend, even after you told the truth. You just wanted to use me to get to Mateo, since you knew we were talking!"

"That's not—"

She doesn't give me a chance to defend myself. She talks over me but this time to Tisha. "And you," Camila snaps. "I told him all about you, too. Sensei Decker said you're a leech and a drama queen. You stir the pot. You got me all confused that I was the bad guy, but where were you when Aiden broke my heart? I got beat up by my stepmother. I got lied to. I looked for help, and I found it. I'm not the bad guy here. *You* are."

Our jaws drop. It's like I've been sideswiped out of nowhere.

My eyes turn to Mat, and I stare at him in disbelief. He didn't just go behind my back, then. He went behind Mr. Samuels's back, too. They've been training with Decker and keeping it a secret. "Why?" I ask him. "Why would you go behind our backs and train with that guy? The same guy who threatened us. You remember that?"

Camila lets go of Mat's hand and gets in my face. "See! There you go again. You don't care about me. I tell you all this, and the first thing you do is turn to Mat. He's all you care about. My stepmother is terrible, you know that? I told you all about her. But you never listened." She shakes her head. "I told you about her when we dated, but when you came over that day with Tisha, it was like you were seeing me for the first time. You were never my friend! You ignored me. Your mind was always somewhere else."

My heart sinks. How many stories had she told me while my mind wandered? When we were "dating," she'd talk on the phone to me for hours some nights. She's right—I didn't listen.

"How long have you been training?" I ask. It's a stupid question to ask, perhaps. There are much bigger things to worry about, but I think I'm in shock at everything.

"That's all you care about!" She laughs. "This stupid tournament! See—look in the mirror. You're too obsessed with yourself to care about anyone else."

Maybe she's right. My heart is breaking.

"Why you?" I ask Mateo.

"I told you once before. I work with the best to be the best. You should see what this guy knows. He taught Samuels everything, but he knows so much more."

"You lie. You lied to me!"

"And you didn't lie to me?" He steps off the bench. The wrestling team makes an *oooh* sound.

"Mat, you don't—"

"You lied to me! You... you...." He bites his lower lip, but the word is on the tip of his tongue. His eyes widen, full of fury. Then he says it. "You *queer!*" He hisses the word through gritted teeth. "Decker told me what you're trying to do. He told me you'd try to manipulate me. To turn me into... whatever you are. He says that's what you people do, and he's right. Look what you tried to do to me!"

If my heart wasn't broken before, it just imploded. Tears race down my cheeks. I can't hold this back, even as Logan and the rest of them laugh at me.

The room spins. My knees wobble. I release a sob, unable to control it, and the wrestling team laughs even more. Everyone laughs but Camila. She glares at me with vengeance.

Tisha steps toward him. "You're an asshole!" Then turning to Camila, she snaps, "And you're a bitch!"

Then Camila throws a sidekick right into Tisha's stomach.

59

Fight

TISHA TWIRLS WITH the momentum—my mind flashes to the first lesson we learned, rock versus water. She counters with a spinning back fist. Camila blocks, and my jaw drops. That's not a lucky block. She wears the confidence and executes the technique of an experienced fighter.

Mateo steps in between the girls.

"Enough. You'll get us in trouble," he says to Camila. She snarls, and Tisha keeps her guard up.

The rest of the lunchroom stares at us. Where are the teachers? There doesn't appear to be anyone watching us.

No, that's not true, I realize, my eyes catching a glimpse of the truck-sized douchebag in the corner. Coach Krake strokes a whistle around his neck, much like I'd picture a villain petting a cat on his lap.

I picture taking that whistle and choking him. Of course, that's a laugh. He'd break me in half if I ever fought him.

Could Mr. Samuels take him? That's a showdown I'd love to see.

"Save it for the competition," Mateo continues. The girls look like they're ready to plow right through him.

"You were my best friend!" Tisha cries. "Why would you do this?" She relaxes her guard by an inch. My heart doesn't slow down. I look at Mateo, who avoids me.

"You chose *him!* When he lied to me, you chose Aiden!" Camila says. "I had to smile and nod and pretend to be happy. But I wasn't. You ruined our friendship. You weren't there for me, either."

Camila takes a deep breath. Are those tears in her eyes, too? "Do you know what hell I've been through at home? No, you don't, do you? Just like Aiden. All you cared about were boys." She wipes at her eyes. "You know who was here? Who saw me right away? Mat and Captain Decker. But I couldn't tell you that, could I?"

"You could have," I say, stepping forward. "You could have told us you were in hell at home. You could have just said it if we weren't picking up onto it or whatever."

"I *did* tell you, Aiden. I talked about it multiple times on the phone with you. You apparently weren't listening."

Her words cut through me like a knife.

"What about you?" Tisha asks Mateo.

Mat's spine stiffens. "You know, people are who they are. I tried to understand that. Tried to be cool. But you made a move on me. You tried to make *out* with me! That's not cool. It's exactly what Decker said people like you would do."

"Gross." Logan spits on the cafeteria floor. I search for anyone other than Krake—where is Mr. Samuels? I want to run away and die.

I have no words. My stomach clenches, and nausea rises in my throat.

"Oh, shut up," Tisha shrieks. "Please! You're so full of it. Say you have feelings for a girl, and you try to kiss her. She accepts or rejects, and you move on." She shakes her head. "I don't know what world you live in, Mat. Or any of you jerks. And clearly Decker is serving you one giant homophobic glass of Kool-Aid." Tisha scans the table looking at each of the wrestlers. She steps close to Mat and whispers in his ear. It's loud enough for me to hear, but I don't think anyone else does.

"He liked you, Mat. It's a compliment. You don't have to act like this," she tells him.

His eyes flash, and for a moment I see my best friend inside them. Then he glances to the side, catching Krake's eye.

"You just don't get it," he says to both of us.

"Boys are so stupid," Tisha says. "Ugh!"

"I don't wanna fight anymore," I tell them.

"Of course not," Logan says, jumping up. "Cuz you'll lose."

"Screw you,"

"What's that, homo?" He steps right up into my face. I try to swallow the fear in my throat, but it's a lump that won't go down.

"I said *screw you!*" I clench my fists and step back.

He lunges at me, but Tisha extends her leg. Logan falls hard on his face, tripping over Tisha's sweep.

Camila throws a punch at Tisha, but Tisha blocks. Mateo jumps in the middle again.

I rush at Mat.

I don't know what I'm doing. Anger surges through every vein. I forget everything I've learned, and I dive like a spear straight into him.

He catches me, twirls, and tosses me on the floor of the commons. He locks me in a scarf hold. "Why do you make me do this, Aiden? Why?"

"That's enough!" It's the loud voice of Mr. Samuels, and I couldn't be more grateful to hear it.

Mat lets me go. Logan brushes himself off. Camila and Tisha quickly step away from each other.

"What's happened to you?" Mr. Samuels glares at Mateo. Mat looks down and refuses to answer. "Clearly, you all can't get along. Save it for the tournament. In the meantime, we're all going to have a nice talk with the principal. First order of business—new class and lunch schedules for all of you. You'll be separated while you train. Is that understood?"

"Yes, sir," I say, relieved. Honestly, I'd prefer to switch schools.

"Good."

DeMarcus, the only boy on the wrestling team I ever liked besides Mateo, raises a trembling hand.

"Yes, DeMarcus?"

His lips form a tight line. "Can I come with you?"

The team and Mr. Samuels look at him curiously.

"I mean, um, I'd like to switch, too." He stands and looks stronger than I've ever seen him. "Switch to be with you guys." He avoids the glares of his teammates. "Sorry, guys," he says, glancing briefly at Mateo. "But not sorry. All this is B.S. I don't wanna be a part of it anymore. I didn't sign up to be on a hate club."

They scowl. I am sure they're biting their tongues. Mateo looks like he's been smacked in the face. It's the first wrestler, besides me of course, that has quit the team.

"Absolutely, DeMarcus. Come with me."

DeMarcus gives me a quick, subtle smile.

Maybe there's hope after all—hope that the world isn't full of jerks who look the other way when people do stupid stuff.

We follow Mr. Samuels to the principal's office.

60

Cleaning Up Bull

I SIT OUTSIDE the principal's office and listen to an exchange of words. Mr. Samuels raises his voice one time, and it's the only phrase I hear of their conversation.

"There's a lot of B.S. in this school, pardon my language, sir. You either add to it or you help clean it up."

After that, their voices soften, and I can't make out what they say. DeMarcus sits across from me and Tisha next to me.

"Thanks," I tell DeMarcus.

"For what?"

"You know. For just being real," I answer.

"I got tired of it, man. It's been so much worse since you left. Like you leaving ripped tape from their mouths. The whole team is, like, poisoned." He bounces his knee. "I should have left when you did."

"Does, uh, Mat say bad things, too?"

DeMarcus shakes his head. "He's the only one who didn't besides me. But he never told anyone to stop."

"What do they say?" Tisha asks.

"You don't wanna know," DeMarcus mutters. "But, man, I've learned one thing. Once you tolerate intolerance, it's like opening a door to some crazy, bigoted past. Except it's not gone. It's here. And I can't be a part of that."

We sit in silence for a minute, digesting his words.

"So, you like karate?" DeMarcus asks after a bit.

Tisha speaks up immediately. "Hell yeah. I never thought I'd be a karate kid or something, you know? The movies can make it look all weird and nerdy. But it's nothing like that. It's totally badass." Her lips stretch from ear to ear, and it's infectious.

"Yeah?" he asks, his eyes sparkling.

"Yep," I say. "So, you'll join us? If we're really doing this tournament, we could use more people on our side."

"Heck yeah. I'm in!" He laughs. "Let me tell ya. There are a few guys I'd love to kick in the balls. Some of those guys—it wasn't just sexuality that they mocked. Hate breeds hate."

He rubs his dark skin, like a chill rushes through him.

The world is just so confusing I don't get a single thing.

I look at DeMarcus more closely than I have in the past. He was always nice to me during practices. Is he—could he be—?

No, don't even think it or ask it. Because it doesn't matter, I tell myself. He's a friend.

Try not to lose this one. You don't have to stay in the closet, but for the love of all that is good in the world, you could try to keep your hormones locked up.

The door opens, and I sit up straight. "Thank you for your time, sir," Mr. Samuels says. The principal grunts, and Mr. S closes the door. "The principal agreed to cover my classes this afternoon. The three of you will be excused, unless you'd rather go to class?" He raises his eyebrows and chuckles.

"Nope. Totally cool!" I say. We all laugh in unison.

"Then it's a field trip. Go to your lockers and get your stuff. Meet me in the faculty parking lot by my car."

TISHA TAKES THE front seat. DeMarcus and I take the back. Mr. Samuels checks to make sure we have our seat belts buckled, and we drive away from Washington High.

"Tisha, in my bag on the floor, there's a green folder. Will you pass out the schedules in there?" Mr. S asks.

Tisha pulls out the folder and hands each of us a schedule.

"Your principal and I rearranged your class schedules to do two things. First, you'll be in classes together, so you can look out for each other," Mr. Samuels tells us. "Second, you won't see Logan, Mateo, or Camila in any of your classes. I wish I could say the same for the entire team, but there are just too many damn wrestlers."

"No crap." Sensei smiles at me through the rear-view mirror.

"We have a few months to get ready. So, from now until the first of March, we eat, sleep, and breathe training. We will still do the club after school, but for anyone entering the tournament—morning sessions every day before school and private training every evening after dinner. That's the commitment I need. Think about that while we drive, okay?"

We ride in silence, and I try to digest everything.

I won't see Mateo for *three months?*

No more weekend sleepovers, that's for sure. Now, my schedule's been rearranged, too. I know Mr. S did this to protect us. Even though Mateo's behavior sucks, that doesn't mean I've lost all hope. To catch his eye in one of my classes—to search for a little of my old best friend—now, all that's gone.

I rub my temples.

"Why did you ever wanna join wrestling?" DeMarcus asks, interrupting my thoughts.

I tug at the safety belt and sigh. I have been asked that question so many times that I don't know if I even know the truth anymore. "I wanted to get strong and to make some friends. That's all."

"Me, too. It made me stronger, but my friends were fake. Not my kinda friends." He looks out the window.

"Why karate?" DeMarcus asks me.

Mr. Samuels glances at me through the rear-view mirror. It's like both he and DeMarcus are in my head.

Do I really want to eat, sleep, and breathe karate? All this for what—to face my best friend, um, ex-best friend in a tournament where he will no doubt kick my ass? He's miles ahead of me. No amount of training is going to make a difference.

I don't want to face him. It will break my heart all over again, and it may break a lot more of me than that.

61

Why Fight?

"SO?" DEMARCUS ASKS again. "Why karate?"

I look DeMarcus in the eye. "It somehow gives me strength and peace. Wrestling may have given me strength in time, but the way Krake coaches it, it's strength and anger. It made me feel pissed off all the time. Karate—the way Sensei teaches it—comes with more. Strength and peace," I repeat.

Mr. Samuels keeps his face stoic in the mirror, but there's a twinkle of approval in his eyes.

"Strength and peace. That sounds nice," DeMarcus says.

"So why fight? Why go through this just for a tournament that we will probably lose?"

Tisha turns around. "Because they stole our peace. He's right," she says to DeMarcus. "I've never felt so strong and yet so calm until I started training. But Camila, Logan, Mateo, and that stupid team—it's like they don't want anyone else to be happy. Sometimes you have to fight to achieve peace."

"These are all interesting perspectives," Mr. Samuels says. "As you know, karate is for self-defense only—"

"Sir, if Decker was your teacher, I mean, did he teach it this way to you?" I interrupt.

"No," Mr. S shakes his head. "Decker was the kind of man who hopped out of a car to pick a fight with a stranger if they looked at him funny."

"How did you turn out the way you did then?" Tisha asks.

Mr. Samuels turns down a side street. "When you're young, it's easy to pick up the attitudes and behaviors of those who teach you. When you're a child, it's your parents, typically. As you get older, you look for other adults to provide you with validation, whether you are conscious of it or not. It's a part of life. Some kids find good leaders. Some find poor leaders, but even poor leaders can provide the validation kids need outside of their parents." He takes a deep breath. "But at some point, you have to reflect on what you've been taught and ask yourself who you really want to be. I left Decker's school because I didn't want to be Decker. It was really that simple. I spent almost every evening with that man. One day, the question dawned on me—do I want to be like him? Does he have the values that I want to have? The answer was hell no. So, I knew I needed to leave, or I would risk becoming someone I didn't like. I stopped doing martial arts for years—that was the saddest part of it all." He looks back at me. "Until Aiden reminded me of the true potential of karate."

"Me?" I ask.

"It's because of you that I'm teaching karate. Because of all of you. I had to reflect on what I was taught and how I thought it should have been taught. Not Decker's way. My way." He grips the steering wheel hard. "Is there a little bit of Decker in me? Of course. Maybe that's why I like the idea of the tournament. I try to be aware of his influence on me, even now. Yes, karate is for self-defense only. But I agree with Tisha. Sometimes, we have to stand up for what's right. If we constantly turn our backs, the world gets run by bullies. Look at our school. Hell, look at this town."

"I'm in," I say. "One hundred percent in. Mornings, afternoons, nights. Whatever it takes."

"Me, too," Tisha says, as if I had a doubt about her. "I wanna do it right, though. Like, I mean, if I'm being honest, I was ready to tear Camila's head off today. That scares me a little."

"Me, too," Mr. Samuels says, frowning. "We must discipline ourselves. Find the peace, the calm you all talked about."

"I'm in, too," DeMarcus says. "I know it's a quick decision. But I've been training every day in wrestling. I wanna fight for something good. With good people."

Mr. Samuels pulls into a driveway of a modest house. "This is my home," he says. "It's time I show you my personal dojo. And then we train."

"SHOW ME *WANSU*," Mr. S commands.

Tisha and I perform the kata. I try not to think about the night I showed Mateo the form and my favorite part of it—when I tossed him on the floor, when my head rested on his stomach.

Moments before I ruined everything.

DeMarcus watches. We do the form a dozen times. He asks, "When will you teach me that?"

"What do you see?" Mr. Samuels asks. DeMarcus wears a blank expression. "Perform the end again," Mr. S tells Tisha and me.

We step into tiger stance, sidestep and strike the air, then execute the final spin.

"What do you see?" Mr. S asks DeMarcus again.

"It looks like they're pushing someone?" he suggests.

"Show him," Mr. S tells me. I take DeMarcus through the movement, just as I had Mateo. My stomach feels weird. I'm tired. Our training started so early, and it has been a long day.

"Woah," DeMarcus says, after I demonstrate the strike and throw that follow the tiger stance.

"But that's not all," Mr. S says. "There are hidden movements in forms. Secrets. Some that Decker may not even know. He wasn't the biggest fan of *kata*. He preferred pure fighting over the traditional forms. He taught us the forms because they were promotional requirements, but then we spent most of our time fighting. No surprise, right? Each form holds hidden movements that you must discover. Run the *kata* again."

Tisha and I run through it another time. "What do you see?" Mr. S asks us. A throbbing pain in my temples makes me want to go to bed. I'm not sure I could do basic arithmetic right now, let alone complete some weird martial arts scavenger hunt.

"Run it again," Mr. S says.

"Sir, I'm—uh, I don't know how much more I can do," I confess.

"I can't feel my legs," Tisha says.

DeMarcus observes, and Mr. S looks disappointed. I'm not getting the lesson. I'm not uncovering the secrets.

"I want you both to teach DeMarcus the *kata*. Then I want you to go home and get some sleep. We start again at six in the morning. You dream of the *kata*. Dream of the secrets. There are many to find."

"Why can't you just tell us?" I ask.

"Finding the secrets is part of the journey," he answers. "It means you've practiced the form enough that it's pure muscle memory and a part of your subconscious. So, we'll run it until that moment comes. Teach DeMarcus. Then go home."

"Yes, sir."

We walk DeMarcus through the form. I bet Mateo could see the secrets. He reads martial arts and wrestling moves like they are a natural language he was born with.

How am I ever supposed to compete with someone like that?

62

And So It Goes

THE DAYS BLUR. I only get to sleep in on Sundays. Six in the morning practices consume the rest of my week. Then school—where, thanks to Mr. Samuels' schedule changes—I no longer see Mateo, Camila, Logan, or half the wrestling team. Now and again, I bump into Krake or Jeff. Their eyes fill with an intensity I still don't understand.

After school, it's the club, stronger than ever with over thirty high school participants. Only five of the thirty have decided to enter the tournament, including DeMarcus.

DeMarcus learns quickly. He's athletic, strong, and fast, better than me on all three accounts. But when we spar, I win. Even with wrestling rules, I win against him. Mr. Samuels has us rotate between karate and wrestling rules. Then he mixes them up—mixed martial arts is the name of the game, after all.

After the club, it's dinner with Mom. Sometimes Mr. S joins. Sometimes he doesn't. I think he likes to give me a little space with Mom, especially since I'm training so much. Mom smiles more, not only because Mr. S makes her happy, but because as the weeks pass, I'm less bruised. My skin has apparently thickened.

Then it's private training with Mr. S—those competing in the tournament come to my house in the morning, and then we meet at Mr. Samuels's home for the late session.

I've done *Wansu* ten thousand freaking times by now, and I'm about to scream.

"What are the hidden movements?" he asks.

I want to cuss. Sometimes I want to cry. It feels like a nasty trick he's playing on us. There's no magic in karate. It's awesome, and it's effective, but that's science, not magic. I'm not Harry Potter or Luke Skywalker. I'm Aiden Rothe, and I'm exhausted.

We perform the *kata* in the air against imaginary attackers. Then he makes us perform it in slow motion. Our stances get deeper than ever, our legs tremble, and we perfect every movement. Then we do it as fast as possible.

"Relaxation and continuous motion," he shouts. "Those are the secrets to speed. Go!"

He says I'm fast, faster than ever. But could I ever be quicker than Mateo? I don't think so.

"I'll tell you one secret. One secret to hopefully open your mind to the kinds of secrets that are hidden in your training. Are you ready?" He raises his eyebrows. We nod like rabid hyenas. "All blocks are attacks. Think about that. A block is not a block. A block is an attack."

Huh?

Secrets. Hidden movements. Advanced martial arts principles that aren't making sense to my stupid brain.

"Do you understand, Aiden?" Mr. S asks.

I shake my head slowly, embarrassed.

Mr. S tilts his head, then a smile suddenly forms. "You remember when I first asked you why *kata* begins and ends with a block?"

"Yes, sir."

"Go on." He gestures. "What was the answer?"

"Um, well, to symbolize the defensive nature of karate."

"And?" His eyebrows stretch to the top of his forehead again.

What else had he told me? Oh, yeah! "Um, if you can end a fight with a block, then there's no need for additional strikes!"

"Exactly. So how is a block an attack?"

"It's two-in-one," I tell him. "If you block an attack hard enough, or use it to both block and strike at the same time, then that could be enough. Game over."

We train hard like this for weeks. Then, in January, a surprise—at the end of a session, he brings in five green belts and a small box.

Tisha, DeMarcus, Tony, Amanda, and myself, the five who have decided to enter the tournament, we're all promoted to green belt.

Mr. Samuels opens the small box. When he removes the item, my lips stretch so wide it hurts my face. Mom must have told him, of course.

He lights two candles—a giant one and a giant five. Turning, he gives me a warm smile. The class sings "Happy Birthday," and Mr. S walks toward me with a cake.

I'm fifteen today. I tried not to think about it all day because there's really only one person I wish were here to celebrate with me. He's not, though, and the next time I see him, there's a good chance he'll be kicking my ass.

"Thank you, sir."

Mr. S cuts the cake, and we take a break to enjoy it.

When we finish, he calls the new green belts to move forward. "Now, your next gift, for all of you."

Mr. S shows us a new *kata*.

"This one is called *Anaku*. Whereas *Wansu* teaches power, *Anaku* teaches speed. If you master both, you will do well in the tournament."

So, we practice this new form that has a different hip motion—a side to side for speed instead of an inward thrust for power. It has a beautiful ending, too. "Tell me the hidden movements," Mr. S demands.

He receives no answers.

I dream about karate. Seriously. I can't even escape it in my dreams.

I wish I'd have a dream about Mateo, but I don't. I don't even get to see him when I close my eyes.

I don't know if that's a blessing or a curse.

And so it goes.

On some Sundays, we get to hang out with each other, those competing. Mr. Samuels wants some team bonding. Today is one of our final Sundays before the big tournament. We choose to go to a movie and then a Chinese buffet.

DeMarcus tries to use chopsticks and fails.

He smiles at me, and for just a second—no, I can't think like that. I get one day off and hormones start messing with my mind.

Do I like DeMarcus?

Yes.

Do I like him like that?

I don't know. But it doesn't matter. He's straight. Every boy I've ever liked is straight. I'm cursed.

"So, are we ever gonna talk about the elephant in the room?" Tisha asks.

"Huh?" Amanda doesn't look like she could hurt anyone. She's tiny, with arms like chopsticks, but she's got some crazy, inner power. When those little things make contact, they hurt. Long, ash-blonde hair, very similar to my mom's color, sits on her shoulders.

"About the hidden movements? I don't have a friggin' clue what Mr. S is smoking," Tisha says.

"Oh, yeah," I mumble. "What do you think it means?"

"I've even Googled it, and nothing comes up. I don't get it," DeMarcus says.

"He said that the masters hid secrets in the forms," Tony adds. His hair has grown even more. It's long, dark, and messy, but it suits him. He's still thick. Maybe not chunky like when I first met him, but he's got thick arms and legs. "How does he expect green belts to figure out the secrets of the masters?"

"Assuming it's not all bull," Tisha says. She twirls noodles on her chopsticks and eats them, taunting DeMarcus with her skills. He scowls at her but then cracks a smile.

"He wouldn't make it up," I defend, but I have my doubts, too.

"There's nothing secretive about what we're doing," Amanda says. "A punch is a punch. A kick is a kick. What's hidden about that?"

"But all blocks are attacks," I repeat the only secret Mr. Samuels has ever given us. Puzzled looks form on our faces, but no one has an answer.

"Can we just enjoy a day without thinking about it?" Tony asks, taking a bite of crab rangoon. We nod, everyone craving some kind of distraction.

DeMarcus stabs his orange chicken with the chopsticks. We laugh.

"Delicious no matter how you eat it," he says, with a mouthful of food.

His cheeks grow like little balloons when he smiles. I look away. I don't want to feel what I feel. But there's something undeniably cute about him.

I scoop up a bite of fried rice, but it falls on my plate. Not because I lack chopstick talent. But because of who walks through the door to the Chinese buffet.

It's a group of guys on the wrestling team, all wearing new Hornets Wrestling T-shirts. They turn and glare at us. I squeeze my chopsticks so hard they break.

63

Chinese Fight

IT'S A SMALL group, only five of them.

Five of them, and five of us.

There's Jordan, Anthony, and Jeff—I recognize the faces of the other two, but I don't know their names.

Jeff flips me the middle finger.

"Oh, hell no," Tisha snaps. She leaps up and gives him the finger with both hands.

"Can we get out of here?" Tony asks.

"We have to face them all soon enough," DeMarcus says. "Might as well be today." He cracks his knuckles.

"So much for a recovery day," Amanda adds.

"What makes you think we'll fight?" I ask. "Everyone has strict orders to leave us alone until the tournament." I try not to think about my bathroom encounter with Jeff and whatever Tanner promised them. That was a long time ago. Our schedule changes must have helped.

"Look at 'em," Tisha says, shaking her head. "They walk like they're better than everyone. I hate that they're so mean. For what?"

"I dunno," Amanda says. "I'm not hungry anymore. I'm with Tony. Let's go."

"Fine," I say, pushing my plate away. My favorite part of the Chinese buffet is getting ice cream at the end, along with one of the unique-looking cakes. It's another sacrifice to make because of the wrestlers.

We paid when we entered, so we grab our coats and exit. Tony, a sophomore, is the only one with a license and a car. We hustle to the rusted Ford Focus he drives.

But I stop in the middle of the parking lot.

"You know what, guys?" I shout. "Our lives have been nothing but training for the last couple of months. We get one day to have a little fun, and we're running away like scared kids. What are we training for?"

Tisha turns around and walks back to me. "Aiden's right. We train so we don't have to be the losers who run and hide!"

DeMarcus nods. "They're eating, anyway. Look." He gestures toward the restaurant. I zip up my coat. Flurries scatter in the air. I wipe away the snowflakes that land on my face.

"What are we doing?" I ask. "All this training—what's it been for if we're still running away?"

"It's not running away," Amanda says. "It's just not wanting to fight."

"Well, good luck with that." The voice is deep, and we jump. It comes from behind. Tanner McQueen, the varsity captain, steps out from his Dodge Ram. "It's too bad this club just started. I'd have loved to face some karate kids." He makes silly karate chop gestures and laughs.

"What do you want?" I ask.

Tanner's alone. Did someone text him from inside the buffet?

"A preview," he answers. A terrible smile grows across his face. He waves at the wrestlers inside. Jeff exits the Chinese restaurant and stands next to Tanner. "How about a little one on one?"

"We're not supposed to fight before the tournament," Tony says.

"Scared, little boy?" Tanner grits his teeth, and Tony's skin turns whiter than the snow.

"I'll take him," Tisha says.

Tanner throws his head back and laughs. "I certainly don't want to be—what? Un-feminist? If you wanna face Jeff, let's do it. There's an empty parking lot in the back. Follow me."

Tisha takes off, and Amanda grabs her hand.

"What are you doing?" Amanda asks.

"Showing these jerks that we're not afraid," Tisha answers. "Or at least that *I'm* not."

"This is *not* self-defense," Amanda says.

Tisha shakes her head. "Yes, it is. It's self-defense for our mental health." She follows Tanner to the parking lot behind the Chinese buffet.

I chase after them, clenching my fists. What if Mateo shows up? Although it's cold out, sweat glistens on my forehead.

When we get to the back, Jeff and Tanner face us.

"Tisha versus Jeff. It's a warm-up for next month's tournament," Tanner says, laughing.

"Why the hell are you doing this?" I ask him. "Why not save it for the tournament?"

"Because I don't wanna." He spits on the ground. "Now, shake hands, competitors." Jeff's blue eyes fill with menace, but he extends his arm and smiles. Tisha looks skeptical, but after a moment, she takes it. Jeff pulls her forward and kicks her in the stomach.

Tisha grunts, and I rush to help her. Tanner stops me with his huge arm. It slaps across my chest like a four by four. "Let them have their one-on-one."

Turning, Tisha grabs Jeff's jacket. She goes in for a sweep, but Jeff counters, throwing her on the ground. When she tries to get up, he performs a spin kick, connecting his foot right in her face. She yelps.

"C'mon, Tisha!" DeMarcus yells. Tanner glares at the former wrestler. My heart skips a beat. Jeff knows how to kick, and he kicks incredibly well. Too well. He's showing off. Is that what this is about? A little intimidation before the big tournament to show us how much they know?

Tisha leaps up. Jeff throws another kick, but Tisha scoops his leg in one hand and nails him right in the balls with a front kick. Then she sweeps his standing leg. Jeff falls, and Tisha jumps on him, her elbow driving right into his throat. Jeff screams, and Tisha bounces right back up, facing Tanner.

"How about you?" she asks. *Damn, she's tough!*

"Not bad." Tanner laughs. "Okay, team. Now!" he shouts.

From the side of the building, the entire wrestling team steps out.

Leading the pack, Mateo runs toward us and takes his place next to Tanner. To Mat's side stand Logan and Camila. A dozen other wrestlers fall in behind them.

"Let's have some fun," Tanner says.

The wrestlers charge us.

64

Wrestlemania in the Parking Lot

MATEO DOESN'T MOVE, but Logan dives at me, tackling me to the ground. He punches my ribs, and he elbows my jaw. He leans back to gain momentum for another punch. He throws his right fist at me, but I grab his arm and roll him over.

It's my turn.

I throw a punch and it connects with his lips. Blood shoots from his mouth, and I throw a second punch. Then someone grabs me from behind. My body flies in the air. I manage to land on my feet, but muscular arms grip me from behind.

I know the feel of these arms. It's a bear hug, and I can't move.

Camila and Tisha exchange blows. Jeff has DeMarcus tangled up, and other boys take turns kicking him. Amanda and Tony are buried under another group of jerks.

We don't stand a chance, not against numbers like this.

"Why?" I snarl and grab the arms that wrap tightly around me. "Why, Mat? Because I liked you? You were my best friend!"

He squeezes me harder. His hot breath blows against my neck. "You haven't figured it out? I thought you were smarter than that."

"Figured *what* out?"

He laughs, and I grunt as he squeezes me harder. Two boys grab Tisha from behind. Camila kicks her in the stomach.

Anger burns inside me. I can't let them get hurt like this!

"You really don't know?" he asks.

"Know what?" I kick at his shin, but it doesn't even phase him.

He huffs. "I guess I thought you were smarter than you clearly are."

"What?"

"What we did in the beginning—me training with you and Samuels, me befriending you—that was what Decker and Krake wanted, not me. They wanted to know what Samuels was teaching you."

Bile rushes into my throat. "No! Why?"

"I don't know what beef your teacher and mine have. I just do what I'm told," he says and pushes me away with violent force.

I fly forward but spin around the second my feet hit the ground.

"The whole thing—our friendship—all of that was a lie?"

That hug when you said I was your best friend? How could that have been a lie? *No!*

Tanner watches me with a sloppy grin that I want to kick off his face. He stands next to Mat, listening to every word.

Mat glances at Tanner, then back to me. "It wasn't real, Aiden. None of it was real."

He turns away.

I charge, jumping on his back and wrapping my arms around his throat. I squeeze with all my might, but Mat flips me over his shoulders like I'm a bag full of nothing.

Tanner laughs, but Mat's face remains stern.

I stand and punch him.

Mat blocks easily.

I kick and punch, but I can't connect a single one. He doesn't hit me back, which is even more insulting. It's like he's telling me he doesn't even need to waste the energy on me.

Angry tears rush down my face.

"What a baby," Tanner says.

"Enough! Everyone stop right now!" The voice is loud and unmistakable. My tears stop, and hope springs to my chest for the first time since the parking lot brawl started.

It's Mr. Samuels.

"Not here, loser," Tanner says. "Walk away now, and your students will leave with bruises. Stay and they'll have broken bones."

Mr. Samuels doesn't back down. "You will stop right this second. No games. *NOW!*"

Tanner rushes at him, diving into his stomach like a football tackle. Mr. S takes the blow and somehow picks Tanner off the ground. He swings the biggest, strongest wrestler and tosses him on the ground with ease.

Tanner grunts. "Mateo, help. Now. Everyone!"

Fear flashes in Mateo's eyes. Disappointment runs down my teacher's face as his former student charges him. Mr. Samuels deflects Mateo's tackle, sweeping him and tossing him to the side, too.

Logan, Jeff, and a series of other wrestlers jump my teacher. It's a blur of light, but Mr. S moves faster than I ever thought any human could. He doesn't once strike a student. He dodges their attacks. He sweeps and throws only when necessary. In seconds, the wrestlers are all on the ground. Mr. Samuels remains standing.

Tisha, Tony, DeMarcus, Amanda, and I walk to his side.

Mr. S shakes his head. "Look at who you have become." He says this to everyone, but his eyes focus on Mateo.

Then a police siren blares a quick woop woop from behind. The cop car shines its bright light on us. Decker steps out from the driver's side, but he's not alone. Krake exits the passenger side.

"So, a grown man picking on teenagers. You must be proud of yourself," Decker tells him.

"Self-defense," Mr. Samuels states. "And I didn't hit a single one."

Decker's mouth opens in a near gasp, but he catches himself. He looks at all the wrestlers, then back to Mr. Samuels. "Looks like a violent attack to me. Wouldn't you say?" Decker asks Krake.

"Absolutely."

Decker takes out his handcuffs.

"There are witnesses," Mr. Samuels says.

"You're right about that. We have an entire team of wrestlers who say you violently attacked them. Isn't that right?" Decker asks.

"That's right," Tanner says, brushing himself off and standing.

I glare at Mateo. He doesn't speak.

"You have the right to remain silent," Decker starts, and he handcuffs Mr. Samuels.

65

Sunday Night Sleepover

A CROWD FORMS in the parking lot behind the Chinese buffet. Mr. Samuels sits in the back of Decker's police car, and Decker drives our teacher presumably to jail.

"Enough fun for one night," Krake says. "Everyone go home. Save the rest of your energy for the ring." He cackles as he walks away. I'd love to see Mr. S kick his ass one day. His *and* Decker's.

"You guys okay?" I ask. The five of us huddle together.

"Yeah," Tisha says, but she holds her stomach. "I think they're trying to intimidate us."

"You think?" Tony's voice is high and sarcastic.

"Yeah but not like just as jerks," Tisha says. "They've got real moves. Real karate, on top of wrestling."

"Yeah. They're showing off and tryin' to hurt us," DeMarcus says, "to throw us off our game before the tournament."

"Let's get home. We gotta help Mr. Samuels," I say, thinking of the one person who will burn this town down if she had to. Mom.

"I'll come with you." DeMarcus looks at the rest of the team. "You guys go home and tell your parents. Tell them everything. We can't hide from this crap anymore. We may need all the adults we can get."

We get in Tony's car, and he drops DeMarcus and me off first at my house.

Tony takes the girls home. DeMarcus and I march toward my front door. When we enter, Mom's in the kitchen.

"Hey, did Lloyd find you? He said he got a text from one of the kids, that something was wrong." Mom approaches us, takes one look at our roughed-up bodies, and gasps. "Not this crap again. I'm calling the police."

"That's what we need to talk to you about, Mom," I mutter. "Decker arrested Mister Samuels."

"*What?*" Her eyes light up with rage. "Tell me everything."

We share our story, and Mom paces the kitchen.

"Okay. Here's what I'm gonna do. I'm gonna march to your principal's house and drag him out. He's coming me with me, and he's helping me. If not, I'll burn down that fucking school, starting with the wrestling room. You hear me?"

She's yelling, not at us exactly, but yelling nonetheless. I've never seen her so enraged. It's terrifying in the best way possible.

DeMarcus and I nod enthusiastically at her question.

"You boys stay here. I don't want you involved in this any more than necessary. That includes that stupid tournament, all right?"

We nod again. Mom storms out the front door. But there's no way I'm missing the tournament. Not after tonight.

Mateo told me our friendship was a lie. That he was what—some kind of spy or something? That he was doing what those douchebags Krake and Decker wanted.

But he was so nice at times. I slept next to him. Multiple times. He was accepting and understanding until—

Until my lips betrayed me.

How could he lie and fool me like this?

"Whatcha thinking about?" DeMarcus asks.

"Nothing." I sigh. "Everything."

I walk up to my room, and DeMarcus follows. We sit on the edge of my bed. I turn on the TV.

"Anything you wanna do?"

"Nah. Just hope your Mom can help Mr. S."

"She will. Or she'll end up in jail, too."

DeMarcus laughs, and it makes me smile. "Your mom is pretty B.A."

"Yeah, she is."

"What did Mat say to you tonight?" DeMarcus asks.

I don't know if I want to tell him, but I also need someone to talk to about it. DeMarcus smiles sympathetically. Can I trust him? I trusted Mateo and look how that turned out.

"He said he was only friends with me because Krake and Decker wanted to know what Mr. S was teaching us."

"Oh, man. That's terrible. That's some super B.S. right there! Are you okay?" He leans a little closer. It's nice to see a friend get pissed about Mat, too.

"Yeah. I mean, I dunno."

"You really liked him?" DeMarcus asks.

Our eyes lock. How honest can I be? "Yeah. A lot." Screw it. If he doesn't like it, he doesn't have to be my friend. It wouldn't be the first I lost. I'm tired of worrying about who I can be honest with and who I can't.

"Sorry, Aiden. That sucks." He puts an arm around me, and my body freezes.

He likes me for me.

"Yeah." I swallow hard. "You ever like someone like that?"

He shrugs a little, but he doesn't take his arm off my shoulders. A lot has happened today, and I don't trust my mind. I like DeMarcus—he's adorable. How could anyone not like him? Have I wondered at all if he could be like me? Of course. But I'm scared, too. How does one boy ask another boy if he's gay without offending him? And hell, it shouldn't even be offensive, but it always seems to be.

Right now, it just feels nice to have someone comfort me.

"So, um, you like like Mateo, right?"

My nose runs, and I sniff back the apparent allergic reaction I have to my own embarrassing stupidity. "I guess."

"Even after everything he's done?" DeMarcus asks.

I shrug. "I hate that I like him, especially after all this crap. But yeah. I do. Maybe that's why I—you know, did what I just did. I wanna forget about him. Completely."

"That's what our training is for."

"What do you mean?"

"I like the discipline, the focus Mister S teaches us. You gotta clear your mind and focus on the real fight."

"The tournament?"

"Yeah," he replies. "We gotta win, man. We just gotta."

"But Mat's better than all of us combined. How can we win?"

"We train when they're not. Run *kata* with me?" DeMarcus bounces off my bed.

He's right. I know I should focus on the tournament. I need to focus on the fact that the one guy I love is going to kick my ass in front of everyone.

DeMarcus extends a hand. "C'mon."

I take it, and he pulls me off my bed, grinning. I'm sure it's my imagination, but his hand lingers longer than it needed to.

"You trust your mom?"

"Absolutely."

"Then let's not worry. Let her burn down the city. You and I might as well train."

We practice our *kata* together. We perform it repeatedly, stopping only to get a drink or to stretch. DeMarcus calls his parents to let them know what's going on. He talks to them in the hallway. I keep practicing. I don't have to think about the movements anymore. My mind has deeply memorized each technique.

I think about the *kata's* secrets. What are the hidden movements? I still don't know the answer.

It's late, and it's a school night, but I have a feeling our parents will let us skip school tomorrow.

That's good. I'll train all day. I'll train until the hidden movements scream in my ear.

Around midnight, we take a break for food. DeMarcus and I search through the fridge. We decide on a late-night breakfast. I scramble some eggs, and DeMarcus makes pancakes.

"What are you doing?" I ask when he takes out his phone.

"Watching a YouTube video on how to make pancakes."

"Are you serious?" I laugh.

"I've never made them before!" he defends.

"I can't believe you have to Google that. Directions are right on the box!"

"I'm not Googling. I'm YouTubing!" We both laugh. DeMarcus ruins the first pancake, but the second one isn't bad. We each take a few bites of it, sharing the pancake, while he makes another.

The garage door opens, and Mom finally returns.

She's not alone.

Mr. Samuels is with her!

I run to him and throw my arms around him.

"Hey, boy. I'm glad to see you, too." He chuckles. I step back, slightly embarrassed. I don't know what came over me. I'm just really glad he's okay.

"How did you do it?" DeMarcus asks.

"Your principal helped. As did my threat of lawyers and other things." She winks at me. It's a wonder Mom wasn't arrested, too.

"They wanted to scare you guys and me. But they won't scare us," Mr. S says.

"Lloyd and I had a good talk," Mom says. "As did the principal and me. I want you to promise me one thing, Aiden." She walks over to me and puts her hands on my shoulders. Then she takes a deep breath. "You kick the jerks' asses. Do you understand? You give this your all.

You beat these bullies at their own game. Okay?" She pulls me in, hugging me tightly.

"Yes, Mom," I say. "I will try."

"Oh, don't make me say it," Mr. S says.

I pull away from Mom. "Huh?"

"Do or do not," he says in his best Yoda impersonation. "There is no try."

I laugh on the outside. On the inside, fear creeps in. Even Mom wants me to win.

But it doesn't take away from the fact that I have to face guys like Logan, who may genuinely want to rip my head off because he's a homophobic dick. Plus, of course, there's Mat.

How do I fight someone I love?

66

Final Training

"I'M VERY PROUD of all of you," Mr. Samuels says. We line up after the Washington High club session, the second of three practices those entering the tournament have each day. The karate club has grown. Thirty students, their friends, their parents—it means we'll have our own cheering section at the mixed martial arts tournament.

Of course, wrestling has decades of history and state championships. They'll have an entire gymnasium of supporters.

The newest white belts get promoted to yellow. Some of the yellow belts get promoted to green.

Mr. Samuels calls the green belts—the five of us—to the front of the room last.

"Finally, one more promotion," he says.

It's what I had been hoping for, nearly holding my breath, but my mouth still pops open in surprise. If these promotions feel this good, what would black belt feel like?

"Tony, Amanda, DeMarcus, Tisha, and Aiden... Remove your green belts."

We do as Sensei instructs. He stands in front of each of us. A fresh blue belt awaits—hard, crisp from having never been worn. A little white string holds it together. Our teacher faces Tony first. With a strong hand on each end of the new belt, he pops it open. The string flies in the air. Tony dives, his big, messy hair spreading out like wings, but misses it.

Mr. S ties the belt around Tony's waist. "As is tradition, the instructor puts the belt on the student for the first time, symbolizing the passing of knowledge from teacher to student." He extends his hand. Tony shakes it, and then they bow.

Continuing, Mr. S moves down the line. Amanda and DeMarcus both miss the string, but Tisha catches hers. She grins, and I know what she's thinking. She's got a one-on-one match with her former best friend, too. The string is good luck.

Mr. Samuels stands in front of me last. He pops open the fresh blue belt. The string shoots behind me. I turn to catch it, but no luck. It landed straight on the floor. No chance at all.

I hope that's not a premonition of things to come.

Mr. Samuels ties the belt around my waist.

"A black belt is a white belt who never quits," Mr. Samuels states, one of his favorite mantras. "The tournament is this weekend. We have one final lesson before the competition." My heart rate increases. How is it already time for the tournament? "Aiden, come stand in the middle." I approach, albeit hesitantly. "Everyone else make a circle around Aiden."

My eyes grow wide. "Um, what for, sir?"

A mischievous grin forms on his face. I don't like that look. "You'll see," he whispers, the corners of his lips twitching.

He turns to the rest of the students. "Fighting stances, everyone." They jump into their *kumite* guarding positions. "Everyone versus Aiden. Right now. Ready?"

I gulp. "What?"

"Hajime!" When Mr. S shouts "begin," everyone rushes at me. I run, but Tisha catches me. She grabs my shoulders, attempting a throw. I reverse it and toss her into a few other students. Tony throws a strike combination at me, but I dodge. I kick him in the stomach

and then sweep him. He hits the ground. Amanda makes her move. She jumps on my back! Then DeMarcus dives from the front. He grabs me, and he laughs. He's having a blast, while I'm trying to figure out how to defend myself against thirty people.

With Amanda on my back and DeMarcus at the front, they take me down. The rest of the team jumps on top of me, forming a great big pile of martial artists.

"Yame!" Sensei yells "stop," and one by one, each of my fellow karate-ka get off me. DeMarcus is the last. When he stands up, he offers me his hand. I take it and smile.

I wonder what the wrestler's final practices are like. I'd guarantee no one is helping anyone else off the floor.

We line up. I raise my hand. "Sensei, what was the purpose of that?"

He chuckles. "Two reasons," he says, facing all the students. "First, remember that no matter how hard something is, the odds could always be worse. You give your best fight no matter the odds. Do you understand?"

"Yes, Sensei," the class says.

"Good," he says. "The second reason—because sometimes you just have to have some fun! Tisha—your turn. Class, gather around Tisha."

I still don't know what hidden movements and secrets my kata were supposed to teach me. I still don't know if I'm anywhere near good enough to face Mateo or even Logan. All I know is that if I put up a good fight, if I don't show fear and I give them my best, that maybe they'll leave me and all of us the hell alone. Maybe that's going to have to be a good enough reason to fight.

The team laughs and chases Tisha.

Yeah, it would be worth it if we could just have a normal-ish life. Because this is a lot of fun. Life should be full of fun. Not full of fear.

67

Round One

ALTERNATING BLACK AND red wrestling mats line the Washington High gymnasium. The wrestlers warm up—wearing their ridiculous singlets, that stupid uniform that got me in trouble on day one.

Apparently, the crowd is as big as the state wrestling championships, which the Hornets won of course. Mateo took first in JV. Tanner took first in varsity. Both teams also scored winning titles this year.

The state championship banners hang proudly over the bleachers. How do five rookie martial artists stand a chance against a wrestling team that dominated the entire state?

Captain Decker and Coach Krake both wear suits. So does Mr. Samuels, but something about Decker and Krake looks so fake.

I tighten my belt. Mr. Samuels bought us new uniforms. They are black and red to match the school colors. Full black pants with a top that is black in the torso and red down the arms. My blue belt clashes, but that feels appropriate somehow.

Even local media appear. Krake walks to the center of the gym floor and speaks into a microphone. *"Good morning, ladies and gentlemen. Thank you for attending Washington High's first-ever mixed martial arts tournament. I must give thanks where thanks are deserved. Thank you to the school's English teacher, Mister Samuels. Today's event raises money for our boosters to support all school athletic programs. Thank you, Lloyd."*

Mr. Samuels waves, but I pick up on the double insult. Krake does not refer to him as the martial arts instructor. And, of course, the karate club is not an official athletic program, so we won't see a dime from today's event.

"But now, let me introduce the main man of the day, the Washington police captain and our very own striking instructor, Captain Claude Decker!" Everyone applauds except us. *"Mister Decker joined the wrestling team specifically for this event, to give the wrestlers a fun break from their real work. In between winning championships, he taught them strikes. You know, those little quick things that happen before a fight turns into a grapple."* He chuckles. *"No one knows how to strike better than Mister Decker. Sir, would you like to say a few words?"*

Decker takes the mic from Krake. *"My brother-in-law and I like to joke about what's better—my striking or his wrestling. Fun rivalry aside, I'd like to use today to announce something very special to me."* He glances over at us and grins. *"My brother-in-law and I would like to announce an investment in our community. We will be opening the first ever mixed martial arts studio. We officially open next week! Today, we will show you what real mixed martial arts training can do for young athletes."* Decker glares at Mr. Samuels. My heart beats faster than ever. They don't just want to win. They want to destroy us. *"To celebrate, we open our doors to all of you, all ages, kids and adults. The first month is absolutely free."*

The crowd erupts in applause.

Tisha touches my shoulder. "Just what we need—an entire town trained to be bullies," she whispers.

My heart sinks. She's right. It's not a school of bullies we'll have to worry about. If anyone can train with these jerks—well, it will be like the pandemic happening all over again.

"We *have* to win," DeMarcus says from the opposite side of me. "Winning is the only chance we'll have to stop this."

Mateo and Logan jump side to side, continuing their warm-up.

Mateo doesn't make eye contact with me. Logan, on the other hand, snarls at us.

"Now, please stand for the singing of our National Anthem," Decker says. Students from the Washington High choir sing, and then Mr. Samuels gathers us in a huddle.

"Everything they're doing, even with these announcements, is to distract you. To get in your head and make you lose focus," he tells us. "I need you to clear your mind. Lose yourself in your karate. Think of nothing else. Do you understand?"

"Sensei, can we win?" I ask.

He puts his strong hands on my shoulders. "You're damn right you can win!"

"Yeah!" we cheer.

"Hands in," he says. *"Kiai* on three, two, one."

We all yell in unison.

Krake takes back the microphone. *"Our first match—Tony of the kung fu club against Jeff from your Washington High Hornets wrestling!"*

"Krake's an asshole." Tony bounces, up and down, thick hair dancing.

"You can do this!" I cheer him on.

Tony and Jeff enter the ring. Jeff's skin looks paler than normal, like he hasn't seen the sun in months. They shake hands and get in their beginning positions.

A referee blows the whistle.

Jeff charges. He strikes Tony in the stomach. He wraps his arms tightly around Tony's neck, whipping him in a violent throw. Tony smacks the mat, and we gasp. Then Jeff locks Tony in a rear choke.

Tony hits the floor repeatedly with his hand, tapping out.

The fight is over in a blink of an eye.

What the hell?

Tony is better than that. How did that happen? Suddenly, a deep sickness hits my gut. It's a simple, nauseated realization. They're better than us. They've been training longer. They've got multiple coaches.

They didn't take time out for fun. Every second was spent so they could annihilate us in the blink of an eye.

Just like Jeff did to Tony.

Tony walks back over to us, his head lowered.

"Are you okay?" I ask.

His eyes glisten with tears, but he doesn't answer.

"I have to run to the bathroom." I rush, worried I'm not going to make it. I'm going to get sick right in front of everyone.

Sprinting, I find a toilet just in time. My guts are in knots.

We're going to lose. We were stupid to think we had any chance. What the hell are we doing here? This entire thing is ridiculous, all based on false hope.

The audience applauds loud enough that I hear it all the way in the bathroom. Krake's words reach all the way into the stall, too, thanks to the microphone.

"*Next up,*" Krake announces, "*Amanda of the tai fu club against Camila of Decker's Mixed Martial Arts Academy.*"

Oh, Amanda. Please win.

Please, don't let this be one giant embarrassment.

I'm so tired of losing.

68

Quite a Crowd

I WASH MY hands and run back to the gym, just as Amanda and Camila walk onto the mat.

Amanda offers Camila her hand. Amanda has her long, blonde hair pulled back. Those tiny arms may not look like they can do any damage, but I've been on the receiving end. I hope Camila gets a taste of Amanda's power. Camila shakes her hand briefly. Her dark hair is also pulled back. The whistle blows, and Camila jumps into a fighting stance. She releases a kiai, then grits her teeth. Spinning, Camila executes a tornado kick—turning three hundred and sixty degrees in the air, her fight foot crashes into Amanda's face.

Amanda falls on the mat. The ref blows the whistle again and gestures for the fight to stop. It's a knockout. Game over.

That's two losses. Two losses in less than two seconds.

No, this isn't a loss. This is an absolute humiliation.

"What is happening?" I ask Tisha.

"They've just gotten lucky." Her voice shakes, though. That kick Camila performed—that's something we've only seen. That's super-advanced stuff. How did Camila learn that? I hate myself a little for feeling this way, but I wonder if our training is inferior to what they've experienced.

Mr. Samuels puts his hand on my shoulder. "Feet low, hands high.

You maintain a strong stance and keep your guard up, and you can block that. That's flash used to distract you."

Tisha and I nod. *"DeMarcus versus Mateo,"* Krake announces, and DeMarcus swings his arms, pumping himself up for his match.

"What?" I ask. "Mateo? Why would you be facing Mat?"

"I got this," DeMarcus says. I hide my fear the best I can.

"I thought Mateo would be in the final round or something," I whisper to Mr. Samuels.

"It's all tournament style. Even Mat has to win to continue and advance," he says.

"Why DeMarcus?" I ask.

He doesn't have to answer. When I look over at Krake and Decker, their expressions say everything. DeMarcus left the team. Krake wants him annihilated.

DeMarcus and Mateo shake hands. Mat's face is stoic but not mean. My best friend has to be in there still. My best friend would not hurt DeMarcus. Now's his chance to reveal his true self and let DeMarcus win. Turn and laugh at Krake. Walk over and join our team, instead!

DeMarcus leaps in with a series of punches when the whistle blows. Mateo dodges and blocks. He grabs DeMarcus and throws him to the floor. DeMarcus looks like a pillow in Mat's arms. Mat slams him on the floor and then jumps on top of him. He's not just trying to pin DeMarcus—he's stifling him. DeMarcus doesn't stand a chance, and Mat isn't taking it easy on him, not at all.

Mat moves his arms around DeMarcus's neck, forming a chokehold. Mat's biceps bulge, as do DeMarcus's eyes. DeMarcus tries to bridge, but his legs collapse. He slaps Mat's arm repeatedly, tapping out.

Mat rolls and performs a kip-up. He looks like he hasn't even broken a sweat.

"We're in trouble," Tisha mumbles.

"So much trouble." I wish I could turn back time. Why did I ever

try wrestling in the first place? If I hadn't walked in that door, would my life be different? Maybe I'd have never been friends with Mat, but life wouldn't be full of bullies and bruises. I wouldn't have to get my ass kicked by the boy I love.

Could it really be that simple?

I risk a glance toward Logan, who cackles with his mouth wide open, his tongue flopping through his teeth like a dog.

No. I can't worry about past decisions. If it wasn't me who had joined the wrestling team in the first place, Logan would have picked on someone else.

I stand taller and take a deep breath. I can stop this, here and now. I can stand and face my fears. Win or lose, I can take the beating that some other kid may have received in the locker room or in the parking lot of our worthless high school. Someone needs to teach these jerks a lesson.

Or they'll never change.

So, why not me?

"Logan versus Aiden," Krake announces.

Good. I'm ready.

Mr. S leans in to say something, but I move forward without waiting to hear his words of encouragement. If I lose to Logan, I'll never have to face Mateo. That would be okay with me.

But if I lose to Logan, then he will always think he's better than me.

Maybe it's not always about winning or losing. But sometimes it is. I have to win this match.

When I enter the ring, I don't look at Logan. My gaze wanders toward Mateo. Finally, he looks me in the eyes. What is he thinking? I will my eyes to say everything I feel. *I hate you. I love you. You were my best friend. Who the hell are you, really?*

"Shake hands," the ref instructs when neither Logan nor I move.

Mateo's eyes tell me nothing. Slowly, I face Logan.

Here's the first boy who ever gave me hell. From day one, he insulted me. He laughed at me. He hurt Tisha. Who knows what he's said or done to the team, but I know he's helped fuel their hatred.

He leans in. "You're gonna lose, homo."

His breath stinks. I put in my mouth guard. I want to say a thousand things, but I choose to show him how I feel instead.

We touch hands, just briefly.

I glance at the stands. Do I have a cheering section? I could use that right now. Mom stands and claps. She looks nervous. Behind me, Mr. Samuels catches my eye. He bows slightly. I bow back. It's time I show my teacher what I learned.

The referee raises his hand. I scan the gym's audience. I've never been in a situation like this before, with hundreds of people cheering and screaming. Some for me. Some against me.

Who am I kidding? It's mostly against me.

The referee blows his whistle.

69

Logan vs. Aiden... Again

LOGAN KICKS ME in the stomach. Pain rushes through me, and I can't breathe.

I know I need to focus on the match. If I lose this, everything I've worked on so hard over the last few months is all for nothing.

Logan grabs me. He turns me like a steering wheel, stepping in deep with his right leg. He swings it up high, and I know where it's going—he's going to take me out with a huge outside leg sweep.

I jam my right knee into Logan's stomach and step hard and deep in between his legs. As he swings his right leg down, I shift my weight, lock his leg with my own, and reverse the sweep.

He falls hard on his back, and cheers erupt behind me. Adrenaline surges through my veins. I drop down and slide into a scarf hold pin.

Logan bridges and rolls me over. He's strong, and I shouldn't have expected to win easily. I jump off the ground and get in a fighting stance.

Logan swings at me. I step outside his arm, closing off the attack. With quick hip shifts—straight out of my current *kata*—I jab Logan twice in the ribs. He steps toward me, and I sweep his stepping leg while pulling the arms that reach toward me. He tumbles forward but performs a summersault, standing right back up in a fighting stance.

He snarls, but I've surprised him. He didn't expect me to last this long. He expected me to be an easy win.

Well, I've got news for him.

He punches at my face, and I throw a step behind sidekick to the same ribs I just jabbed. Logan drops his guard, and I leap in with a back fist, nailing his temple. He howls, his hands racing to guard his face, but I'm a step ahead of him. With his hands high, I swing a roundhouse into his belly.

Settling in my strongest horse stance, I watch Logan struggle to catch his breath.

I don't want to smile. I don't want to be the person who celebrates revenge. "This is for everyone you ever hurt."

Prying my heels off the mat, I bounce on the balls of my feet. Then I spin, hitting Logan with a spinning crescent kick right on the side of the head.

He falls over. The referee gestures and blows the whistle.

It's a knockout.

My section cheers, and Tisha runs for me, embracing me tightly. Mr. Samuels pats me on the back.

I turn to Mateo. Anything? Is he impressed? Shocked? His face is expressionless, and he looks away when my eyes meet his.

"Thanks, guys," I say to the rest of my team.

"We need you to win next. Okay?" I say to Tisha.

"Absolutely!" She hugs me again.

"Tisha versus Alyssa," Krake says.

Tisha enters the ring.

I don't know Alyssa. She's not dressed like the wrestlers. Her shirt says *Decker's MMA*. The fist logo and those letters—a memory of Camila's hidden shirt flashes in my mind. She trained in secret, and then she told Decker everything about me. I'd like to think the good person I once knew is still inside her. It's Decker who has poisoned her, right?

Right?

Alyssa fakes a punch to Tisha's head and kicks low. Tisha sees it, though. She executes a low block and performs an incredible reverse punch that sends Alyssa flying out of the ring.

Alyssa falls. She holds her stomach. She bends over, and I can only think of one thing—she looks like....

And then she does exactly what I picture. She throws up, her mouth guard falling out with projectile vomit, her body convulsing.

I bite my lip to keep myself from screaming in victory.

The referee whispers something in Alyssa's ear, but he looks like he's going to get sick at the sight of her. Then Decker approaches and examines Alyssa. In a huddle, they exchange information I can't hear. Decker's face twists with anger.

The referee walks away, points at Tisha, and declares, *"Winner!"*

We scream with excitement!

"One punch!" I yell, hugging Tisha. "Oh, that'll send a message! One punch! You're a rock star."

Krake takes the microphone. He tries to hide it, but there's frustration in his voice. As far as he's concerned, the tournament should have been over by now—a clean sweep.

But we're still standing. Two of us have won, and one of us did so with a single punch.

We're not a total embarrassment, after all. No matter what happens next, at least we have these moments.

How great would it feel to win this tournament? What if there's a chance I could take Mateo? No matter how talented someone is, there's always luck. Mr. Samuels said that before. Even a little kid has enough strength to poke someone's eye out. Anyone can get lucky in a fight. It was his way of teaching us to never get cocky, but right now it gives me hope.

Anyone can get lucky.

"What a great first round. Let's give our first-ever MMA competitors a big round of applause!" He pauses to let the crowd cheer. I look over at Mom, who claps and screams. *"Now, let's take a fifteen-minute in-*

termission. Give our athletes a short break before we do it all over again. One final round—Tisha from Mr. Samuels's Kung Do Club"—he pauses to laugh. I know he's mispronouncing on purpose—*"will face Camila from Decker's Mixed Martial Arts Academy. And then Brayden, another student of Samuels, will face this year's JV state champion wrestler, our very own Mateo!"*

"Let him screw up your name, Aiden. He's just trying to get under your skin," Tisha tells me. "Everyone will remember your name when this day is over."

"Yeah, but what will *I* be remembered for?"

I don't give her time to answer. Now that we get a little break, I run over to Mom. I could use her enthusiastic support, as I'm terrified right now.

"Oh, Aiden, you were wonderful. I am so proud of you!"

"Thanks, Mom."

She hugs me. In this moment, I understand why pride is so important, especially to people like me.

When you grow up thinking you're abnormal, when you have to lie about yourself, when some people hate you because of who you are... having someone take pride in you can make all the difference.

I hug her back.

Mom releases, and Mr. Samuels approaches. "Aiden, I'm so proud of you." He reaches for my mother's hand. She gives it, her smile unwavering. Win or lose, I've got two adults who are proud of me. It feels darn good.

"Don't you have a pep talk with the team to give? This break won't last long," Mom says.

"Yes. That's why I was getting Aiden. C'mon. We don't have much time." Mr. S releases Mom's hand and puts an arm around my shoulders.

The happiness I felt at their pride fades too quickly. In minutes, Mateo will face me in the ring. There are more imminent things that require my focus.

Mr. S guides the team out of the gymnasium and into his classroom. "Have a seat."

We each take a desk in the front row.

"How are you feeling?"

Tisha leans forward, her elbows on the desk. "I want to kick some major butt. Krake's ridiculing us. Camila's going down."

Mr. S looks at me.

"Nervous," I answer. "Terrified."

"Now, I want to tell you something, something from the heart before you continue. I'm scared, too. It's all right to be scared," Mr. S says. "It's all right to want to kick some butt. Fear, revenge—these are very human emotions. Our goal isn't to deny ourselves these feelings. Instead, our goal is to learn from them. How does this make you feel?"

"I don't like it," I answer.

"I dunno. I kinda like it, actually." Tisha claws at the desk. "But yeah, maybe I'd rather not feel this way."

"So, why are we here? Why are we fighting today?"

Silence fills the room. DeMarcus takes a deep breath. He's clearly still disappointed in his loss, as are Amanda and Tony.

I raise my hand. "I think that it actually doesn't matter if we lost to another person today. That wasn't who we were fighting."

Mr. Samuels gestures for me to elaborate.

"I mean—our opponent is fear. Our opponent is whatever negative thing we feel in ourselves. If we face that in the ring, then we win, even if we lose."

"Yes," Mr. Samuels says. "DeMarcus—you put up a good fight. A *great* fight! You won against your own fears, and you held your own against an incredibly talented athlete." His voice softens, and I wonder what Mr. S really thinks about Mateo. Mr. Samuels gave Mat extra time and teaching, too, after all. "Amanda and Tony—you entered a huge competition after only a couple months of training. You showed courage and strength. You all are winners today. Do you understand?"

They smile for the first time since leaving the ring. "Yes, sir."

"Tisha and Aiden—you still haven't won. Do you see? You still have fear and revenge to face. No matter what happens in that ring today, you walk out of it having conquered yourself. That's what is most important. That's more important than the person you have to face. Do you understand?"

"Yes, Sensei," Tisha and I say.

"Good," Mr. Samuels says. "But if you happen to kick some butt while you're at it—well, all the better!"

70

The Final Matches

WE RETURN TO the gym. Krake holds the microphone. *"Our final women's match of the day—Camila versus Tisha."*

They enter the ring. Krake walks off to the side, standing next to Mateo and Decker.

The referee blows his whistle, and the girls jump back into a fighting stance.

Camila yells, kicking at Tisha's face. Camila throws a front kick with her right, a roundhouse with her left, and spins with a right hook heel.

Tisha dodges each kick.

"Go, Tisha!" I yell. Adrenaline surges through me, and my heart leaps into my throat.

Camila bounces in a high horse stance. Tisha steps in and performs a tornado kick—the same kind of kick Camila did against Amanda.

I gasp! "How did she learn that?" I ask Mr. Samuels.

"She picks up quickly," he answers, laughing.

The tornado kick connects with the side of Camila's head. Her body hits the ground, and Tisha jumps on top of her.

Tisha goes for an armbar. She locks it in, applying all her weight on Camila's joints. I cover my mouth, scared that a bone will explode right before our eyes.

But Camila rolls right into Tisha, escaping from the lock. They stand back up, hands rushing to guard their faces, snarling. My body shakes, and I'm scared to even blink.

Camila charges with a series of punches, and Tisha stomps forward with a thrust kick to Camila's chest that sends her flying backward.

"Yes!" I cheer again.

Camila drops to a knee, and Tisha moves into a grapple. But Camila leaps off the ground, throwing a flying sidekick right into Tisha's neck.

Tisha drops to the floor, and Camila rushes in for a pin. Her hands go under Tisha's neck and legs, trying to lock down her shoulders and hips. Tisha throws her body weight into Camila, and then quickly snaps the other way. It's rock versus water—Tisha uses Camila's momentum against her, escaping the pin.

The girls get back up, each breathing heavily. Camila executes a jab-cross, but Tisha blocks, turns, and performs a spinning back fist to Camila's temple. Then Tisha steps, side-kicking Camila in the ribs. Tisha rotates, whipping a spinning hook heel to Camila's face.

Camila falls. Tisha dives on top, going for the armbar again.

She locks it in, and Camila screams. So do I!

In seconds, Camila taps out. Tisha performs a reverse summersault, jumping up on two feet. Camila holds her arm in pain. Krake and Decker look away, shaking their heads.

I rush the ring and hug Tisha. "You were awesome! Oh, my gosh!" She laughs and hugs me back.

Then she takes a deep breath and removes her mouth guard. "Mister S is right," she whispers to me. "It's not about beating Camila."

She examines her former best friend, then walks over and puts out her hand. Tears run down Camila's face.

"I'm sorry," Tisha says. "I don't know who is right and who is wrong, honestly." She pauses, taking in several more big breaths. "Can't we understand that we were all hurt? I want you to know I'm sorry. Okay?"

"Easy to say when you just won the match," Camila's mouth guard shoots out of her mouth. She slaps Tisha's arm away and marches over to Decker, who whispers something in her ear.

My heart drops. She'd prefer Decker's words over ours. I scan the gym, looking for her father or stepmother. I can't find either one. Maybe that's why she's so taken to Decker. She finally has a strong father figure who believes in her.

When this is all over, we need to have a big talk.

Mr. Samuels approaches and puts his arm around Tisha's shoulders. "You did the right thing. No more revenge. Okay?"

Tisha nods. "Yes, sir."

Mr. S turns to me. "Now, we have one more opponent to face. Time to destroy your fear, Aiden. Be the person you always wanted to be."

Krake approaches the microphone, his face twisting with disappointment. *"Ladies and gentleman, the winner of our first MMA women's division—Tisha."*

The crowd cheers, even though Krake's voice was curt. Tisha takes the trophy and waves at her parents. Then she walks back, standing next to me.

"You can do this, you know. Look at me," Tisha says. "I mean it. You can *do* this. Mateo knows he's good. You know you'll have to give it everything you've got. That can make all the difference."

"Next, our boy's championship—Mateo versus Aiden," Krake announces. The crowd claps when we enter the ring.

I offer Mat my hand first. He shakes it without making eye contact. There are so many things I want to say to him, but right now I want to show him that I'm not scared, no matter how tough or talented he is.

The referee blows his whistle, and Mat and I jump into our fighting stances.

71

Mateo vs. Aiden

MAT AND I freeze in our stances. He doesn't move. I don't think I can move. I steady my breathing, and I wait for Mat to make a move.

He takes a step forward. Lowering my shoulders, I focus on relaxation. He's close enough for a kick, should he choose to do that. I'm pretty sure I know what Mat wants, a though—a grapple to end the match quickly.

When he steps again, I slide in tiger stance. It's the move I taught him the last night we spent together.

Mat flinches when I move. My stance does the trick. It provides a memory and an emotion I want him to feel. The distraction lasts only a second. Mateo makes his move.

He's fast as a snake, one arm flying at my shoulder, the other near my leg. As he reaches, I step forward into a deep opposite side horse stance and throw a low block that strikes his thigh.

Mateo winces, but he doesn't move back. His strong hands sink into my flesh. He goes for a takedown. I move with him, letting him fall right on top of me.

Right before I hit the matted floor, I press a foot into his chest. As he falls on top of me, I perform a sacrifice throw, water moving rock.

He rolls forward, popping right up on his feet, unscathed. Blinking, he tries to wear a poker face, but there's the slightest cringe.

The state champion wrestler tried to take down the karate kid and failed. My section grows with more applause. Apparently, everyone loves an underdog story.

Mat races for me from across the ring. I jump into horse stance and extend my arms into a knife guard position. He dives for my chest. My body moves counterclockwise, spinning so that I'm right next to him in mid-air. When Mateo lands, I've used enough momentum to flip around and land on his back.

He smacks face-first on the floor, and I'm on top of him! Quickly, I put him in a rear chokehold. My form is good, but Mat's strength is overwhelming. He stands, and I'm hanging on his back with my forearm digging into his neck.

He pushes his chin into my arms, creating a gap between my forearm and his neck. It's enough for him to swallow a mouthful of fresh oxygen. Then his hands grab my arms, and he flips me over.

It's a beautiful throw, and he lands on top of me. He slides right into a scarf hold. He's got the pin, but it's not a pin he wants. His arm flexes against the back of my neck. Mat wants me to tap out—it's a choke disguised as a pin. It feels like my spine is about to snap in half.

"Why?" I gasp, nearly inaudible. It's a big question—there are so many "whys," and now is no time for a conversation.

But now, I want to conquer my fear—and I want to conquer Mateo, too.

Water.

No, water won't work when my neck is about to break. Water needs to become rock, long enough to trick it.

I bridge with all my strength. With a scream, I bridge high enough so it's obvious Mateo doesn't have me in a pin. That's not the impression he wants. He uses all his might to slam down the bridge I made with my legs.

That's when I turn back to water. As Mateo forces my lower body down, I roll with it.

I reverse the hold, pinning Mateo! My own scarf hold tightens around his neck, but with his strength, it doesn't even last a second. He throws me off like I'm a weightless bar. He runs a hand through his sweaty hair, and his eyes sparkle with surprise.

Mateo puts his hands into a fighting position. This is now a street fight. He's going to take my head off with his fist.

My nerves swell. My adrenal glands work overtime, more energy surging through every inch of my body.

I step back into tiger stance.

I visualize Mateo's punches before he throws them.

Hidden movements. Secrets. What does the kata *teach you? Visualize it! What are the secrets, Aiden?* Mr. Samuels's voice echoes in my mind.

Yes! Maybe it's the crowd screaming or the adrenaline heaving through my veins, but I see something I've never seen before—not in the thousand times I performed the *kata.*

I see the secrets.

72

Secrets and Singlets

MATEO JABS AT my face. I switch into an opposite side tiger stance, blocking with my upper tiger palm. He throws a punch at my body. My other arm blocks that as it moves into position—it's not just a form or a stance. Each movement is a block. No, each movement is a strike. Each movement is many things. Mateo pushes me, but my arms move and tangle him as I continue with the tiger form. With his arms all tied up, I twirl him.

He spins away from me, struggling to catch his balance. He looks like he doesn't know what just happened—like he's fighting Spiderman.

The biggest grin grows on my face.

He sprints toward me.

Seeing more than I ever have before, I use the tiger form, not to strike his throat and groin, but to once again tangle up his arms. With no arms, he can't strike or grab me. Then with one arm low and one arm high—much like how he first tried to throw me—I execute a takedown.

An uproar ignites the crowd.

The little karate kid just took down the state champion wrestler.

I dive for a pin, wanting to beat him at his own game!

But he flips me over, a quick reversal, showing his strength and expertise. Sweat trickles down his singlet, and he growls as he flips me over, slamming me like he's taking a sledgehammer to one of those carnival games.

The gymnasium crowd gasps.

Mat pins me hard. No tricks. Just a perfect pin. I can't breathe. I can't escape. There are no secrets or hidden movements out of this one.

The referee begins to count. I don't hear the numbers. The crowd is too loud for me to concentrate.

I only know one thing.

I just lost.

Mateo releases me. He sits up, sweat racing down his face. I move slowly, every muscle in my body still twitching from the adrenaline.

He stands, looking over at Krake and Decker. Expressions of surprise and relief cover their faces. They nod at him, though, and they clap. The hundreds in the gym cheer, too.

Mateo looks down at me. His lips move, opening into a gentle smile. And he offers me his hand.

I gulp, worried it's a trick. Will he try to hurt me?

Carefully, I take his hand.

Mateo lifts me off the floor. We stand side by side. He adjusts his singlet, and I tighten my blue belt.

The hundreds in the gym holler. It's a loud cacophony of cheers and screams that make me cover my ears, which in turn makes them laugh and scream even louder.

They're cheering for me, even though I lost the fight.

I look at Mateo.

Then he does something that surprises me and makes my stomach drop all over again.

He hugs me. He hugs me tightly. His sign of affection makes the crowd yell even more.

I can barely hear my own thoughts, but Mateo whispers in my ear. "I'm sorry."

I put my arms around him and hug him back.

"I'm so sorry." He starts to cry. It's a sob I've never heard from another boy. I don't know if the crowd can tell what's happening. I hug Mateo harder. "They made me, Aiden. They threatened me. Threatened my future. My scholarships. College. *Everything!* I never wanted to hurt you. When I said I lied, well, that was a lie they made me tell you. Tanner watched my every move. I'm so sorry!"

My eyes well with tears.

What? Say it again! I'm too dizzy to speak. I just listen.

"They told me I had to lie to you, to say I was never your friend. I'm a coward, Aiden. I'm so stupid. Can you ever forgive me?"

He doesn't look me in the eye. He hugs me tighter, with more affection than ever.

I can't believe what I'm hearing. Then he says something else, and my knees turn to Jell-O.

"I love you," Mat tells me. It's a whisper, and certainly the crowd can't hear, but they continue to cheer.

"Huh? What?" It's all I can manage to say. My world is spinning faster than a Tilt-a-Whirl.

"I said I love you, Aiden. I love you, and I'm so sorry."

A warmth hits me like a tidal wave.

"I love you, too," I manage to say. His grip loosens just enough for me to find air and speak. "You were always my best friend. All this time—I've wanted nothing more than to have my best friend back." Tears fall down my face and drop on his shoulders, but he doesn't let me go.

"No, you don't understand." He steps back enough so that we are face to face. "I have so much to apologize for. You thought I was strong. No, Aiden. You're so much stronger and braver than me." He wipes away the tears from his eyes, but they keep on coming.

"I love you. You're all I've thought about. You and how to be strong like you. And also how to be honest like you."

My arms shake. The crowd begins to quiet. I see Mom from over

Mat's shoulder. She covers her mouth, eyes wide, and she's ready to squeal and scream for me all over again. Decker, Krake, and Camila stare at us with confusion, and Camila's face also shows pain.

"What do you mean?" I mumble.

"Don't you get it?" He wipes at the stream of tears rolling down his beautiful face. "I'm, um—like you. And I like you. No, not like. *Love.* I love you, Aiden."

He pauses for a moment, biting his lip.

"Can you forgive me? Oh, man. I'd understand if you couldn't. I was so weak. Such a coward! I couldn't accept who I was. I fought that as hard as I've fought anything else. That whole time—when I was trying to help you learn wrestling, you were helping me learn real strength. It just took me forever to get here." He sniffs and wipes his eyes. "Can you forgive me for everything? I would understand if you never wanted to talk to me ever again."

Maybe I hit my head too hard, and I'm hallucinating. Everything I have ever wanted feels like it's about to come true. I don't care about the hundreds of people watching. I care only about this moment.

"I forgive you. What we feel—there's so much. And it's so hard. People don't know what it takes, and coming-out is different for all of us. I get it, Mat. I really get it. I forgive you." I wipe away my own tears, but there's a huge smile on my face. "And I love you, too."

He lips open and he moves impossibly close to my face. He pauses long enough for me to nod, and I can't believe what's about to happen.

He kisses me, his lips pressing hard against mine. I kiss him back, throwing my arms around him, forgetting that like a hundred people are watching. Although quiet at first, the crowd erupts with cheers after we kiss. I'm pretty sure the first scream came from Mom, but it's contagious.

The crowd applauds for us again. A powerful thought hits me as hard as anything has ever hit me—most people, most are cool. They really are. The most ignorant and the most hateful voices are simply often the loudest. But that doesn't mean they speak for everyone. Far from it.

Mateo holds me close. I kiss him harder, tasting sweat and tears and feeling every emotion imaginable.

When he lets go, he takes my hand. We look around the crowd. "I don't know what to do from here."

"We'll figure it out together. Okay?"

He smiles. "I'm not scared with you by my side."

I smile back. "The feeling's mutual."

We walk into the crowd.

73

Let Us Be Us

FIRST STOP AFTER the tournament—a pizza buffet.

Plate after plate of Hawaiian pizza, sausage, extra cheese, and more arrive at our table. Mateo laughs about something Mr. Samuels says. Mom laughs, putting her hand on my teacher's knee. Tisha and Amanda joke about something, too.

Mat catches my eye and smiles. I can't believe everything that's happened tonight.

Mr. Samuels raises a glass. "To all of you. Today, you made your teacher and your families proud. You *all* won today, in my book. Congratulations!"

We clink plastic cups full of soda.

Mat sits across from me, and his foot touches mine. Neither of us moves away. If anything, our feet get closer.

"Now what?" Tisha asks. "Do you think there will be a tournament like this every year?"

"If there is, there's no need for us to fight again," Mr. S says. "Decker can have his school. Krake can have his wrestling team. We have each other. That's all you need."

My gut tells me Krake and Decker have a lot more up their sleeves, especially with Mat leaving their team like he did. We may not have the luxury of not fighting.

But I don't want to worry about that. Not today.

Today, I want to be with my boyfriend.

Isn't that an incredible word? *Boyfriend, boyfriend, boyfriend.* I want to say it over and over again.

"Mom, can I spend the night at Mat's?"

She looks at me like I just asked if she'd buy me beer. "Um, Aiden—"

"How about one night with *us?*" Mr. S suggests, squeezing Mom's hand. "Mat can stay with you. The bedroom door stays open all night. Understand?"

My face burns with embarrassment, but I smile. "Yes! That would be great."

"Yeah," Mat says. "Thanks."

I swallow hard. We've got a lot of catching up to do. But I also hope we don't spend the entire time talking.

Mateo smiles at me, and my heart fills with absolute joy.

MR. SAMUELS DROPS Mom and me off at home. Mateo also went home so he could shower and get his stuff before coming over. He told me that he came out to his parents last night. He said that he didn't know what he'd do in the ring, not for sure. He wasn't sure if he'd have the courage to do what he really wanted to do—take my hand, apologize, and come out in front of Krake, the team, and the entire school.

But there was something I didn't know about Mateo. His older sister—the one I had seen only in pictures at his house—she's gay, too. She's in college now, and when she came out, Mateo's parents fought with her and resisted. They almost lost a daughter, but eventually they started talking again. Mateo was terrified of what it would mean to his parents if both of their children were gay.

Everyone's journey to truth is different. I know being honest can be terrifying. But I guess I didn't know that everyone would have different obstacles, or that there could be variables that no one on the outside could even guess or understand.

I was scared to come out to an accepting, loving mother. I can't even imagine what all went on inside Mateo's head as he prepared to come out to his parents.

"Any luck with Camila?" Mom asks softly, taking me away from my thoughts.

"No. She's completely blocked me, Mat, and Tisha online."

"Aiden, put yourself in her shoes for a minute. She's had two boyfriends. You and Mateo. What else do you and Mateo have in common?"

I look down at the floor. "I know. She has to be heartbroken."

"More than that, I bet," Mom says, patting my knee. "Everyone cares what others think about them, even if they say they don't. You guys got in a fight because she thought you lied to her."

I stir uncomfortably. "And her teacher isn't going to help. It's just fuel for his homophobia. You know he's told her that I used her and probably blames me for Mateo?"

Mom nods. "Lloyd told me about Decker. He's not a good man. You, Mateo, and Tisha need to do whatever you can to help her, make it better with her, get her away from him. Promise me you'll do that?"

"Yes, Mom."

"Good." She kisses me on the cheek. "It's the right thing to do, even if it's hard."

"I love you, Mom."

She smiles. "I love you, too, Aiden."

WHEN THE DOORBELL rings, my heart races. I pace the room, triple checking that I've picked up all my clothes and trash.

"Hi, Mateo," Mr. Samuels greets him from downstairs. Apparently, Mr. S is spending the night, too.

"Hello, sir," Mat says. "Aiden upstairs?"

"Yes," Mom tells him. "You can head on up."

I sit on my bed. Then I stand. Then I sit back down and cross a leg. Then I roll to my side, put an elbow under my head and try to look cool. None of it feels right.

"Hey," Mateo says from my doorway.

"Hi," I say back, swallowing the lump of fear and excitement that's grown in my throat.

"You were amazing today," he says, sitting next to me. "That fight—you almost won." He reaches for my hand.

"I *did* win." I squeeze his hand back. He leans in and kisses me gently on the lips. Every inch of my skin tingles.

"You gotta teach me those moves," Mat says after a few minutes, in no hurry to end the kiss. "That thing you did to my arms when you tangled me up? That was amazing."

"You'll be training with us now, right?"

"If that's cool."

"What about wrestling? What about scholarships and college?"

Mat shrugs. "I'll figure it out. I don't wanna think about it right now if that's okay. I just...." He shuffles even closer to me, putting his arm around my shoulders. "I hated myself, you know that? I hated myself for months. Some days I thought I'd rather die." His eyes gloss, and he wipes away a tear. "I'm so sorry. I never wanted to be that person. Decker was very persuasive at times. He seriously had me doubting who I was and even blaming you."

My face reddens. I think about what Mom said and how we've got to make every effort to help Camila. "It was hard. It hurt a lot. But, you're here now. Let's just, you know, be us. The *real* us. Now and always."

He smiles. I lean in and kiss him. Mom clears her throat from the hallway and pokes her head in the room. "Door open, all night. Okay? And Mat—I've got an air mattress you can sleep on. I'll bring that in later."

"Thank you," he says.

Mom leaves. Mat and I kiss again.

Eventually, we turn on the TV, but we spend more time with our lips locked and eyes closed than anything else.

"What do you think Krake and Decker and everyone's gonna do now?" I ask, later in the night.

"Oh, I should show you this." Mat takes out his phone. He scrolls through some social media pages and finds one for Decker's school. "Look at the cover photo."

Tanner McQueen stands front and center, with Logan and Camila on his sides in a freshly updated cover photo.

"Tanner's training with Decker now?"

"Yeah. Plans on joining the UFC circuit after graduation. Already got a contract. He's the best."

"Not in my opinion." I roll my eyes. "You almost beat him. You could beat him again. Maybe I could beat him, after a dozen years in the weight room." I laugh.

"I'd like to see that."

"You never know." We lay back on my bed and watch some TV. He puts his arm around me. "We've got to make it right with Camila."

"We will. No matter what it takes. The poison Decker teaches—it's bad," he tells me.

Mom brings in an air mattress and fills it up. Mat rolls off the bed and lays on the mattress. "Thank you."

She smiles and looks at me with curious eyes. I can tell she wants to say something, but she holds back for now. If my eyes could talk, they'd say *"thank you"* and *"please leave."*

Mom exits without any final words.

We turn off the lights. I listen for Mat's snoring, but I never hear it. A few minutes pass, and then my bed moves, just a little. "Um, do you mind if I join you?"

"Not at all."

He gets in bed, putting his arm around me. We snuggle through the night.

I close my eyes and welcome sleep. It's been a long day. Before sleep comes, one final thought surfaces. Please let life always be this good. Please let us always be happy. That's all I ask for.

Just let us be us.

Author's Note

THANK YOU FOR reading *Singlets and Secrets,* and I sure hope you enjoyed the story. Before you even started this book, I am excited to say I've already been working on the next ones. Book two will be ready to go right around the corner, see keep an eye out for that (subscribe to my newsletter at www.joechianakas.com). I am so excited for you to see where this series is going, and I hope you will stick around for even bigger surprises in book two. There are many places in the country where our community is under attack from "Don't Say Gay" laws to anti-trans legislation to even banning drag. I wish these things were not happening, but they are inspiring some events in the rest of this series. If you are a queer creator, I hope you enthusiastically share your work with the world. We need representation more than ever to help combat the rise in hate and anti-LGBTQIA rhetoric.

If you want to see more of my work and more of this story, please recommend it to your friends. Sign up for my newsletter at www.joechianakas.com to get an email when the next book hits stores. Or search for me on your favorite socials.

Thank you for your support, and I wish you nothing but joy.

JOE CHIANAKAS is an author and a college professor. He's won multiple teacher-of-the-year awards and inspiring students in his greatest passion. He loves long walks with his furbaby Bailey, a mini-Australian Shepherd. He lives in Peoria, IL with the love of his life, Brian.

Joe's known for his horror series *Rabbit in Red*—a three book trilogy that became a huge hit after multiple subscription boxes bought and mailed thousands of copies to horror fans around the world. Joe's next horror novel, *Darkness Calls,* will be releasing soon.

Chianakas is currently represented by Amy Brewer of Metamorphosis Literary Agency and has multiple publishing contracts with Roan & Weatherford Publishing Associates. Learn more about Joe and send him a message at **www.joechianakas.com** or follow him online at www.facebook.com/chianakas or search for him on your favorite socials.

Printed in the USA
CPSIA information can be obtained
at www.ICGtesting.com
LVHW052304080124
768489LV00035B/261